RODERICK DAVIDSON

PALLITINE RISING

PALLITINE'S PATH
BOOK ONE

This book is dedicated to my pillar of support, my wife.

Special thanks to:
Angela, Jim, Joe, Jolene, Josh, Kim, Nikki, and Pam

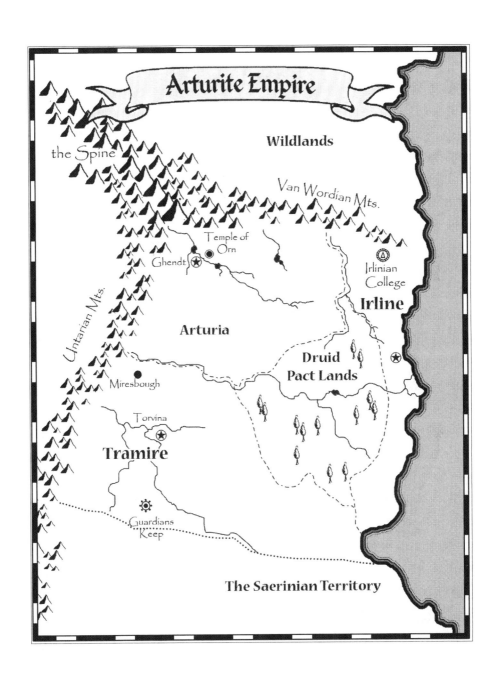

PROLOGUE

SHARP RAYS OF LIGHT FILTERED through a break in the otherwise overcast sky, blinding Thoman. The apprentice squinted and lowered his gaze toward his two new riding companions, both Arturian knights, as they rode to the village of Kengston.

Pallitine Janos seemed all right in Thoman's eyes. He was serious and down to earth, which Thoman respected. The slender man kept his dirty blond hair closely cropped, and with the exception of the bits flaring out around his narrow ears, looked as orderly as the man's demeanor.

Pallitine Markel, however, was quite the opposite in nearly every aspect. The muscular, thick-necked brute's hair was the color of midnight and curled out in thick, loose twirls in almost every direction. A scraggly beard sprouted from his face and ran a hand span's length past his chin, stretching out in an unruly mass. He bore the tanned complexion of some foreign land Thoman could not place. The one thing that struck Thoman, however, was the smile that graced his face, prefacing one of the many jokes he kept prepared for any occasion.

The two men were partners assigned to accompany Thoman

and his mentor, Pallitine Hadrian. The small group was tasked to investigate rumors of a large beast near the mountains. The beast was purported to have sacked farms, eaten local livestock, and devastated several stores of grain in a remote village.

Markel noticed the sidelong glance and grinned a toothy response. "Aye, lad?" The depth of his voice gave it a rich timbre, which sounded smooth when he spoke in his typically laid-back manner.

During their short time together, Thoman grew comfortable with the man's unabashed and friendly demeanor and decided to voice his thoughts. "I was trying to peg your heritage, actually. You don't appear to be of Arturian blood, nor Tramirian. You certainly aren't of Irlinian descent, you are *far* too broad in stature for that, and your coloring is a bit darker than I've seen before. And you are far too civilized to be Saerinian."

Markel raised an eyebrow and smiled to himself for a moment before responding. "Aye, my blood is mixed. Although, I daresay that I take after my father more so than my mother." He urged his horse to slow so he could ride side by side with the apprentice. "My father's folk hail from the southern deserts by the mountains, but his clan has been known to..." the man pondered his next words carefully, "philander when they travel about." A rare glance of seriousness splashed into his explanation as he continued. "Nothing untoward mind you, just the usual infatuation with foreigners in a foreign land, rest assured." He shrugged toward Thoman, who remained silent as the pallitine continued. "As you may suspect, our bloodline is somewhat diverse. It's said that I have some dwarven ancestry, and if one were to dig back far enough, you would find the blood of a fierce and mighty dragon, which explains my hardy strength." He waggled his eyebrows and flexed a thick arm to accentuate the point.

Thoman grinned at the dark giant who rode next to him. In his twenty years, he never met anyone who was more of a living contradiction. The pallitine, like all pallitines, possessed a steadfast and honorable spirit with a fierce sense of duty, yet his mannerisms showed a clear lack of regard for all sense of propriety and decorum. To have lived such a life in what was typically the prim and proper society of Arturia must have been hard indeed, unless he took a small amount of joy in having offended certain sensibilities. An amused respect for the large man began to emerge as he chose to believe the latter.

Markel's companion raised an eyebrow at the exchange and turned to Pallitine Hadrian. "So how are our young friend's preparations coming along for the trials?"

Hadrian looked along the trail ahead thoughtfully before responding. "He has been doing very well actually. He excels in his studies as well as the more rigorous demands of the position. He has grown as a man more than I could have expected from him. He will have no troubles with the Trials of Honor in any regard. As long as the praise doesn't go to his head." He made sure to speak the next part more loudly, as if he did not know Thoman was listening, "If that happens, he's doomed." He turned back to look at his apprentice and smirked.

"The only thing that would doom me is the lackluster training I've received these several years past." Thoman ribbed back. He brought a hand up to touch his father's ring which he still wore on a chain around his neck and took comfort from its familiar touch. He enjoyed these trips, and as much as he was looking forward to moving on from apprenticeship, a strong part of him looked with uncertainty toward the future.

The four figures rode into a village which seemed much like any other along the edge of the mountains. It cropped up close to a river, dotted by feeble and worn buildings whose wood grayed from age, and carried the heavy air of austere despair.

The village looked typical enough in its meager décor and

calm undertone. This appearance of a calm tranquility was shattered when the group reached the southern end of the village where the granary resided. The front wall to the village's granary stood decimated, laying the interior open to the world before it, revealing several temporary support beams propped to maintain their grip on the cracked ceiling within an otherwise empty shell of a storehouse. What remained of the wall now sat strewn outside in a haphazard pile.

The new arrivals urged their mounts to stop near the granary and waited for one of the workers outside to draw near as they carried the stones from the side of the fractured building.

Hadrian held up his hand in greeting. "Well met. I am Pallitine Hadrian. Is there an elder nearby to speak with?"

The haggard and sinewy man raised a hand to block the sun, pointed a grime-encrusted finger to the other side of town by the river, and stared at the group through empty eyes.

"My thanks." Hadrian waved as he pulled on the reins and urged his mount on toward the river.

Several minutes later, the four riders found themselves near the water where a small gathering of people sat on the river's bank talking. A few villagers turned toward the new arrivals, and watched the group as they were greeted by a young man who offered to hitch their mounts to a nearby tree.

Once dismounted, the pallitines came closer to the congregation.

The villagers stood and gawked at the approaching armored figures.

As the group got closer, they made room around a central figure so the newcomers could approach.

The elder was a broad-shouldered man who barely looked older than Hadrian, but held himself with an aura of commanding confidence as he looked warily at the group.

"Greetings. I am Pallitine Hadrian," he started. "I trust you are Kengston's elder?"

The elder looked reassured with the introduction and moved

forward to offer his hand in greeting. "Aye, that's me. Call me Joseph. Yer here for the troubles, I hope?"

Hadrian nodded and turned to his companions. "Yes, sir. My companions and I are here to assess the situation and take care of the beast we've heard about." He pointed toward his associates as they stepped forward to greet the elder. "This is Pallitine Janos, Pallitine Markel, and my apprentice Thoman."

The elder eagerly greeted the party members and motioned the group to walk with him as he led them to the northern side of the village. "Praise the god, ye've come. We've been struck no less'n three times in the past month. Each attack worse'n the last."

"What happened? Has anyone been hurt?" Hadrian asked.

Joseph shook his head. "Naw, thank Orn. Not directly, at least. The beast has taken its toll on our herds and crops." He stood and let his concern for the village slip through as he continued, "Though, if'n this goes on, I think we're in a heap o' trouble, I'll tell ya. We can't take much more without fearin' o' starvin' in the winter."

Janos stepped next to Hadrian and frowned. "That would be unfortunate, indeed. We shall do everything in our power to help however we can, but we must know all you know of this beast." His countenance took on a stark earnestness as he listened expectantly.

Joseph turned to face the pallitine as he answered, squinting while the sun shone in his eyes. "Well, it's been said by the few that've seen it, that it looks like a dragon, 'cept smaller, and with no wings. I've been told that it breathes fire like one, but that's about all I know. Don't sound like no dragon I've heard of, but then again I ain't ne'er seen one." He shrugged. "All I care 'bout is this menace ending."

Along the way, the elder pointed out a few of the local farms where the beast took advantage of the abundance of food present in the gardens and pens. Just past the farms, the elder pointed along a craggy mound nestled in the base of the foothills and the surrounding trees. "That, my friends, is where it's been seen leavin' to every time. If you'll find it at all, it'll be up there."

Hadrian's face creased as he cast a stern eye up the hill and nodded. "We'll take a look up there once we get our gear in order." He glanced toward the sun before looking down on Joseph. "I'm not sure what we'll find with what's left of the day, but we'll set up camp at the base once we've checked it out and continue in the morning."

By the time they made it up to the top of the mound, the sun had already started its slow descent through the darkening sky. From this vantage, several pockets of trees dotted the landscape in the distance along the hills as they continued off to the west and into the mountains.

"How about we try up there?" Markel suggested, pointing up to a nearby rocky slope that seemed to give a good view of the area.

Janos started up before anyone else could react. "Looks to be as good a place as any around here, I suppose." He was the first to reach the ledge at the top and, likewise, the first to set up watch as he scouted the hills around them.

Thoman found his perch, as did each member of the group along the ledge, and drew in a breath of the crisp mountain air as he looked about the rocky landscape. From his vantage alongside Hadrian, he clearly saw the mountains as they led south and the sparse grasses laid in patches along the rocky terrain as they wound their way to the forested foothills. He leaned forward on a knee and watched vigilantly for the source of the village's fears, his breath streaming out in faint wisps in the cool air as he flicked his gaze across the landscape. In the time searching, he found no visible sign of their quarry, or of anything that would speak of a place where it would likely retreat to.

The sun's light began its descent across the horizon and struck the upper reaches of the mountains in deep gold which was growing fierce with orange as time passed, dimming the land below them considerably when Janos stirred.

"Markel, what do you make of this?" He pointed off toward a break in the lower foothills near a previously overlooked outcropping.

Thoman, relieved there was something to break up the monotony, moved to where Markel joined his partner and looked out to the area Janos pointed out along the northern reaches.

"I think I see what you mean," Markel commented while he stared ahead. His motionless gaze bore no hint to what he saw, much to Thoman's chagrin.

Thoman squinted and tried in vain to see what the two pallitines watched. After a minute, he thought he saw some movement between the hill and a stray outcropping.

"Nice catch, eagle eyes." Markel laughed as he squeezed his friend's shoulder. "Hadrian, I think we found our beast." He pointed toward the darkening landscape which held the moving creature, and leaned in toward Thoman. "Do you see it?"

Thoman nodded. "Yes, it looks like a big lizard, with scales ranging from tan to red, quite unlike the green pond lizards near the keep."

"He probably bites harder as well, I'd imagine." The large man quipped while he watched the creature saunter down the hill.

"How big do you think it is?" Janos asked as he examined the reptile.

Hadrian pulled out his bow and adjusted his quiver. "I'd say the body is about as big as a stallion's. It'll be put down like anything else, I'd imagine."

Markel eyed Hadrian as he prepared his bow and followed suit. "Good idea, might as well get some target practice in. Though we might want to get closer. I'm not sure if I can hit it from this far away."

Janos laughed. "What, the almighty Markel can't hit an oversized lizard from a mere half league away? For shame." He scoffed while equipping his own bow.

Thoman chuckled and turned from the pallitines. His breath

caught in his throat as he saw the lizard scampering up the rocky slope toward them. "Slag it, he's seen us."

Markel stepped toward the edge of the slope and drew his bowstring back while he took aim. His shot looked true, but missed as it gradually veered to the left.

"You aren't taking the wind into consideration. Here, allow me." Janos nocked an arrow and let it loose. The arrow glanced across the advancing beast, causing it to wince slightly as it ran up the hill.

Hadrian joined the two pallitines and began to release his arrows at will. Of the four arrows he managed to loose off, only two stuck into the beast's scaled hide, and neither seemed to affect the creature at all.

Markel and Janos both had similar luck and abandoned their bows as the creature drew near. Each of the four men drew their blades and backed away from the ledge, fanning out as they prepared to flank the beast.

The moment the creature's head peered over the ledge, Janos's eyes opened as if revelation struck. "I know what this is." His face flashed with uncertainty as he continued to watch the beast climb onto the leveled ground and face them. "This is an adolescent wyrm. Not a full dragon, but close. We're in for a fight, guys."

Thoman grew wide-eyed at the proclamation and turned to Hadrian.

His mentor looked upon him confidently as he reassured the apprentice. "You'll be fine. Let us draw his attacks and you strike him when the opportunity presents itself, all right?"

The three pallitines pulled their shields off their backs, and held their swords up defensively, just in time to watch the wyrm charge in.

Janos headed in to face the beast and held his shield high as the others flanked the wyrm.

The giant lizard snarled, its deadly gaze focused on its confident adversary, drew its head back, and breathed a fiery burst, striking the pallitine.

Were it not for the quick use of his shield, Janos would have been crippled. His shield glowed a bright red from the heat and he cursed while trying to shake it off his arm as he drew back away from the beast.

Charged with fear, Thoman dove in and swung his blade, striking the wyrm soundly across his scales. The blow did little but to scratch the thick armor and reinforced the sinking feeling taking root in his gut. He looked up in alarm at his mentor.

Hadrian cursed as his strike proved equally futile.

The wyrm reached out to both figures and swiped at both Hadrian and Thoman, knocking them down in alternating strikes with its claws.

Markel watched the first two attacks on the beast, and wedged his broadsword under a scale before shoving it through the softer skin underneath with all his might. A loud tearing sound broke across the area as the creature's muscles ripped along its backside from the attack.

The wyrm howled in pain as its hindquarter slumped in agony, and again when the blade was ripped free from its flesh. The wyrm lashed out with its tail, knocking the pallitine over the ledge, and sent him tumbling down the rocky slope it scrambled up not moments ago.

Janos ran back to the melee, the glowing shield still stuck on his arm, and grimaced while swinging his blade at the creature's snout. "Stab the creature; impale it with your blades!" he shouted while distracting their quarry. The pallitine's blows were easily dodged by the wyrm, but he moved too quickly about for it to focus its fiery attack a second time.

Adrenaline surged through Thoman, and gave him the energy to shoot back on his feet. He stepped toward the distracted wyrm and started to advance.

Hadrian pointed to the ledge. "No, get Markel and help him back here," Hadrian commanded the younger man.

Doubt filled the young man at the command. He glanced at

Janos, who tripped in his backward retreat and barely dodged a strike from the creature, and then back toward the ledge, where he heard the cursing and scrambling of the other pallitine as he worked his way back to the fray. The immediate threat forced him to action as he stepped into the creature's view and bore down on its brow with a mighty swing of the steel blade, knocking off one of the ridged spines from above its eyes.

The wyrm turned to face the apprentice and puffed its chest outward as it pulled in a deep breath.

"Get off him!" Hadrian shouted as he charged in and impaled the creature's shoulder with his sword.

The beast toppled slightly as its attack was interrupted. It roared with a vengeance, twisted its head toward Hadrian, and spat out the searing burst meant for Thoman.

Hadrian's arms flew up to protect his face while his sword clattered to the ground. The pallitine dropped to his knees as he screamed in pain and fell to the side, curling as he shook from the pain of the brutal assault.

Shock swept through Thoman and filled him with regret. *That should be me.* Guilt fueled his limbs and forced him to fight. He charged in, mustering the loudest cry he could and swung his blade under one of the armored scales. Before he knew it, he impaled the creature's side and prepared for another strike.

The wyrm stepped back and turned from Thoman to Markel as the large pallitine pulled himself up from the ledge and ran to join the battle. It twitched for the briefest of moments and rushed past both figures to run over the side of the ledge and down the rocky slope of the hill, followed only by a splattering trail of blood.

Markel rushed to the ledge when Thoman's gaze fell upon his mentor. His confidence shook when the smoldering form of Hadrian came into focus. The pallitine's convulsions weakened as Thoman knelt next to the fallen man. Regret, fear, and guilt enveloped him as he saw his friend dying before his eyes.

"Thoman," Hadrian coughed, "is it dead?"

Thoman shook his head. "No, it ran away as soon as Markel climbed back up the hill."

Hadrian breathed out the faintest wisp of a laugh. "Figures that it'd take Markel's ugly scowl to chase it off." He grimaced while he tilted his head to better look into his apprentice's eyes. "Promise me something." He raised his burned hand and set it on Thoman's shoulder.

"Anything," Thoman said as he fought off the sea of despair from the overwhelming guilt. *If only I listened and helped Markel up the ledge, none of this would have happened.*

"Swear to me you will be the best man you can be. Promise me you will never falter in aiding the weak. Promise me you will take all I've taught you and hold it dear in your heart."

"I swear," he stuttered.

Hadrian's face relaxed as he leaned back.

"Good. I've always been proud of you, Thoman. Since the day I first saw you, I knew you would grow up to be something great. I've never been prouder in all my life." Hadrian clasped his hand on Thoman's and closed his eyes. The pallitine wheezed his final breath as his soul relaxed its grip on the mortal coil.

Tears streamed down Thoman's cheeks as he silently mourned the loss of the one figure who helped him through so much in his life. He looked up and across the mountains, filled with doubt and regret. Then his oath to Hadrian came to mind, and his resolution grew firm as he knew what must be done. His thoughts were interrupted as a large and rough hand graced his shoulder.

"I believe this is yours," Markel said gently as he held out the horn Thoman broke off the wyrm's brow.

Thoman took the horn, and ran his thumb across the coarseness of its dark red surface. From the moment he touched it, a fire lit inside his breast, twisting his guilt into rage and melding it to his sworn oath until both became irrevocably intertwined with a hatred for the beast that slew his mentor and friend.

CHAPTER 1

MOTES OF DUST DRIFTED THROUGH the sole shaft of light streaming into the cramped shack from a shuttered window, illuminating the dark and cluttered room. Taryn moved with a stubborn determination as she rushed through the rear of her mother's modest home. She passed the old kitchen table and the haphazard pile of dirty dishes and grimy spoons that needed washing from the night before. The young, charcoal-haired girl bore an edge beyond her years, an edge that rusted with disappointment as she watched her mother and sister grow self-consumed in their own affairs. Annoyance hung heavily in her mood already, made worse by the need to escape.

"Where do ya think yer goin'?" Serra, her sister, asked as she stepped through the front door.

She turned and looked back, hiding her anxiety. Being the youngest sister, weeks away from her fifteenth year, it was her responsibility to make sure that the house was taken care of while her mother worked, though she wanted none of it. "Out for a bit," she barked, and instantly regretted the harshness of her tone. "They let me off early from cleaning the bathhouse and I need some air." Her eyes let a fleeting hint of regret slip past before she willed herself into her typically stubborn scowl.

Serra pointed toward the black pot resting in the ash covered and dirty hearth. "Don't forget about dinner, Ma's going to be back soon and I'll be out looking for coin." She shook her head and frowned. "Best be glad I don't need you today, or you'd be out there with me."

"No, I wouldn't." Taryn bit back a harsh retort and cringed inside. After watching her sister Serra get dragged down by her mother, there was no way she would let herself get sucked into wasting her life chasing easy money like they were.

Her sister scoffed. "Yeah, we'll see. Good luck doin' somethin' else." Her smirk faded. "How many times do we gotta say it? Look around ya." She waved her hand toward the door and the world outside. "There ain't nothin' for our kind 'sides what we make of it. Ya can't trust no one but those who've been there. Ain't no one but no one's gonna do nothin'. We're all ya got, 'bout time ya figured that one out and accepted it." She held up a sack, one that likely held a clutch of the dreamseeds she had grown so fond of as of late. "I'll be off for a bit. Don't even think of botherin' me." Serra turned to duck behind the shabby curtain hanging from the ceiling which cordoned off her corner of the room. "Don't forget dinner. I mean it," she barked from behind her wall of cheaply patched fabric.

"Ugh!" Taryn spat out, exasperated. The very nerve of her sister telling her what to do set her on edge. *Like I'm going to end up wasting my life like you and Mom? Doing anything to get a coin with no thought to the future? Not a chance. I'll get out... someday.* She headed for the rear door in the corner and stepped out into the alley.

Dull, yellowed light struck her from the overcast autumn sky. Diffused streams of black smoke swam down from the bathhouse and mixed with the area's veil of waste and refuse, an odor often referred to as the alley's charm, not that it bothered anyone much, save for the occasional patron who wandered too far down Velvet Alley. Taryn squinted up at the oppressive clouds toward the solitary orb hiding overhead and sighed. *At least it's not raining.* She grabbed the rusted latch and closed the door behind her before she turned to head toward the river's side of town. The sun above marked the time as somewhat past midday, allowing her a couple hours to herself before she needed to return.

"Ah, there's the pretty one." A familiar and drunken drawl called out from the side of the home.

Revulsion for the man she knew waited for her mother swamped her. Her shoulders slumped as she turned. "She's still in the field. You'd best get to the bathhouse and clean up before she gets back if you want to see her." As she expected, Donald, one of her mother's many acquaintances, sat leaning against the shack. His leathered skin looked even more pallid and sunken than usual, probably from a late night nursing a bottle, much like the one he coddled in his arm.

The worn, thin dwarf pushed himself upright from the wall and stumbled across the grayed earth toward Taryn. "How 'bout Serra— " His dry, rank breath filtered through his pitted teeth and filthy beard, and carried the bitter stench of someone who had been drinking far too long.

"I said go." She turned, repulsed by the man and nauseous from his rank aura. Taryn cared little for what her mom thought of the man, but she needed to leave before something happened that either of them would regret.

He stumbled forward and reached out to her shoulder to steady himself. His hand squeezed gently as he tried to coax her into staying. "Hold on now," he slurred, "no need ta run off."

Shivers wracked her back as she fought off the bile creeping up her throat. "Don't touch me!" She jerked her shoulder away from his calloused touch and squirmed out of reach. *I think I'm going to be sick.* Taryn ignored his attempts to gain her attention and call her back as she rushed out of the alley. Her heart pounded with every step, measured relief found in each of the rickety shacks she passed. The corner was met with a welcomed sigh as the sight of indifferent strangers throughout the area brought their distractions. The casual conversations and clatter of everyday life helped fight off the worst of the feeling when she turned down the street.

The girl's quick pace brought her near the river as the last vestiges of the man's ghoulish touch faded from thought. The approaching sound of rushing water babbled loudly, and nearly drowned Trent's taunting voice as it rang out from near the bank. Not even the cool, soothing breeze that swept out from the river helped to ease her mood when she heard him. Her ire found a focus when she found the source of his voice. He stood laughing as he tormented two younger boys, brothers who lived outside the alley, near the edge of town.

He grabbed one by the scruff of the neck and held him to the water's edge, threatening to send him in. The other boy sat there, sniffling as he watched his older brother flail helplessly against his much larger opponent. Trent's rounded and freckled face turned to watch Taryn as she came into view. "Lookee here, right in time to watch the little flea swim." His blond locks framed the cold and cruel blue gaze as he teased Roy with a push toward the edge.

What little patience that still clung to her anger disappeared with the motion. "Why do you gotta be such a slag? Leave them alone." Her tone sharpened as she continued walking toward the brutish boy. "Don't you think they suffer enough without havin' to look at your face?"

"Yeah? It's just a bit o' fun." He spouted in defense. "Not like you can stop me."

"Pull him back and we'll see." She stood and drilled a defiant stare into the bully's dull gaze. "Or are you scared that you'll get whooped by a girl?"

His lip curled in a sneer, creasing his face in spite as he stepped forward, shoving Roy toward his younger brother. "Scared o' you?"

Taryn relaxed, glad to see the boy released, and watched as he scampered away before turning back to Trent. Up close, his meaty frame towered over her and sent a shiver of doubt down her arms, filling them with nervous energy. Her cheeks flushed as she drew on the frustration and anger from earlier and swung at his face, hitting it with a resounding smack across his cheek. "*Don't* do that again." She fumed. "Those boys have never hurt anyone; they don't need your trouble."

Trent's eyes shot open with disbelief from the unexpected blow. "You hit me." He lifted a hand to his cheek and touched it. His brow furled in anger as he struck her in a backhanded slap.

The force of the blow pushed her back. A second later pain wracked the side of her face. The rage she felt earlier dimmed compared to what now coursed through her veins. Venom flowed through her eyes and shot seething rage, startling him into a nervous step back. She took advantage of the hesitation and plowed forward, pushing the bully over.

Trent stumbled and landed in a heavy thud on the bank, wheezing as the air got knocked out of him.

A hint of satisfaction spurred her on, and before he could react, Taryn leapt on top of him with her fists clenched and pounded the surprised boy. After the first round of strikes, Trent lowered his guard. She paused as she glared down on him. "Don't you *ever*," she punched Trent in the eye to stress the point, "hit me again! Understand?" She leaned over him and waited for his response.

His arms flew up defensively and tried to push her off, only to have his hands land awkwardly on her chest.

The dimming fires of retribution instantly blazed anew with that ill-placed gesture. She grabbed both hands and pushed them off her and got up, slamming her foot in his gut in the process. Her leg hung poised to strike Trent again when two hands gripped her arms from behind and pulled her back from the bully, who lay on the ground curling from the pain of the assault.

Fear mixed with the anger as she shook off the hands that held her. Taryn's fingers curled into a readied fist as she turned to look at the person holding her.

Jacks stood there, laughing and held his hands up. "Hey! I'm on your side." He looked at Trent and laughed, wincing in sympathy from the pain he was still groaning from.

Relief to see the sole person she counted as a friend there, with her, drained the anger away. "Don't do that!"

"What happened?"

She shrugged. "He was being himself. Again." She looked sheepishly up to Jacks. "And I had a bad day."

"Serra?"

She nodded. "Partly. And Donald. And life."

He winced.

Lee fidgeted, drawing her attention to the boys who still sat nearby, watching.

"Oh! I almost forgot you." She rushed to Roy and Lee and looked them over with a concerned eye. "You two all right?"

Both boys nodded fervently and mutely stared in awe at her.

"Good." Her tone softened as she knelt beside them. "If you see Trent, try to avoid him. And if you can't, let me know he's bothering you two, all right?"

They quickly nodded and stood up to scramble back toward their home.

Jacks watched the brothers run off with a hint of amusement. "Where to, the tree?"

She nodded and moved past Trent to where Jacks stood. Together, they walked along the river to her favorite place to get away from the stresses of Miresbough, and all who lived in the area. The tree was an old growth, one of the few left standing near the town, and provided the perfect amount of shade during midday. It rested on a small knoll overlooking the river and gave Taryn the perfect excuse to lose herself in the comforting sound of its rushing waters and forget her dreary and dismal troubles of everyday life.

Once they settled in their familiar spots at the base of the tree, Jacks leaned his head against the trunk. "Are you going to tell me what happened?"

Her dour mood returned as strong as ever, sinking the tension in her neck. "It feels so hopeless. I want something more for myself." She shuddered. "I love her, but I can't stand seeing Mom go downhill. Working in the fields all day, then coming home to..." Her voice lingered listlessly.

"But she's gotta, right? What else is she gonna do? It's not like there're many choices."

He still doesn't get it. Taryn scowled at Jacks. "I don't care. There's always another way."

He raised his hands defensively. "Hey, we've hashed through this before. Back to Trent. You really gave it to him good." He grinned.

She sighed. "Don't get me started. I just wish I didn't have to."

He peered quizzically. "You wish you didn't have to? You *hate* Trent. He's a creep. It had to feel good to knock some sense into him."

"*Yes,* I hate him, and *yes* he's a creep. Doesn't mean I want to thrash him." Taryn lost herself in the rhythm of the river's mildly turbulent current and watched the babbling waters roll by as a smile crept up her lips. "It *did* feel good, though."

CHAPTER 2

ARYN WALKED IN HER HOME and, for once, was glad to be there and away from the bathhouse. The light from the overcast sky behind her cast the dingy kitchen in a harsh light, illuminating her mother's wiry form as she sat at the table.

"'Bout time you came home."

Her shoulders slumped as she prepared herself for yet another of her mother's demanding tirades. "I was working."

"Not enough. You need to go out with Serra more and pull your weight." In the last year, her mother's eyes had sunk into her skull as her angled features poked out from her emaciated figure, which had grown more pronounced the deeper she fell into her addiction. Even with as gaunt as she had become, her eyes still burned with a vitality and assuredness that was just as strong as the vindictiveness and spite that had grown inside her.

Pull my weight? Taryn gaped in disbelief at the words she was hearing. She was done watching her mother waste away in her perpetual torpor, drooling in her corner and wasting her life away for those blasted seeds. The stench that rose from the corner was unbearable and she was the only one who even cared to clean it. "Maybe if *you* weren't too busy *dreamin'* and spent more time out in the field pulling *your* weight, then we'd *all* be better off."

Anger flashed from the sunken eyes as her mother bolted from her chair, stepped forward, and slapped her. "Don't you *dare* talk to me that way. I brought you into this world and by the gods—" She pointed her finger at Taryn in frustration. "You know them dragon attacks up north are the problem. With none of the northern coin comin' down things aren't as good as they used to be."

"Oh, yes. The rumors of dragons now." She rolled her eyes and tilted her head as she looked at her mother. "Who *couldn't* see how two dragon attacks this last year in remote villages in Arturia, not even the same province, would stop you from working. It makes perfect sense."

Her mother's hand opened and shook for a minute before she relaxed. Her eyes softened as she stepped forward conspiratorially. "But you're missing the point, sweetie." She nodded, smiling and looked out toward the street. "You'd have the world open to you. Just *think* of the freedom you'd have. No one to answer to. Go where you want, when you want. Just livin' the life with Serra. She's got it, ya know. Follow her lead; she'll go places. Just watch." She nodded, her eyes bearing the torch of irrational conviction.

"Never mind that she chews the seeds almost as much as you do." *Why did I even bother coming in?* She was regretting coming back more and more as the conversation wore on.

"Look, this ain't no choice. I bore you through these times and now it's your turn. Get out; I've only a few seeds left and Donald's comin' over."

Finally.

～⚶～

"Ready?" Jacks asked, as he sat bored against the back of the old oak.

"No, I *really* don't want to go back yet." Taryn griped. "Mom's still working, and I don't feel like interrupting." She ran her fingers through her short, black locks while looking out onto the road as it led back into town. She drifted halfway through her fifteenth year and *still* found no hope, no clue on how to escape the fate looming before her. She sighed and looked to her longtime friend.

Jacks leaned over and turned to face Taryn with a mischievous grin. "So, what do you want to do then?"

"To not be home right now." She looked away, glancing down the river and watched the water pass them by. "Mom wants me pilfering the streets with Serra, but I won't."

Jacks shrugged. "Why not? You're good at it."

"It doesn't feel right stealing from people."

"Pah, it's not like they'll catch you. You're good. One of the better shades, if Serra's right."

She shook her head. "I don't care. That's not the point. There has to be a better way."

"Work the fields then. I do." Jacks stared at her, half-listening to what she said.

"I can't. Mom won't let me. She thinks I'll make more money picking pockets with Serra. Besides, I already help to clean the bathhouse. That earns her almost as much as I would out in the fields."

"Then find something else to do."

"Like what? No one wants an alley rat around."

"For starters, *I* have an idea how we can pass the time." He scooted closer and leaned in to Taryn.

"No." She flared as she backed up. *Gods, for once just stop.*

"Why not?" He complained, the perceived insult wore thin in his dull green gaze.

"Look, I just *don't*, all right? We've been friends for years, *please* don't."

"C'mon." He rolled his eyes. "We'll still be friends after this. I mean, really. Besides, Serra has practically thrown herself at me. Why not you?"

"Look, I'm not like my sister. You know this. Just stop, all right?"

Jacks put a hand on Taryn's arm. "You'll like it, I promise." He leaned in with an intent gaze as he puckered his lips.

Taryn's heart started beating faster as his grip tightened. "Look, I said stop!" She pushed him away and started to stand so she could walk home.

"Come back here." He spat out while he grabbed her arm again. "If I had the coin, don't you think I'd see your mom?" He spouted angrily. His tone softened as he drew closer. "You must've known I've always liked you. Now come over here."

Adrenaline kicked in as the threat solidified. "I said I'm not like her. Just because my mom's a whore doesn't mean I am. Now back off!" she demanded, and then punched him in the face. Taryn stepped back as he grabbed his nose. She clenched her other fist, hoping he would come to his senses.

Blood started to seep through his fingers as he looked up in seething hatred. "My nose, you broke it. You–"

She didn't bother to wait for him to complete his sentence as she swung a second time and struck him with an uppercut in the stomach, causing him to bowl over and retch on the dried grass. Rage at the betrayal, and the loss of what she thought had been a good friendship, boiled inside her. "You jerk! I trusted you." Tears streaked down her cheek as the one last and good reason for her to stay had burned to ash. The early evening's shadows stretched over the alley by the time she came home. She waited until Donald walked out of their small shack, and as she watched him stagger away, the cold realization of how alone she truly was sunk into her thoughts. Her choice became clear. She needed to leave.

The sun set long before, and shadows lingered throughout the shack that she, until this night, had called home. Taryn crept to the back door and reached out for the handle. The one assurance she expected to find before she left was gone. The small pouch of coins she set aside for herself had disappeared and she knew who took it. Even with no money, she had to go. Her mother was growing more irrational with each passing day, and she couldn't take her sister's selfish and snide attitude any longer.

"Where are you going?" Serra asked from a shadow.

"Out, away from this place. What's it to you?" She sneered.

Serra placed a hand on the table and braced herself as she stood, then walked to Taryn. Her typically vindictive gaze held a depth of sadness not seen before. "Where to?"

Her mood softened in response to her sister's sorrowed manner. "I don't know. I just need to get out of here." Her frustration and loathing vented as she whispered. "Out of this cesspool of a town."

What little moonlight filtered in from the outside lit her sibling's face, highlighting a new bruise on her cheek as she got closer. Serra sniffed as she composed herself. "Good, you go and make a better life for yourself."

Taryn gazed deep in her sister's eyes, pleading. "You can come with. If you want."

She shook her head. "No. I'm not strong enough. Not like you." Serra placed her hand on the younger girl's shoulder as her lip drifted up into a half-smile. "You've always had the stubbornness to do what you felt right, not like me. I'm too much like Mom." Her eyes swam in guilt, and brightened slightly, breaking her morose demeanor for an instant. "Here, I'll be right back."

The dark bruise revealed in the moonlight further reinforced Taryn's resolve to leave and quelled any doubt she may have entertained. She waited as her sibling crept behind her curtain and came back with something clutched in her hand.

"Take this," she said while handing her a small pouch. "I'm sorry for taking it earlier. I... I took it because I needed the seeds. It's what's left over from earlier. It's not much, but it might buy you some food for a couple days. I'm sorry."

Taryn clasped her hand on Serra's. "Thank you." She was still upset that she took the money, but it made her feel better knowing that there was some amount of remorse from the act. Her eyes misted as realization dawned that she might not see her sister again for years, if ever. She moved in to give her one last embrace before heading back toward the door.

Serra watched as she turned. The look of envy and a sorrowful happiness followed Taryn out the door as she left. "Good luck."

CHAPTER 3

TARYN'S EYES SPRANG OPEN, AND her stomach growled in protest as she shifted to her side. She desperately tried to cling to the rapidly fleeing tendrils of sleep. A yawn forced its way out as hunger pushed those wanted tendrils from her mind. For three days she had traveled and all she thought of was eating the last of the food bought with Serra's money the day before.

The sun fled the night's grasp too long ago to recall, its rhythm refusing the simple mercy of sleep with its various chirps, calls, and rustling from the trees around her. After several unsuccessful attempts at rest, Taryn resigned herself to resuming her journey. She looked out from her improvised perch in one of the trees close to the road and made sure no one lurked about before climbing down.

Once her feet landed on the root-covered ground, she checked to make sure she still carried her only possession, a burlap sack, which held a pouch with three coppers, and crumbs from the last loaf of bread she ate the day before. She headed north again, toward the only place she knew of bearing a decent reputation, Ghendt. Being the capital of the Arturian Kingdom, and home of the Prime Temple of Orn, it represented freedom from the sort of less scrupulous people she had known throughout her life.

After an hour of walking and fighting the beginning of hunger pangs, the dim light of a dying campfire flickered in the distance. Taryn stepped more softly as she drew near the fading light and crept to the outskirt of a camp.

Once there, she found a break in the trees circling a flat of ground where someone partially cleared the bushes to make way for a fire. Off to the side, a horse stood tied to a nearby tree outside the small clearing where a slumbering man wearing a worn set of plate armor sat propped against another tree. Her eyes quickly focused on the one item of note that hung above the far side of the small clearing. A sack was suspended by a sturdy rope, and teased her with the possibility of her next meal.

She followed the rope to where it rested on a nearby tree. Faint snoring drifted from the man, so she kept her steps light as she crept carefully to where it sat tied around a thick and sturdy branch. The convoluted knot constricted the thick cord, securing it in place, and once Taryn thought she loosened it sufficiently, she found her initial efforts only tightened the knot itself.

The glint of the sleeping figure's sword caught her eye. For a moment, she considered using the weapon, but thought better of it. The size and weight would make it too unwieldy and all she would do is wake its owner. She eyed the weapon, unhappy with how close it rested to him. When she turned back to the knot, all she could think about was him waking up. *Coin purses are so much easier than this.* Her frustration gave way to thoughts of hunger as her stomach grumbled loudly, making her flinch from the noise.

After several more attempts, repeated glances, and too many hushed curses, she finally pulled the knot free. Once loose, the rope slid quicker than she anticipated and it nearly flew out of reach if not for her quick reflexes.

"Would you like some help?" came an amused voice from behind her.

Taryn jumped and let go of the rope, sending the bag, and its contents, crashing onto the ground. *How did I not hear him?*

She smiled coyly as she turned around, looking for his sword. "No, thank you."

The man stood much taller than she'd imagined. He moved with a grace she wouldn't expect for someone wearing such heavy armor. Stubble adorned his face and his unruly brown hair needed tending more than he probably cared to admit. He chuckled softly as his gaze followed hers. He sauntered over to pick up his sword and set it behind him near the tree he rested against moments ago. "You know, a knife would work far better."

She anxiously looked around for avenues of escape, and regretted the very idea of trying to steal the man's food in the first place. "You don't say."

The ground crunched softly under the step of his boots as he moved forward and opened his arms peaceably. "Are you hungry?"

Her intimidation and fear instantly flared as he stepped closer. "Don't you dare touch me."

His eyebrows rose at the reaction and he held his hand up reassuringly. "No, I have no intentions of harming you, rest assured." He stepped back slowly, away from the fallen sack of food. "By all means, if you are hungry, have something. Unfortunately, there's only a sparse amount of bread and cheese, and some dried fruit. If you want the food, it's yours. There's also a spare waterskin tied on the horse's pack leaning on the other tree there." He pointed to the tree near where the horse rested.

Taryn hesitantly stepped toward the bag of food and opened it while she watched for any sudden movements. As he said, food rested inside.

"I'm Pallitine Thoman. What's your name?" he asked as she reached inside the bag.

She didn't take her eyes off of him as her hand rummaged through the sack. "You don't look like a pallitine." She sneered. "Aren't they supposed to have shining armor?"

Thoman leaned back against the tree and shrugged. "Not if it's used."

Taryn pulled out a hunk of cheese and grunted doubtfully. *Makes sense, I guess.*

"And your name is?"

She looked warily upon the pallitine as she bit into the cheese, unsure if she should trust him. "Taryn."

"Well met, Taryn. Where are you headed in the middle of the night?"

"North."

Thoman nodded and accepted the answer. "I see. I hope where you are going isn't far." His brow furrowed with concern as he continued. "With you walking and having so little food, it might take quite a while. Depending on where you're going. I'd offer to travel with, but I'm traveling south toward Miresbough for supplies, then to Guardians Keep."

"I am *not* going back to that cesspool." Taryn said firmly.

The pallitine's eyebrows quickly raised. "Miresbough isn't that bad. Is that where you were from?"

She nodded curtly, looking at Thoman as she pulled out a quarter-loaf and broke a piece off. "Velvet Alley."

Comprehension flowed across Thoman's face as she looked up. "I can see why you wouldn't want to go back. I wasn't aware it was populated by those so young."

"I didn't work there," she barked defensively. "My mom does. I just don't want to end up like her, or my sister."

"I take it you're the youngest?"

Taryn nodded reluctantly.

"I'm glad you had the guts to leave. Not many do." He sympathized. "I came from Harker's Row, quite the different area from what you are used to. Other side of Miresbough, literally and figuratively. At least I did until my father died. I moved to the seminary in Millstown shortly thereafter."

"Very different. The men aren't, though."

"Not all men are bad, Taryn." He paused thoughtfully, and after a moment spoke up. "In fact, I know you aren't going south." Thoman sat down next to the tree and leaned against it. "But if you like, you should come with me. I'm only stopping by a shop near the markets on the other side of Harker's Row to get supplies. Once my business is done, I can take you down to stay with some friends near Guardians Keep. They're good people who will make sure you're fed and safe. If you like it, you can stay. If not, I can arrange a ride for you to head north. It may not be exactly what you're looking for, but for now it would provide something Miresbough can't offer, and I fear, the road would be unable to as well." He nestled against the tree to get comfortable. "Think about it. I'll be leaving at first light. If you choose to come, I welcome the company. If not, you will at least have a safe place to rest tonight and some food in your belly." Having spoken his piece, he leaned his head back against the tree and closed his eyes.

Taryn wanted to believe the supposed pallitine. To have found someone who cared more about a stranger than his selfish needs ran against the grain. She mulled the thought over as she looked around the campsite for any signs he wasn't telling the truth. She wasn't comfortable having to rely on someone else; it went against all she'd ever known. Throughout her life she couldn't rely on those around her. The only friend she cared to trust betrayed her. Her mother who once loved her showed little else but a casual disregard, and until she left, her sister grew too concerned for her own needs to give her a second glance. Anger and bitterness engulfed Taryn as she pushed the past out of her heart and stared at the stranger who showed more kindness in the one simple act than the many she'd known for much longer. She sank against the bark of the tree on the far side of the camp as she fell asleep amidst the cacophony of doubt threatening to swallow her thoughts.

Taryn woke with a start at the sound of crackling wood and the sight of Thoman sitting and prodding a pan over the fire. Within a moment, the scent of eggs wafted in her direction. "I thought you said you didn't have any other food?" she accused.

"I didn't. Doesn't mean I can't hunt." He pointed past the trees. "I found a pheasant's nest not far from here. You don't need to bring much food on your journeys if you hunt for what you don't have." He smiled in reply. "There's some roast pheasant that's about ready, and the eggs are nearly done. Would you like some?"

Taryn nodded reluctantly and edged toward the fire. She accepted the tin plate offered and quickly ate the pheasant and eggs. Though it wasn't seasoned, it tasted like one of the best, most succulent meals she had savored in forever. She was not sure why, but a growing trust sparked for the pallitine. She handed the plate back to Thoman and licked her fingers clean.

"Have you decided if you wish to join me?"

Her defenses went up at the thought. "No, I can't," she said regretfully.

Thoman's head lowered at the response. "Fair enough." He started to pack the cooking utensils and clean up the campsite.

Taryn sighed, cursing her inability to trust him, but she needed to trust her initial instincts. "Thank you for your kindness." She started with as she prepared to leave. "It's a rare thing to find in this world."

The pallitine reached into one of his saddlebags and pulled out a sheathed knife. "Here, catch." He called out before throwing the tool in her direction.

She deftly caught the knife and examined it. The weapon sat tucked in a firm, brown leather sheath. She pulled out the blade, and saw a piece of steel unlike any she had seen in her life thus far. "Thank you." She stammered, caught off guard from the unexpected gift.

"If you're to venture out on your own, you'll need at least one tool. Judging your skill with knots, it might serve you well." He quipped, grinning. "Even alley cats need claws."

Taryn couldn't help but smile at the jab made toward her difficulty untying the rope the night before.

"I'll be riding south. However, I fear I've been riding my horse a bit harder these past few days so the going may be slow." Thoman smiled hopefully toward Taryn. "Once we've reached Miresbough and I've had a chance to resupply, he'll be rested enough to continue, I think." He patted his mount after tying the saddlebags in place. "Are you sure you don't wish to join me?"

Taryn offered a quick affirmation and turned to leave before temptation changed her mind. The sound of hooves clattering away sounded within moments after leaving the camp. The fading noise echoed in her thoughts, followed by a flash of regret that welled as the clattering grew faint.

After she hiked a fair distance, realization dawned on her about why she declined Thoman's offer. She needed to make sure she could trust the pallitine and to see if he would let her go. Now that she knew she could trust him, he was gone. She hated to admit her stubbornness, but he made a good point. Ghendt loomed more than a few days away by horse, and even longer on foot. With no food, it seemed hopeless.

Taryn stopped in her tracks and turned around cursing before she rushed off to catch up with the pallitine. She prayed her luck would hold and she could catch up to him before he traveled too far.

After a disheartening hour of following the road, she finally caught sight of the pallitine in the distance. He stopped on the side of the road and was looking in one of the saddlebags on his horse. She drew closer and thought she saw a flicker of movement on both sides of the pallitine, but dismissed it as the shadows playing games with her eyes.

She hastened her pace, glad to finally have him in sight. Once she covered half the distance, he drew away from the horse and stepped into the base of the underbrush, probably to relieve himself. After a moment, a silhouette stepped out of the shadows and came upon him.

She saw Thoman react to the noise behind him and pull out his sword. Fear for this man sped her feet even though she could do little to actually help. She felt helpless being so far away and unable to do anything as she watched the two men bear their swords against one another. Her heart raced as she saw a second shadow come out and flank the pallitine, striking him from behind as the first rogue dropped to the ground after being struck by Thoman's blade.

Fire fueled her legs, burning them from the effort of running as a surge of panic forced her to move faster. She pushed the bleakness of the moment aside and pressed forward in the hope she could get close enough in time to help.

Again, blade clashed against blade as the pallitine fought the new assailant. By the time the second strike rang out, the first highwayman drew himself up on a knee and stumbled toward the trees. Her legs strained from the effort and as she drew near, she found the man leaning against a tree, blood dripping down his side as he gripped a bow, drew an arrow, and pulled the string back to take aim.

Taryn changed direction, rushed to the man, and slammed into him, getting the wind knocked out of her in the process.

The cutthroat yelped in surprise as they tumbled to the ground. The impact set the bow loose, and let the arrow fly off, away from Thoman.

Taryn's breath slammed out of her from the impact. She focused on the ground and gathered her wits in time to find the vagabond lurching forward to push her down. She fell on her back as he leapt on top of her, pressing down on both of her shoulders.

"My, you're a pretty one aintcha?"

Adrenaline surged at the sight of the man looming over her, flooding her with panic. She lifted her legs and kneed the man in his injured side, knocking him off-balance.

He cursed in pain and clutched the wound as more blood streamed out of the gash Thoman gave him earlier.

Enraged, she pounced on him and drew her knife, stabbing him in the shoulder.

The cutthroat cried out and covered his face, trying to defend himself from the girl's rage.

Distraught from the amount of blood coming from the man's wounds, Taryn fell back on her hands, still grasping the blade, and scooted away from him.

"Are you all right?" The strong but soft tone of Thoman's voice called out from behind her.

She stood and turned, sighing in relief at the sight of the pallitine as he stepped away from the second figure who lay slumped and unmoving on the ground. Taryn nodded and pointed to the man as he rocked back and forth, cradling his wounds.

Thoman strode forward and grabbed the vagabond by his shoulder and propped him up. "This didn't go the way you planned, did it?" He turned to Taryn and motioned toward his horse. "Get me the rope from the left saddle bag. We have a prisoner."

Within moments, with the prisoner's wounds tended, a leash secured his bindings and forced him to walk behind them as they traveled to Miresbough.

"You've got some guts." Thoman complimented Taryn as she rode behind him on his horse. "I appreciate you watching my back. Nice work."

"Thanks for not heading straight to town. I wondered if the talk about your tired horse was intentional, but I'm glad you didn't rush."

He shrugged. "I had a feeling."

She looked at the man, and wondered what would be so important as to pull a pallitine so far out of his way. "So what brought you out here?"

"I was to bring a man in for questioning."

"Oh? What'd he do?"

"He belonged to a group called the Absolutionists, and was suspected in a number of activities against the crown."

Taryn frowned. "Who are they?"

"No one to be concerned about. Just a group that takes

Orn's teachings to an extreme, using him as an excuse to pursue whatever goals they have."

"So where is he? Or have you already interrogated him?"

Thoman turned to his side and looked back. "The man managed to get free before I arrived. He murdered his guard and died trying to escape."

"Oh, at least he can't hurt anyone now."

The pallitine nodded. "There is that. I just wish we could've had the chance to get more information out of him before he died."

"To help stop whatever he may have been involved in. That makes sense."

"Indeed."

After a few moments passed, he glanced over his shoulder. "Are you the religious sort by chance? Do you believe a higher power can show us our paths or guide our hands?"

Gods I hope he isn't trying to convert me. "Not really. I believe in the gods, but I'm not what you'd call overly religious. As long as you know who you are and treat people as you'd want to be, that should be enough, right?"

Thoman surveyed the area ahead, past the trees to the fields beyond as they rode. "I'm not particularly religious either. As far as that being enough, perhaps. But that's a different debate entirely."

"As far as destiny goes, we make our own. I haven't seen anything to think other powers guide us. Only petty greed."

Thoman nodded as he turned to look back. "And for many, you're absolutely right. Just don't discount the true of heart. There are many who desire good for the world." He turned back to watch the road as the horse trotted toward Miresbough. "Once, there was a time when I'd also doubted we could be steered by fate. It's not until the one time out of many, when you least expect it, that you feel fate has pushed you to a specific course for a specific purpose. That's when it strikes."

Taryn grew curious at the confidence behind the words.

"And you've felt this?"

With absolute certainty, Thoman nodded. "Yes. Yes, I have."

Taryn grew silent, unsure of what to say, and watched the countryside pass her by as they rode back to the place she worked so hard to escape.

"Can I ask you something else, Taryn?"

"Sure," she answered, curious again about where the question led.

"Do you always fight so fiercely? I don't think he stood a chance against you," he asked, voicing his obvious amusement at their prisoner's predicament.

Taryn laughed self-consciously, and agreed. "I've been known to stand my ground for what I want."

"Excellent, glad to hear it. Steadfastness, valor, and ability are great assets in an apprentice."

CHAPTER 4

THE TREES GRADUALLY BROKE AS the two rode toward a small village that gave way to a keep in the distance. The village was simple, uniform in its rugged Tramirian charm, with heavily accented doorways and eaves. Where it lacked in the gaudier showmanship prevalent in the nicer parts of Miresbough, it reflected a warmer quality, rich in simple, but personal touches. Villagers dotted the various farms along the landscape, and milled along the main street going about their business. The single building that stuck out from the blanket of quaint uniformity was the blacksmith's shack, and even this shack held a charm she wasn't used to, aside from the familiar sight of an apprentice nursing a bottle barely out of sight from the forge.

In the week since they dropped off their prisoner, Thoman showed a genuine interest in Taryn. While disarming, it set her on guard with how willing he was to help her. She was unfamiliar with being around a person who had no apparent ulterior motive. As the days progressed, a cautious respect grew for this man who showed an interest in her future. The thought of being given a chance to be apprenticed to him, to one day become a pallitine herself, seemed foreign to her. She liked the idea of being trained to protect not only herself, but others. These ideas, however, clashed with the uncertainty of what to expect and filled her with unease that made her wonder if this was really happening at all. *If nothing else*, she figured, *I'll have some warm food and a roof over my head for a while.*

As soon as they drew nearer to the village, she felt her familiar defenses spring back into place. Her muscles tensed as much from the unfamiliarity of these people as it did from her instincts for self-preservation.

Thoman turned his head to the side and spoke. "This, Taryn, is Durston. The people here are kind and true. Much different, I believe, from what you've been used to."

She nodded while looking around the area and up ahead to their destination, the keep that was looming ever closer.

Guardians Keep stood as a monument to the will and perseverance of the Tramirian people. Constructed some three hundred years earlier, it was built from large granite blocks mined from the Untarian mountain range. The keep had the distinction of being built from a vein of granite with rich streaks of dark basalt running through it, which gave the otherwise gray exterior a subtle marbleized tone. Stretching two stories high, its ceilings loomed over the tallest of men. Two towers flanked the keep, and jutted from the keep's southern wall, one each on the eastern and western corners. Both towers provided not only a fine view of the area, but allowed a defensive edge as well.

Since the keep's creation during the Old Wars, when the Irline mages and druids banded with Tramire to fight the Saerinian clans, Durston had cropped up around its perimeter. In the last century, the village had greatly prospered under the care of the pallitine's guidance and protection. Several farms dotted the landscape, with a chapel, an open-air market, and a handful of homes that rested nearby.

"This here," Thoman started with a hint of pride in his words, "is Guardians Keep. This is my home, along with several other pallitines. It serves to house the Tramirian High Pallitine and acts as one of the places where we train some of the more aspiring squires who wish to one day join the order. In the past it's served as a barracks as well as a home for the Orn priesthood. For now, however, it will be a place you can call home." He glanced behind him. "Assuming you still wish to learn our ways."

Taryn was caught off guard with the question and nodded, surprised by her quick answer. "Yes, I would."

A smile broke out across Thoman's unshaven face. "Good. If you do change your mind in the coming weeks, however, we have a home for you." He pointed across the land to a farm which rested along the far side of the stone structure they neared. "The Almsfords are good, grounded people who have helped the keep on similar occasions in the past."

The uneasy distrust she felt still clung to her breast. She kept quiet and looked apprehensively at the surrounding community. The concept of kindness and genuineness that matched his in such a wide area seemed unthinkable, and forced her to peer skeptically at everything around her. She found herself clinging guardedly to the pallitine's back as they rode to the keep's stables and only after Thoman's gentle prodding did she dismount once they came to a stop.

Thoman handed the reins to a stable boy who ran up as they arrived. The boy was followed by a mangy, but energetic dog whose shaggy fur curled over both eyes, nearly masking them completely. He was a lean, but wild breed, the kind often seen in the lowlands. But this one was much friendlier than most. The dog ran up to Taryn, and sniffed her in curiosity while his tongue lolled out lazily.

Taryn laughed at the humorous sight and knelt down to scratch him behind his ruddy brown ears until he nipped at her hand and rolled on his back.

"I see you've met Asher." Thoman leaned down to pat the dog's belly and growled playfully at the mongrel. "He adopted us a few seasons back. Apparently he likes it here."

The display amused the girl, and helped her to relax in the unfamiliar territory. She smiled as Thoman patted the beast farewell. *There are worse things to walk into.* She walked alongside the pallitine and admired the keep in its sturdy, but simple glory until they came to a set of wide stone stairs that led to an open terrace overlooking the back of the keep and connected to the rear entrance.

The thick wooden doors leading inside the keep were bolted together in grand, stained bands of iron which spoke of a strength and determination not seen in the simple ramshackle buildings along Velvet Alley. The ominous doors creaked as they opened up to a wide corridor which seemed to invite her in with its warmth and quaint charm. The floors were stone, smooth from heavy use and led forward into the keep. The hall was sparsely decorated with banners depicting the symbols of the Order of Guardians and was flanked by another set of smaller doors.

She watched Thoman as he led the way in, and took a nervous step into the cold stone of the keep's hall before her. The air quickly warmed as she moved closer to their destination several feet ahead.

One of the doors to the side was open, and echoed a bright, orange light that flickered with movement as activity bustled from within.

The inviting smell of cooked meat and freshly baked bread wafted her way as she followed Thoman. Taryn cautiously followed the pallitine as he knocked and then led the way through the door. She found that the room held the kitchen and preparation area for the keep. A plump and commanding woman stood with her back to the door as they entered, and spat orders out to two helpers. She was standing by a table with a thick top and scored with a myriad of marks from heavy use. Two fire pits were set in the kitchen's thick walls, one with a lamb skewered on a spit, roasting, while the other hosted a large cauldron tended to by one of the helpers.

"What can I help you with today, Thoman?" the woman

PALLITINE RISING

asked while bringing her knife to bear on a row of carrots she was dicing for the meal being prepared.

Thoman looked reassuringly toward Taryn. "I've brought someone in who might be able to provide some assistance while she acclimates to the keep. I thought you the perfect person to help her get used to our way of life and to show her around. If you've the time, of course."

The cook turned, wiped her sweaty brow with her sleeve, and set her knife down to look Taryn over. "This waif?" A kind wisdom radiated from her welcoming eyes, accenting the mischievous smile she wore.

Taryn looked up at Thoman, her eyes filling with concern.

The pallitine's face broke in a comforting smile. "Taryn, this is Bea. I've trusted her for many years. I have needs to attend to for the moment, but she will show you around and help while you settle in. I'll be by later to make sure you're doing all right."

Terror struck Taryn's heart as she nodded mutely.

Bea walked toward Taryn in a steady, but slow gait as she wiped her hands on her apron. "Is she to be one of our new helpers?" Her voice carried a gentility not present when they first arrived.

"While she is learning our ways and between lessons, of course."

The woman looked at Thoman with a narrowed curiosity. "She'll follow the pallitine's path?"

He nodded. "Yes. I have chosen her to be my apprentice."

The cook let out a grunt of appreciation. "I see. I'll be sure to keep an eye out for her."

Confusion settled into Taryn's limbs as she watched the exchange.

"Bea will take good care of you." The pallitine reassured, smiling as she fidgeted nervously. "I promise."

Taryn nodded and watched her one anchor of trust turn to leave. *What am I doing?* Dread filled her as she watched the pallitine disappear. She glanced back to the welcoming face of the kitchen's matron, then back down the hall. *I should never have come. I don't belong here.* She chewed on a fingernail as she looked past the matron then out the window to the world outside.

"Well then, it looks like you've done something to impress our friend." Bea observed. "It's quite unusual to be chosen so unexpectedly, much less have one like him take responsibility so quickly. Unusual indeed." She nodded while looking Taryn over. She turned to look to where the girl's eyes tracked and smiled.

The girl nodded as she listened, growing nervous in an unfamiliar room, and wrapped her arms around herself.

"Here," she smiled. "Let me show you around." Bea gave some instructions to her helpers before guiding the young woman out of the kitchen.

The older woman walked patiently with Taryn as she looked about the keep. Curious respect and admiration dwarfed her cautious and hesitant manner, replacing it in this world which struck her as drastically different from anything that she had seen while growing up.

Curious, but respectful greetings were given from the few people they encountered, both staff and pallitines alike had shown a warm attitude in greeting the new arrival. Bea had shown her around the grounds, to the stables, the common areas, and casually mentioned the upper areas of the keep as areas she would grow familiar with once she was further along in her apprenticeship, since they housed the quarters for the steward and pallitines, as well as the main office for the High Pallitine.

"Tell me about yourself. Where do you come from?" Bea asked as they walked past the training circle where two men clashed as they swung their swords at one another while they trained.

Taryn turned from the stables they were heading toward and looked at her guide. "Miresbough."

"Oh, where Thoman was raised," the older woman observed

Taryn half-listened as she looked about the area with an anxious curiosity.

The keep, which rested on a broad hilltop, was well tended

and carried a feeling of industrious humility. Almost everyone she met carried themselves purposefully as they all moved about the keep, each doing their part to keep things in order.

The kitchen's matron looked out with a subdued amusement. "Oh, to see everything fresh and new. Enjoy this time, the newness. It will fade before you know it." An eyebrow arched in a friendly, but curious manner. "In any case, what brought you here from your home in Miresbough?"

Apprehension tensed Taryn's steps as they continued to the front of the keep, which presented a nice view of the main village. She was caught between an unwillingness to speak and an uncertainty of what to say. Eventually she spoke as they neared the keep's front entrance. "I needed to get away."

"You don't need to say more if you don't wish. I trust Thoman's judgment. I'm sure he's already cleared whatever story you told him," she stated in a soft, but insightful tone.

The young woman stopped her in tracks, her eyes went wide as it hadn't even occurred to her that she would have been doubted at her word.

"You don't think we take in *every* stray we come across, do you?" Bea turned toward the uncertain girl before her. "Tell me, I'm sure you stopped somewhere right? Maybe spent some time in town?"

Taryn cautiously confirmed the question. "We spend the night in Miresbough. I stayed at an inn and had supper while Thoman brought a man in that tried to rob him."

"I would wager that's when he checked into your story then. He's been around long enough to weed out falsehoods and has many contacts."

She followed the matron while they headed toward the far side of the keep which revealed two gardens. A new sense of appreciation dawned for the trouble Thoman took when they met. While he was trusting and accepting of her, he still was cautious enough to make sure everything was as she said it would be. A part of her felt annoyed and betrayed that he didn't trust her, but she soon realized that she likely would have done the same. Somehow, simply knowing that he took the time to make sure that her story was legitimate gave her a measure of begrudging reassurance.

They walked around to the rear of the keep and meandered back inside. After a turn past the kitchen, they stopped. "This," Bea opened a door near the staff's quarters, "is where you will be staying."

Taryn looked into the comfortable, simply-furnished room and found four beds, two along each side, two desks along the far wall, and a table in the middle. A simple footlocker rested near the head of each of the beds and a small fireplace sat along the wall between two of the beds.

Standing near one of the beds was a tallish boy, barely older than Taryn, who looked up from his footlocker as the two walked in.

"Taryn, this is Arden," Bea started off. "Another recent arrival to our home."

Arden nodded as his face broke in a warm smile. "Hello." His green eyes bore a hint of blue as they held Taryn's gaze. Honey-wheat hair flanked his sturdy, but handsome face. What little light filtered in from the narrow window between the desks seemed brighter as Taryn looked up from the older boy's squared jaw, past the firm lips still curled with a boyish charm, to those warm eyes that teased of something guarded behind the inviting gaze.

A gentle hand settled on Taryn's shoulder and broke her attention as she shied away from the contact.

"This is where the apprentices stay. You'll take one of the empty beds along the wall there, and the boys will stay along these beds here."

Taryn looked again at the suddenly cramped and uninviting room and found the walls too close together for her comfort. Her worried gaze shot back to the kitchen's matron. "I'm to share a room with them?"

Bea turned a serious eye toward the girl as she backed up toward the door. "Don't worry; nothing untoward will happen here. You're safe within these halls," she reassured gently. "Why don't you get settled in here, and get to know your fellow apprentice?" The matron's brow furrowed as she looked back into the hall. "Where's Maddoc, Arden? Have you seen him?"

The light-haired youth snapped to attention and looked at their elder. "Yes, ma'am. I met him for a moment, and he said he had a matter to attend."

The matron let out a skeptical "Hmph" and turned back to the new arrival. "Are you going to be okay here, while I let our steward know you've arrived?"

Taryn nodded briefly and looked gruffly toward the other apprentice, trying to show more confidence than she felt. "I'll be fine."

"Good." Bea stepped forward and set a hand on her shoulder, squeezing gently. "I'm glad you came. Let me know if you need anything. Understand?"

"Thanks." She smiled awkwardly as she watched the matron leave and head down the hall.

"Your name is Taryn, right?"

She nearly jumped as the boy's voice pulled her out of her thoughts. She flicked her gaze back toward the boy who was now stepping toward her. Her instincts kicked in as she stepped back away from him and toward the door. "Yes."

Arden stopped in his tracks and looked curiously at her. "It's all right. I'm not here to hurt you."

"Sorry," she mumbled and glanced at the beds behind her. "I'm not used to this place yet." She took stock of the room and only now noticed a couple of simple, faded tapestries which flanked the narrow window looking outside. A worn rug covered the center of the floor, under the sole table sitting in the middle of the room, its edges ragged from years of traffic over the surface. The room was a far cry from anything she'd ever seen, much less could call home.

"Where are you from, then?" He asked.

"Miresbough." Her voice came out softer than intended.

She spoke with more confidence as her guard came up. "You?"

The boy pulled out a chair from the table and sat down. "I lived on a farm outside of Elmsvale, near the pact-lands. I was presented to the district pallitine there by Father Trevin last fall, when I hit my sixteenth birthday. When my parents consented, I was accepted as an apprentice." His eyes lit up with an eagerness that caught Taryn off guard. "I can't wait to start training. To work *his* will. I've been imagining this for so long."

Taryn set the burlap sack she had still clung to on the bed nearest the door on her side. She was about to respond when another figure stepped through the doorway.

Another tall boy, this one looking older than either of them, stepped into the room and scowled when he looked at Taryn. He had broad shoulders, and short brown hair. His sharp nose hooked down above his thin lips which were now turned down in a frown. "Another newcomer?" He turned toward his bed and plopped himself on it. "I was hoping it was a joke." He grabbed a sack out from the top of his footlocker and pulled out a stack of playing cards, dealing himself a round of some game he didn't care to share.

"And that, Taryn, is Maddoc." Arden laughed to himself as he looked over his shoulder. "Not the warmest person. Personally, I think he liked being the only apprentice around." He turned back around. "I don't care what he thinks. I can't wait to start training and to be assigned to a pallitine once I'm done with the preliminaries."

Taryn's heart sank as she looked at the other apprentice. "Assigned?"

He nodded and leaned back in his chair. "Of course. After a few seasons we're assigned a pallitine to train us in our our duties outside of the keep. Though, with you, it might take a bit longer. Being..." he mulled over his thoughts before settling an internal dispute, "a younger woman, it might be a bit longer to be assigned to a pallitine."

Panic set in as she stepped forward and gripped the back of one of the chairs near the table. "But," she started off, "Thoman said he would train me."

Maddoc choked and looked up from his cards. "The district pallitine said he would train you? A girl? Personally?"

"Thoman did, yes." She nodded after a brief hesitation.

Arden's eye narrowed as he stared at Taryn. "Thoman *is* the district pallitine." He quickly adopted his warmer manner and leaned forward. "For someone who is certain of who is training her, you sure don't know much about the man himself."

"How do *you* rank? Flutter your eyelashes and he falls to your charm?" Maddoc asked incredulously. "I've been here nearly two years and have only recently been assigned a mentor." He threw his cards on the bed and glared at Taryn with righteous jealousy.

"I —" She said, exasperated.

"No, stop. I don't want to hear it." He looked down at his cards and picked them up, turning his back to the room.

She turned to Arden, dumbfounded at the reaction. "What did *I* do?" Shock at such a blatant affront left a bitter taste in her mouth. *What an ass!*

"Oh, don't worry about him. He was just as sour to me when I came in earlier." He smirked. "Although, the question does have *some* merit. How *did* you impress the district pallitine?" He look thoughtfully across the table at her.

Taryn, still on edge from Maddoc's outburst, fumed at the comment and the insinuated meaning behind it. Her knuckles whitened as she clenched the back of the chair.

"Oh, no. You misunderstand me." He waved a hand as he smoothly went on. "What I mean to say is, you and I are going to be *very* good friends, because *I* need all of the help I can get." He flashed a deprecating, if not disarming smile. "And if you're good enough to gain the district pallitine's attention, then I have *much* to learn from you." He nodded seriously.

Taryn looked dubiously at Arden. His boyish charm and

apologetic words had dulled the edge of her anger and brought the barest hint of a smile creeping along her lips.

A knock rang out from the doorway, distracting from the conflict of her lingering anger and the disarming wisps of Arden's light demeanor. Taryn turned and found Thoman standing in the doorway. "Thoman!" She smiled and was surprised at how glad she was to find the man who brought her to the keep standing in the doorway.

The two boys immediately composed themselves and stood, showing proper respect.

Thoman quickly raised a hand to reassure the boys. "Relax. I'm not here in any official capacity. I'm just checking on our newest apprentice and seeing how she is settling in here." He turned to his apprentice. "Do you have a moment?"

Relieved to have an excuse to leave, she quickly agreed. "Of course."

Their steps echoed gently down the stone hall as Thoman led the way through the keep. "How are you doing?"

She looked at the plaques hanging on the stone wall between time-washed tapestries depicting heroics from tales she had never heard. After a few steps, she shrugged. "Fine."

He nodded. "Good. I understand you are not the only apprentice to enter the ranks today. What's your take on him; Arden, isn't it?"

"He seems nice enough. Sure of himself, but friendly. Not like Maddoc." She frowned at the thought of the earlier outburst.

"Ahh, yes. He has a hard time adapting to change. He's been through some rough patches. Give him time; he'll warm up to you."

Taryn snorted in disbelief.

Thoman stopped in his tracks and looked down at her. "Seriously, give him a chance. Don't let a bad first impression get in the way of camaraderie. Okay? After all, the three of you will be spending a lot of time together in your lessons; far better to learn to get along now, than to bicker for the foreseeable future."

Arden's earlier words swept to the forefront of her mind, bringing back her worries. "You won't be training me?"

Gentle compassion pulled Thoman's lips up as he looked Taryn in the eyes. "I promised you I would take care of your training, and that still holds true. I will be around, but first there are other things that I must attend to while you are taught by the brothers and other pallitines here."

"What other things?" Disappointment loomed as she asked the words.

"You've heard of the dragon attacks in the northern villages in Arturia, right?" He watched her reaction, and continued when she nodded. "I have some friends trying to track the wyrm now. This creature has a habit of raiding villages for a few months, then disappearing for years at a time. I've enlisted some help on finding the beast and stopping it."

Taryn gritted her jaw and looked down on the floor. "I see."

"Don't get discouraged, Taryn. There are lessons needing to be taught by those better skilled than I, but you will still see me until I can formally take over the more serious aspects of your training."

"So, I need to learn the basics before you can start." Her spirits lifted as she looked back up to Thoman.

The pallitine's smile filled her with confidence as he replied. "That's a good way to look at it."

"Good." Her movements grew more determined as they resumed their pace. She might have to get used to the other apprentices, but now she had a goal to work toward. Now, she had a chance to prove the faith placed in her was justified. To prove to herself that she was right in leaving Miresbough and the bleak life looming over her there. To forge her own path, needing no one but the man who took her in until her training was done. And just maybe, she could help those who can't help themselves in the process.

CHAPTER 5

TARYN OPENED THE DOOR OUT of the keep and sighed. The morning spent in the scullery had been more arduous than she expected. Though her hands were sore, she found the honest labor more rewarding, though less exciting than spending a day with her sister parting people from their hard-earned coin.

The balcony still rested in the day's shadow, clinging to the scattered patches of damp stone left from the night's drizzle. She breathed in the faint smell of damp earth and vegetation that still clung to the area and took in her surroundings. The blue sky hung invitingly overhead. She looked up and entertained the thought of falling asleep in the fields under the warm sun. While her room was cleaner and more comfortable than what she knew throughout her life, her sleep felt scattered and short-lived. The fresh straw in the bed held a soothing warmth, but even with that, she spent most of the night listening to the boys snoring and stirring. What little sleep she did manage to get lasted no longer than mere moments at a time in a room where she didn't feel comfortable. She knew in her mind she was safe, but the instincts she developed over her life in Velvet Alley took over and refused to let her get the rest she so desperately needed.

She leaned wearily in the doorway near the kitchen and watched two pallitines fighting below her in the training circle, envisioning herself wielding a sword and how she would counter the onslaught of her imagined foes. Watching the men fighting ignited a fire within herself, a need to prove herself in the life that presented itself to her. This need was further bolstered by being mistaken for a new scullery maid instead of an apprentice more than once earlier in the morning. She needed to prove not only that she belonged, but that she could protect herself, and others when the time warranted.

As the moments crept on, her thoughts drifted to Arden, and those warm green eyes which held his charming smile.

"Quite the sight, don't you think?" Bea's sharp, but gentle voice called out from behind her, jolting her out of her thoughts.

"Pardon?" Taryn blinked as she turned around and pulled herself out of her thoughts.

Bea waved a hand toward the men fighting. "The strapping young men, swinging their swords with naught but a bit of cloth between their bodies and the steel they swing at one another."

Taryn nodded absently and turned back to the fight.

"My favorite part's comin' up soon." The matron's voice drew down to a whisper. "When they're done, they'll pull off their shirts and wash up in the trough near the ring. Quite the sight." A subtle giddiness slipped in her voice.

The apprentice turned and looked questioningly at her elder, who winked slyly.

"What, just because I'm older than you doesn't mean I'm dead." She laughed. "Now go on, get ready. It's time for you to meet up with Thoman isn't it?" Bea scolded the young woman and watched her go back to her room before she took up Taryn's roost in the doorway.

Once she was ready to meet with the District Pallitine, Taryn headed toward the eastern gathering room near the foyer.

Thoman was sitting there, dressed in gray pants and a dull green doublet that stretched below his waist, reading a thick and aged tome. Somehow he looked more impressive out of his armor, even with how humbly he dressed. His toned muscles shifted as he moved, and seemed to contradict the gentle and warm attitude he carried since the day they met. The friendly eyes, while relaxed, still possessed their sense of vitality, as if he were ready to react at any moment. He looked up at Taryn and set his book on the small, round table next to him. "Ahh, there you are." He smiled. "You look tired, rough first night?"

Taryn sank into the sturdy, cushioned chair next to him. She nodded. "I'm not used to being in the same room with boys. It's... unsettling."

Thoman nodded. "I can imagine. Unfortunately we have no other accommodations. That is the only room we have for our apprentices. You'll get used to it in time," he replied apologetically.

She nodded and looked around the spacious room. She was not used to the keep's simple elegance and wondered how Thoman could feel so at ease here when he seemed equally as comfortable sleeping on the ground under the stars.

"How has everything else gone? I trust Bea has been helpful?"

Taryn nodded. "She's been the one grace so far." She paused and looked up to her mentor. "I can honestly say I've never seen anyone like her." Her lips pulled up in a smile as she thought of her interactions only a short while ago.

"She has a good heart, and a sharp insight about her."

"I haven't see the others since breakfast, though. So, yes, the day is going well. It will be better once I can get some sleep." Her smile receded as it gave way to the shroud of exhaustion floating about her.

"They're out, working their assigned tasks. They'll be done soon enough. For you, however, there is the matter of meeting your instructor while you're here." He stood and turned toward the exit.

Taryn quickly followed suit, anxiety dripping through her tired bones. The nervous energy met with stirrings of anticipation Taryn only now realized she possessed. Trust started to settle in that there was no axe waiting to fall, no deception to be uncovered, and that's what put her on edge. It was easy for her to deal with deception at every turn; it was what she was used to. Here, however, there was none and she had not yet learned how to deal with that. As unsure as she was about being in such a new environment, she felt just as eager to learn what she needed so she could move on. She appreciated everything that Thoman was doing for her, but lacked the words to properly express the feeling. "What will I be learning here?"

Thoman shrugged. "It depends, really. I'd imagine he'd start by working with you directly and see where you're at and what basics need to be worked on with you alone, and what you can learn with the others."

She stopped in her tracks. "Alone?" Her eyes drifted up markedly toward Thoman.

He nodded, and set a hand on her shoulder with a soft, reassuring squeeze. "Yes, but don't worry, Brother Hendrick is a good man. Truly, no one here will seek you any harm."

Hesitantly, she continued moving forward with her mentor.

Within a few moments, they came to a small library where a man sat next to an unadorned table in the corner. He wore a simple, plain brown robe where even the patches mending the aged fabric had been sewn in a straight and orderly fashion. His countenance held the confidence of certainty and hosted a subtle lack of social politeness. An eyebrow arched as the two entered. His pursed lips parted. "And this must be our other newcomer," he observed.

Thoman nodded. "This is she." He turned to Taryn. "You're in good hands." He looked her in the eyes with an approving nod. "I'm glad you're here. You'll do well." He turned back to the brother and nodded before leaving.

"Now that the farewells are done with, please, have a seat."

He turned in his seat to better face the student. He waited until she sat down before looking her over. "Before your tutoring can begin, I need to know a few things. First thing, can you read?"

Taryn nodded reluctantly. "A bit. One of my mom's… friends taught me when he hung around a couple of years ago."

"I see. Well, that will help make things easier." He held up a small piece of wood wrapped slate and a stick of chalk. "Let's see what else you know, shall we?"

Taryn stepped out of the keep and looked toward the stables to where the boys were to meet with Maddoc's mentor, Pallitine Harrold. Her stride held the newfound confidence from the time spent with Brother Hendrick. She wasn't sure what to make of him at first, but once she was used to his matter-of-fact manner, a fond respect grew for the man. It also didn't hurt that while she didn't have any formal education, she still managed to impress him with her ability to learn quickly. More than once he commented on her aptitude and keen insight.

The next lesson, however, was one she wasn't as confident about. She had always wanted to ride on a horse, but life in the Velvet Alley never gave her a chance to ride one. She eagerly wanted to learn, and now that she tasted success from earlier, she needed to see how far she could push herself.   W i t h enough effort, maybe she *could* prove herself and show that she had what it took after all. She was thankful that both Arden and Pallitine Harrold took the time to give her a few pointers earlier in the morning, since she knew nothing about how to handle a horse, aside from what little she gleaned from watching others ride in Miresbough.

"And there's our last one." The bright-faced Pallitine Harrold called out as she approached. "I'll be back. There are some supplies I need to get before we set out." He turned and pointed toward the stable. "Go ahead and wait there. Maddoc will point out which horse is yours and when I'm back, I'll get you started."

Taryn thanked the pallitine and headed toward the stables as instructed. Within moments, she saw Arden tending to one of the mounts while Maddoc messed with a saddle's buckle on another. She stopped next to the horse and admired the sleek, strong beast before her. "Nice horse. Which one's mine?"

"This one." He stood up quickly and stepped back.

"Oh, what were you doing there?" She asked.

He scowled. "Checking the saddle, I saw Arden playing with it and I wanted to make sure it's secure."

Taryn's eyes rolled at the jab. *Not this again.* "So, is it fine?"

He nodded. "It should be."

"Good." She stood anxiously next to the large beast and traced her hand along its strong neck.

"You've never ridden before, have you?"

She shook her head. "Not once."

He stepped to the side and pointed to a leather stirrup hanging off the side of the saddle. "First, you'll want to put your foot there —"

Arden came around the side of the horse and grinned at Taryn. "Hey, I thought I heard you over here."

Maddoc's scowl returned in full force as he stopped speaking and glared at the interruption.

She smiled at the newcomer. "I just got here. Maddoc was showing me how to get on the horse."

He laughed. "Him? Naw, here, allow me. I can show you everything you'll ever need to know." He strode forward and confidently brushed the horse's mane.

She turned and looked to the older boy apologetically and watched him leave in frustration.

"See? He's fine with it."

After two miserably failed attempts at mounting her horse, she finally made it on top with some help and advice from

Arden, and only a minor amount of laughter at her expense.

Once everyone settled on their horses, and Pallitine Harrold returned with a knapsack of supplies, the pallitine climbed atop his own mount and trotted in front of the apprentices. The pallitine had a pedestrian appeal to him; his manner was nothing but approachable and the warm smile under his brown locks held a disarming charm. He addressed the students in a confident and authoritative tone. "As you know, you're here to show me how well you handle your mounts." He turned to Taryn. "How are you doing? Are you ready for your first ride?"

The pang of being the center of attention hit as everyone turned to hear her reply. She nodded meekly.

"Not a problem." He smiled. "We all began somewhere. Just remember what was taught to you earlier and you'll be riding with the best of us before long." He turned back to address them as a group. "It also doesn't hurt that this provides the perfect excuse to get out of the keep," he commented slyly. "Maddoc, lead the way. Let's go to the northern edge of the village."

Maddoc gripped his reins, nudged his mount on, and darted out in front to lead the way off the keep grounds, followed closely by Arden.

Taryn kept a close watch on the others and tried to follow suit, but had a hard time getting the horse to move.

The pallitine chuckled and sidled up to her. "Here, let me show you."

After a moment of instruction and reassurance that she was doing well, he trotted ahead to catch up with the others.

Once Taryn figured out how to get started, she was surprised at how responsive her horse was to her commands. Within moments, she figured out how the horse responded to the slightest pull of the reins and she grew confident at her command of the beast. She sighed once it dawned on her how far back she had fallen behind.

She urged the horse on and instantly it was galloping to catch up with the others. Wind slapped her face, catching her off guard, and whipped her hair back. Once the initial fright and shock passed, the feel of wind rushing by filled her with an exhilaration and newness that consumed her senses. Her legs tensed as she bounced in the firm leather saddle, acclimating to the rhythmic movement on her living throne. The new view filled her heart with respect for the vantage gained as she sat alone atop the glorious creature. The rhythmic cadence of the horse's hooves clapping on the ground brought about a heightened sense of pace, as if both she and the horse were pushed by the wind to move ever forward, toward her goal. When she finally drew close, Taryn pulled gently on the reins and the creature responded smoothly, stopping near the others.

The rush from the ride still fed her blood and she reveled in the feeling of being swept away on top of the powerful beast. She caressed the horse's neck, appreciating the slickness of the coat in contrast to the coarse hair of the mane itself. The world beamed around her, and she saw possibilities for the first time, possibilities that proved elusive from her view on the ground below.

"If I didn't know better," the pallitine admired, "I'd say you were lying about not riding before."

Taryn couldn't help but smile as she stroked the side of her mount's neck. "This is wonderful. I don't want to stop."

"And you won't have to. In fact, why don't you take the lead." He looked down the road to where the forest met the edge of the village. "Since today's jaunt is going to be short, why don't you head down to the edge of the forest, and we'll be behind you. Just take it nice and easy."

Taryn's heart skipped a beat in anticipation. She was eager to start again, and before it registered what she was doing, she tugged on the reins and the horse followed her lead, and rushed ahead.

Again, the world came alive with the wind as it caressed her skin and flew through her hair. The sheer joy of movement, of freedom, filled her senses as the ground below whipped past her and her mount while they rushed ever closer to the trees. A sharp call from behind her urged her to turn back and look. Behind her, Arden and their pallitine tutor called out to her, their hands raised and motioning as their mounts galloped hard. The sharp cry of her mount's startled whinny drew her eyes forward.

A large wolf stood in her path, its hackles risen and a deep growl grated from its throat. The creature's murky brown fur was sparse, leaving raw, blistering patches splattered along its flank. Its mouth sat open, dripping rivulets the color of dead blood, the deepest of crimson, which poured out in thick strands that clung to its jaw.

Her horse skid to a halt and to the side as the wolf shot out from its menacing stance. The momentum pushed Taryn forward and out of the saddle, throwing her on the ground in a sharp crack with one foot still in a stirrup, twisted in its leathery grip.

The wolf, sensing the fear, leapt at the larger beast, which started to panic and tried to run as the wild-eyed attacker tore at its hind-quarters, ripping the flesh with a barrage of claws and bites.

The horse stumbled under the assault and dragged Taryn with its panicked rush as it carried her along the ground until it stumbled and fell several yards away. Sharp rocks tore into her pants and shirt as the road grated against her skin, scratching it as she tried unsuccessfully to stop her head from pounding on the ground until the beast fell.

Her nostrils filled with the acrid odor of blood and dust as she coughed and struggled to gain her bearings and recover from being dragged across the rough road. She tried to pull her foot out from the stirrup it was caught in and cried out from the effort. The pain from the fall and her ankle twisting when the horse jolted away made moving unbearable, but the sight of the beast tearing into the horse's flesh barely more than an arm's length away gave her all the motivation she needed to get away. With a muffled grunt, she finally pulled her foot free and looked up to find the wolf locking its wild gaze on her with a ferocious, insatiable hunger.

Fear set in, hitting her in the gut as time slowed. She watched a stray rivulet of blood drip from the beast's slavering maw and fall down on the ground below. The sounds of the world crashed around her as the shouts and cries from her companions tore through the moment and pulled her attention to them. The pallitine led the way, bow in hand, and had an arrow aimed for the beast.

The dark wolf glared, tensed its muscles, and charged at her.

Taryn closed her eyes and braced for the impact and grunted when it came. The force of its body as it careened into her forced a shriek of pain as the momentum twisted her ankle and slammed it into the ground. Urgency filled the young woman as the wolf's weight fell on her and pressed her to action. Her eyes shot open and saw the beast struggle as it tried to bite, and clearly was having trouble though it already lay on top of her.

The pungent odor of stale blood and the sour taste of infection and puss streaming from the creature's breath was quickly brushed away by her hands as she beat on the creature in a blind panic, only to realize after several cries from her companions that the creature was dead. Before she knew it, Arden's face hung over Taryn, reassuring her as the wolf was pulled off. Once she recovered, and was gently moved off the road with the aid of both of the other apprentices, she saw not one, but four arrows piercing the wolf's body.

"How are you feeling?" Arden asked, the concern forcing a gentleness to him that betrayed his normally brash and jovial manner.

Maddoc, in an unusually supportive gesture, knelt by Arden's side and watched silently, the same concern etched on his face as was showing on Arden's.

"I don't think I can walk." Taryn admitted after trying to set her weight on the ankle. "Abider's arse, that hurts." She grimaced.

A smile broke out on Arden's face. "And that's what you're

worried about? You should look at yourself, you're covered in scratches and your clothes are a mess."

Maddoc frowned and shook his head. "You need to be looked over. He isn't kidding. You're in pretty bad shape."

Taryn winced from her ankle's throbbing pain as it called out for attention. "How bad can it be?" She forced a smile and reached up to her forehead, which pounded now that she started to regain her senses. Her fingers fumbled over a warmth that oozed out of a swelling gash on her head. "That can't be good." Her stomach sank as she looked at the spots of blood covering her fingertips.

Pallitine Harrold knelt beside the trio and looked Taryn over carefully. "That's going to sting in the morning, but overall I think you'll be fine." He brought a waterskin up to a strip of cloth and moistened it as he carefully cleaned the scratches on her face and arms. "We'll have you checked out by the apothecary once we're back at the keep."

"Why would a wolf stray this close to the village and attack so suddenly?" Maddoc gave voice to the question lingering in the wake of the violence.

Taryn looked to their leader expectantly for an answer to the question that she, too, was starting to ask in the back of her mind.

The pallitine nodded and turned toward his apprentice. "That's a good question." He turned back toward the crumpled body of the wolf. "I suspect that it's the beast plague, judging from its appearance." He shook his head as he continued speaking to the group. "I've heard barely a rumor of it, and until this day, have never seen it." He handed the waterskin to Taryn and urged her to drink as he stood. "Rest assured, I'll have it looked into. If the rumors prove true, it could tell of dark times ahead."

CHAPTER 6

Maddoc walked toward the keep, and recalled Pallitine Harrold's words, encouraging him to drop his guard and give the newcomers a chance. He knew his pride had been bruised when they both came, that it wasn't their fault. He sighed, knowing that his mentor was right. *I just need to go to my room and think things through.*

No. He corrected himself as he walked in. *Our room. Arden's not that bad, a bit cocky, but friendly enough. And Taryn could probably use a friend, after the riding incident the other day. Perhaps another ride, closer to the keep would help us all.*

He looked at the meager flickering of red coming from the hearth. *Odd. It's warm out. Why is there something burning?*

The apprentice walked over to find the remnants of a curled parchment burnt in the hearth. He picked up the last unburnt stretch and read the few words that remained.

...glad to have you join us....
...grace will all be revealed. May he watch over us all.

Maddoc looked at the words, curious as to their meaning,

and tossed the parchment back into the hearth.

He looked about the room and decided that Harrold was right. He needed to welcome his new companions. *Who knows? Maybe we'll even end up mates.* He smiled at the thought of having friends close to his own age around the keep.

The apprentice walked out of the room and saw Arden leaning against the wall, casually near the door of the library. He was about to say something when Arden ducked inside.

The sound of tomes shifting around and pages being moved whispered from the doorway, prompting Maddoc to walk toward the library. The moment he drew near, Arden dashed out, startling them both.

"You got me." Arden laughed as he clutched his chest.

Maddoc grinned. "What're you doing?"

"Oh, here? Not much. Just looking around."

"You know you aren't supposed to be in the library without one of the brothers here, right?"

Arden shrugged. "No, but that's fine. It's all rather dull anyways, right?" He turned toward the hall leading out. "Hey, if you aren't doing anything, let's head out to the circle. The pallitines are training. If we're lucky, we might even get to train with them." He grinned at Maddoc and nodded enthusiastically.

He peered into the library curiously and back to Arden, nodding. "Sure." *Maybe I should keep an eye on him.*

<hr/>

"How's it thickening up?" Bea asked as she looked over the girl's shoulder.

Taryn stirred the shallow pot and watched the off-white mixture bubble. "It looks thick to me." Taryn frowned as she looked dubiously at the fragrant pudding.

The matron leaned in and sniffed. "You sure you put nutmeg in there?"

"Yes, only a *wee spoonful.*" She rolled her eyes as she recited the mantra that she's heard every time she was told to add this or that ingredient to the mystery Bea was having her cook.

"Now, now, no need to get testy," the older woman chided as one of her work-weathered hands deftly swept out to the table she stood near and stole a spoon from its surface. "It's good to get used to measuring. It will help with baking. You see, with cooking like we are here, it's more of an art. As long as you aren't pouring the wrong ingredients in, you can usually get away with putting in slightly more or less of one thing or another and it'll be fine. Baking is altogether different; you've got to be much more precise in your measuring or your breads won't rise or taste like they should, and may not even turn out at all."

Taryn went over the list of ingredients in her mind and couldn't believe how easily Bea rattled everything off. "How do you remember it all? Do you have this written down?"

"Oh, no, there's no need to read a book if you've done it long enough."

"So, what if you come up with a new recipe? Why not write it down for someone else?"

Bea stopped and looked at her. "There isn't anything more annoying than trying to write down a recipe I can easily whip up later. And if anyone needs to know it, I'll show 'em. Writing's a waste of time in the kitchen, too much work to do."

Taryn looked doubtfully at the kitchen's matron and let her continue.

"I think we've let it simmer enough to thicken, let's take a look, shall we?" She scooted closer and scraped the spoon across the bottom of the pot and watched the mixture slowly fill in the trail left behind. "Good!" Bea nodded with approval. She reached out to the cutting block behind her and took a crusted roll in her hand. She pulled it apart and gave Taryn the other half. "This, my dear, is Mother's Pudding. Would you like the first dip, or shall I?"

Taryn looked down into the pot at the still bubbling mass of yellowing pudding then back at Bea. "You."

"So be it." She smiled and tore off a small hunk of bread, and dipped it in the bubbling mass below. Once it was deemed sufficiently covered in pudding, Bea took a bite and looked thoughtfully to the side while she chewed.

"Well?" Taryn asked.

"Where did you get the nutmeg from?"

The apprentice glanced to the jars on the table next to her and pointed to the one she used.

The matron nodded. "That would be the powdered cloves I'm tasting."

Taryn's heart sank.

"And the reason I didn't smell nutmeg at all." A light chuckle split the sour face she started to make.

"Can't we sweeten it with honey, or put actual nutmeg in?"

Bea grinned and squeezed the youth's arm. "I'm afraid, my dear, that won't work. Once something sours the pot, nothing can be done to dress it up. Even honey's sweetness will only mask part of the wretched taste. Sometimes it's best to put it behind you, learn what you can, and start anew. Don't you think?" she asked with a raised eyebrow.

"There has to be something we can do. All the work I put in is wasted if we don't try." Taryn fretted.

"Perhaps. Try it. You'll find out and see I'm right." She urged patiently.

Frustration mixed with the disappointment, forcing her shoulders to sag. "I just want to learn."

"Of course you do," Bea agreed as she gathered the ingredients together, and away from the cloves. "It's why you're here. And once you're fine with starting over, you will. Now then, are you ready to go again?"

Taryn nodded, disheartened with the failed attempt.

A reassuring glint twinkled from Bea's eye. "Excellent. I'll step you through it and keep an eye on you this time. I promise."

Taryn walked out of the keep and headed toward the practice circle, eager to put the torturous reminder that she could not cook behind her.

At least Maddoc's coming around, the past few days have been quiet, now that he's warming up.

Clouds were rolling in, casting a haze over the bright sun overhead. She yearned to be back training to fight. Her first lesson the day before gave her a taste of the excitement, and a focus she hadn't felt since she was on the streets pilfering coin purses with her sister. *Only this is more rewarding and won't land me in prison.* Once she reached the circle, she leaned on one of the fence posts and recalled the moves she witnessed here, imagining she was performing them. She loved these quiet moments and the calm they brought.

"You've lost it." Arden said as he came around the corner, toward the circle with Maddoc close behind.

Oh gods, not again.

"Don't play the fool with me. I've seen you sneaking about. What are you doing here?" the larger boy accused.

Relief washed over Arden as he saw Taryn standing near the circle. "*I* am here to train and one day join the ranks. Why are *you* so insistent on badgering me?" He stopped near Taryn and looked at Maddoc expectantly.

"Because you're up to no good. You've been hiding something since I've laid eyes on you and I mean to find out what."

"What's going on?" Taryn asked as she walked over to Arden.

The blond boy thrust a finger toward the other. "*He's* gone off the saddle." A light chuckle slipped out as he continued. "For some reason he's convinced that I'm here to *ruin his day.*" He held his hands up and waved them about sarcastically.

"That's not what I said at all," Maddoc objected. "I don't know what you're doing, I just know you're up to something.

Why else would you have been sneaking around the keep?"

Arden folded his arms and stared. "I have no idea what you're talking about."

"Yes you do." Maddoc sputtered. "First I've seen you hanging about the library at all hours, and then messing with the saddle on her horse," he pointed vaguely at Taryn. "And now *this*."

"What?" Arden laughed. "Not this again. That was weeks ago. You *know* I've been riding my whole life. I didn't even *touch* her saddle, you were there, next to me while I was looking at it. And in case you didn't notice, it was the wolf who caused her to fall off, not me."

"Look, you're the only one I saw touching my saddle," she said. Annoyance crept its way in, overshadowing whatever sense of calm she mustered from her time alone.

"No, don't laugh at me." Maddoc stepped forward and poked Arden in the chest. "Just because you found the only person here who believes you, doesn't mean you can mock me. Tell me what you were doing!" He stared the other boy in the eyes, threatening him to action.

"I wasn't doing anything." Arden's mood visibly soured as he withdrew from his accuser. "In fact, what were *you* doing with her saddle?"

"I don't need to answer to you." The other boy sneered. "As I've already said, I was making sure it was buckled. Stop lying. What were you doing?" Again, he stepped up and stared Arden in the face.

"Gods, Maddoc, stop." Taryn butted in. "Why do you have to be such an ass? Just leave us alone." She slid between the boys and stared the bully down.

"Oh, now you need a girl to stand up for you. What, too scared that you'll be found out and you need someone to save you?" He placed a hand on Taryn's shoulder and moved her out of his way.

Rage lit Taryn up at being pushed aside. She sneered at Maddoc and shoved back. "Don't you *ever* push me." She threatened quietly, and stared with defiance, daring him to try it again.

He caught himself and blinked at Taryn, unsure how to react at the raw display of hostility. "Hey, this isn't about you— "

Arden chimed in, interrupting the older boy. "No, it isn't. It's about you, and your feeble accusations. What *is it* about you? Jealous we've arrived and stolen your thunder? Is that why you're attacking her?" He stood next to Taryn and clenched his fists.

"No," Maddoc held his hands up, flustered, and defended himself. "I—"

"No?" Arden scoffed. "Stop *lying* to us. You've hated us since we've been here. I think *you're* the one who's up to something." He stepped forward, and poked Maddoc in the chest, mocking what was done to him.

The accuser's eyes bulged with rage at the comment. "Why you!" He raised a fist and struck Arden in the face.

"Hey now!" Brother Hendrick yelled as he ran to investigate the shouting. "That's enough. Stop! All of you."

"But," Maddoc spat out. "He's the cause of it."

"That is *enough*!" The brother warned. "Inside. All of you," he commanded.

⌁⁂⌁

Thoman pulled up a chair and sat next to Taryn in the common room of the keep's dining hall. "Want to tell me what happened out there?" Frustration burned in his words.

Taryn scowled in annoyance and turned to her mentor. "Maddoc happened. That's what. I don't know why he has such a problem with us. If he's not ignoring me and acting like I'm not even there, he's accusing Arden of gods-know what." She shook her head in exasperation. "I don't trust him. He can't, no... *won't* work with us. All he does is try to pick Arden apart."

"Why would he do that? What did Arden do?"

"Nothing. That's the thing. Maddoc has it in his head that he's out to get him or something. I don't know." She shrugged. "First he accused him of trying to mess with my saddle the day we encountered the wolf, and now he thinks he's up to something." She shook her head in frustration.

"Has Arden done what he's accused of?"

She leaned back. "Of course not. It's nothing but slag; he's looking for a way to get him out of here."

Thoman nodded. "I appreciate where you're coming from." He looked into her eyes and continued gently. "But you have to look past your immediate distrust of people. To get to the matter of truth, like all pallitines should try, one must hear the entire story. Do you understand?"

Of course I do, Maddoc's a liar. She nodded, scowling.

"What makes you certain Arden's innocent?"

"Because he *is* innocent!" Taryn spat out. "He isn't the one running around deflecting suspicion by accusing others. He isn't the one acting like he doesn't want anyone around."

"Then you trust Arden's word beyond doubt."

"Of course there's doubt!" She blurted. "There's always doubt."

"What makes you say that?" Thoman's brow furrowed in concern.

She shifted in her seat and folded her arms. "You can't rely on anyone."

Thoman leaned back and mulled over his next words carefully. "No one?"

"No! I want to, but you don't understand. You can't." Frustrated, she leaned forward and put her face in her hands. The tension she felt mounted, and built on the anger that she stuffed down deep most of her life. Her lips quivered as she turned to the pallitine. "You don't know what it's like being on guard day in and day out, waiting for someone to disappoint you, steal from you, hit you, or *worse*." Raw pain from bringing up her recent past came to the forefront as tears beaded at the corners of her eyes. Her voice shook with conviction. "You can't trust *anyone* in this world but yourself. No one will save you. No one will help you." Her lips twisted as her memory sought anyone who stood as a beacon of hope, and failed. "Not your sister, not your mother, no one." Her sharp gaze flicked back toward Thoman as she shook her head. "*Thank the gods* I could defend myself, was strong enough to leave. If I hadn't fought back, I'm not sure I could anymore." The certainty of losing herself in her mother's path like her sister snapped into focus. "I'd be no better off than *my own family*, just giving up and wasting their lives to serve their own petty needs."

The pallitine reached out, but pulled back when his apprentice shied away from the touch. "Look, I know you've been through rough times. I don't know everything you've gone through, but I've seen enough to know you carry a weight." A moment passed as he waited for Taryn to collect herself. "You need to confront it, face your past, and move on. You're strong. You *are* safe and among friends." His voice softened with concern. "We've all had dark pasts, our own trials to overcome. This is yours, and I'm here to help."

She rolled her eyes as the bitterness came out. "Until *you* need something." Regret sank its icy grip into her throat and slid down to her gut the moment the words were uttered.

Anger flashed across Thoman's eyes. "Look, I'm *sorry* you've had it rough." His tone grew harsh as he continued. "But you will go *nowhere* if you have don't have faith in people. Put your past behind, because if you can't trust others, *no one* will trust you. And that is *not* the way a pallitine leads their life." He stood up and clenched his fist, calming himself. His voice lowered and echoed across the worn floor. "You *need* to let others in. I have shown you *nothing* but respect and patience, and you have shown *nothing* but a flat disregard for the faith I put into you. Heed my words, for if you cannot, then perhaps you shouldn't be here."

When he finished, he turned about and left the hall, leaving

Taryn struck by the harshness of the words. Once recovered, she stormed out of the keep and collapsed at the bottom of one of the few trees outside the building. She pounded her fists in the dirt and lost herself in the tumultuous mix of anger and pain from the words spoken. She so desperately wanted to cry, to let go of these feelings, but she could not. *Perhaps he's right. Maybe I can't change. Maybe I don't belong here.*

CHAPTER 7

"OH, CHILD." BEA'S FACE WRINKLED in concern when she caught Taryn's forlorn expression. "What's wrong?"

Taryn leaned against the doorway, unable to move, and when she opened her mouth to speak her lips quivered, letting nothing out.

"Come here." The matron took on a warm, motherly tone and opened her arms. "Just let it out," she cooed while stroking Taryn's dark hair.

The girl sank into the offered arms and held on tight. The reassurance offered brought her back to a time when her sister would still hold her, during those nights when their mother would be drinking too much, and worse yet, leave without warning and not come back for a day or more. For a moment she was a young child again, safe and warm in her sister's arms. But she wasn't. The sister she once knew fell victim to the lure of her vile addiction and money, like their mother. Taryn pulled in a quick breath and pushed her thoughts of the past aside, and focused on the present. The gentle rocking of Bea's arms, and finally feeling safe enough to let her emotions out, if even a bit, helped her calm down and pull herself together.

"You going to tell me what's wrong?"

Taryn pulled back and looked away. "I don't belong here."

"And what makes you say that? What'd those boys do now?" Bea crossed her arms in front of her and tapped her foot.

She shook her head. "It's not them. I," she searched within herself for the right words. "I can't trust anyone. It's too hard. I know I'm around people who care, but my instincts won't let me. I've been disappointed and hurt too much." Her eyes pleaded for understanding when she looked at Bea. "I've said things, mean things, and I don't think Thoman wants me around anymore."

"Oh, please child. It can't be as bad as you think. Heck, it sounds like you've half the battle done already. You know we're not here to hurt you." She nodded. "Why do you want to stay here?"

"Because I don't want to be out *there*." She scowled and wrapped her arms around herself, fighting off the guilt that started to creep in. "And for him. I've let him down, and he deserves better than that."

"That's no way to be." Bea lifted Taryn's chin and looked in her eyes. "If you spend your life doing things only because you think that's what's expected, you won't be happy. Not truly, at least. You've got to look at yourself and ask, is this what you really want?"

Her thoughts were sparked by the words and leapt to her former life and what she went through. The images of Roy and Lee came out, along with others she stood up for in her neighborhood when they'd been hurt. She nodded. "You're right. I need to prove to myself that I can do this." Her back straightened with the realization. *I didn't even realize I was slouching; gods, I must look a mess.* She drew a deep breath. "But not only for myself, but to help others. To stand up for those who can't stand up for themselves. To prove that I'm strong enough to help people from going through what I have, or protect them in some way. To be there like I needed someone

84

there for me, but never had." Her wavering voice faded in her rising confidence as she looked up. "To stand up for those who can't stand up for themselves."

A kind wisdom settled across the matron's wrinkled gaze. "Well, all right. Now, it seems to me that if you want to help others, they'll need to trust you, right?"

Taryn hesitated before nodding, unsure where the matron was leading. "Sure."

"Well, then. How do you expect others to trust you when you can't trust them?"

She's right. Taryn sighed. "I want to, I really do, but you don't understand. People will always do something to hurt you; even if they act nice to your face, they'll steal from you—or worse."

Bea's eyes narrowed. "There's no two ways about this. There really isn't. You've got to move on, to open yourself up to hurt. You *can't* grow if you don't trust. We all have a past, have our hurt. But if you really want to help others, do yourself a favor and get out of the past and live *now*." An eyebrow raised expectantly while she nodded toward Taryn. "You trust me." She shrugged. "Start there and move on."

"Well," Taryn stammered. "You don't want anything from me."

"Of course I do." She scoffed.

Taryn took a step back in surprise.

"I want you to stay. Ain't nobody here can help as good as you. Besides, child, you listen the best." A warm joviality filled her movement as she pulled out a chair from next to the table and settled in. "But look, the only thing anyone wants from you is for you to be happy. Grow into the woman you're meant to, nothin' else."

A noncommittal noise escaped her lips. Taryn wanted to believe, but something wasn't adding up. *It can't be that easy. What is it? Do they grow dreamseeds here? Sell girls like me to the Saerin for slaves? No one just takes people like me off the streets and helps them, do they?* She knew she was being irrational, but it didn't make sense to her.

Bea's hands went up in a shrug. "Maybe he's right. Maybe you can't change."

Taryn's jaw opened with disbelief. "What? How can you say that?"

"Do you really think anything different?" The matron waited for an answer, and got none. "Oh, I see. Thoman *has* wanted something." An eyebrow arched knowingly.

"Of course not!" She burst out without thinking, offended at the thought. Realization hit. Shame sunk in when she remembered her accusation from the day before. Abashed, she crossed her arms and looked down.

Bea's voice softened as she spoke. "Well then, it would seem to me that there's no reason *but* to trust him, and to believe in yourself."

Taryn nodded, reassured by the logic given, and the sentiment behind it.

"You aren't the only one to have had it rough, you know. Your pallitine has had much to deal with." Bea waited for Taryn to look up before continuing. "His father died, murdered when he was a young lad. And as a young man he watched his mentor die in his arms. That, along with other losses over his life, has made it difficult for him form bonds for fear of losing them. The past haunts him much like it haunts you, I'd wager, just in a different way. It's likely why he was so harsh with you. Far easier to push someone away that means something to you before you grow too attached."

Taryn's heart sank. "I knew that he lost his father, but he never said how. And his mentor…. I never knew." She shook her head as a new depth of respect grew for the man she would call mentor.

Bea stood and walked to the firepit, messing with the dying embers with an iron poker. "Not many do. It's why he's so adamant in pursuing this beast he's having tracked down. He keeps most at a distance with his casual and helpful manner. His dedication to the cause and fear of the past repeating itself have kept him too focused to take on an apprentice." She set a couple logs from next to the hearth on the burning coals and brushed her hands off on her apron.

Taryn sniffed, and hugged Bea tight. "Thank you."

The matron returned the gesture with a gentle squeeze. "For what, child?"

"For the talk. It's helped to straighten things out."

Bea smiled and set her hand on the girl's cheek. "Never a worry, dear. Anytime you need something, I'm here for you. Even if it's to set an ornery pallitine straight, I'll be here."

Taryn could not help but grin at the last comment. She stepped back and beamed at the woman who proved more a friend than an elder.

⁓ঽ❊ঽ⁓

The open, blue sky showcased the bright autumn sun as it hung overhead, warming Taryn's skin. She stepped out of the keep and held a hand up to her brow to block the bright light as her eyes adjusted. Thoman and another of the pallitines finished sparring and were cleaning up. She walked up to the training circle and waited for the other pallitine to leave before approaching her mentor.

The older man splashed some water on his face and was toweling off as she approached. He turned to her and nodded soberly.

"Thoman," she managed to get out under the worry from their fight the day before.

The District Pallitine stood and finished wiping himself dry as he waited expectantly.

"I wanted to apologize for what I said yesterday. It wasn't fair. You've been nothing but kind to me and I haven't shown my appreciation." Remorse flowed easily with her words. "I *am* truly grateful that you chose me above all others to walk in your steps, for the compassion that you showed to me when we met, for bringing me here." She fidgeted awkwardly under the scrutinizing gaze. "I'm sorry."

Thoman relaxed and set the towel aside. "I understand. It can't be easy coming from a situation when you aren't sure of people's motives, where anyone might be looking for something from you, even those closest to you."

The weight of their argument started to lift, and with it, her mood did as well.

He leaned against the fence that surrounded the circle. His demeanor shifted subtly as he regarded her. "But those times are past." He waved a hand to the land around them. "Look around you and your surroundings, and draw those that you would have at your side and take pride in the person you are. For this is the person who will shape you into what you are going to become and who you want to be."

"I will. Are we all right?"

A light chuckle escaped his lips. "Of course we're all right." He paused as a pained look crossed his face. "I'm sorry for how I reacted yesterday. I shouldn't have been so harsh with you. You caught me after I learned that the trail for the wyrm I was having tracked had been lost." He clenched his fist and pounded it on the circle's fence. "It's going to be years before we catch up to it now."

Relief swept through Taryn. "Thank you." The depth of the words struck against what she learned the day before. "I'm sorry to hear about losing the trail. I'm sure it'll be found before long and then we can hunt this beast together." She looked up at her mentor. "And avenge *everyone* it's killed."

"You're most welcome." He smiled sadly. "And thank you. It will. I just grow impatient with the hunt." He shifted to his side and looked at her in approval. "You know, with this aside, you remind me a little of myself. Your fire, your conviction. I was very much like that once."

Embarrassment blushed her cheeks as the compliment

sunk in.

"I'm glad that we talked. Let's forget this and move on. We have the future to think of. Now, tell me of your friend Arden." He leaned forward and listened, eager to hear more of Taryn's experiences in the keep.

CHAPTER 8

SHADOWS FROM THE WANING FIRELIGHT melded with the thick cover of trees overhead, providing a firm sense of seclusion in the warm summer night that left Taryn with an even greater sense of isolation than what she felt from being so far from home. She looked across the dying fire and watched Arden settle back and wave away the smoke that drifted to him as it had for most of the night. Her heart would not let go of the warmth she felt when she thought of Arden, nor would it let her forget how irresistible he looked when he let his guard down. These feelings were only intensified by the fact that the sight of him suffering at the mercy of the wind wherever he sat amused her greatly. She turned back to watch the flames flicker, smiling to herself as she picked at the last remnants of her dinner. Her thoughts shifted as she turned to regard her mentor's long-time friend, Hugh, with a hint of caution.

In the two years she lived in the keep, she learned much, especially in the year since Maddoc moved up to the pallitine's quarters and started traveling with his mentor. Now that they advanced in their studies, it was deemed time for both Taryn and Arden to learn what it was like working with one of the

Tramirian Rangers.

The ranger they were with looked about as old as Thoman, and possessed a leaner build than her mentor. The long and once-flaxen hair laid tied behind his back, sported even streaks of gray, and sprouted out in the occasional stubborn tuft that refused to remain bound. The old hunting leathers he wore showed signs of being well-used and in need of repair. Even with this impression of disarray, his eyes bore the sharp, detailed gaze most rangers did, but also held a friendly warmth when he relaxed.

She knew him only briefly from a prior introduction, and until their time together for her training, she had no real interaction with him. Taryn knew in her mind if Thoman vouched for him, he would be fine to stay with for the next fortnight or more, but she was still having a hard time letting go of her wariness. On top of everything, a mage from some council joined with him and pulled them in on a search for some rogue sorcerer.

The man hailed from some mage's college in Irline, and was described as one of the masters. His youthful face gave the impression of a young man, but his eyes spoke of a maturity his appearance belied. His fair and sharpened features, while distinctly elven, bore their own differences from the few elves Taryn met in Tramire. He enlisted Hugh's aid on some matter not yet explained to her, but it mattered little.

She grew restless and the internal conflict soured her mood, so she forced herself to speak with her mentor's friend. "I know Thoman wants us to gain experience working with rangers, but what are we doing here? What exactly is it you do?"

Arden sat up and leaned into the conversation, frowning at the smoke that still trailed him.

Hugh looked up from his food and answered. "Well, ya already know as rangers, it's our duty ta patrol the roads between villages and townships. What ya might not know is there're times we're called in ta do what local guards and constables can't. It's often in those times we work with pallitines, like yer training ta be. These duties can be ugly and may make us unwelcome, but they need ta be done just the same. This is one of those times. As ya know, I've been called ta help our friend here on his hunt for a sorcerer."

Morolinn, the mage that enlisted Hugh's aid, looked up from the thick tome he was reading and watched the banter attentively.

Taryn noticed the attention and turned to the lanky, neatly trimmed blond mage and narrowed her eyes. "Who exactly are we chasing, and why?"

The mage sighed quietly and closed his book. "The sorcerer I am chasing was, at one time, a respected and rising member of the Irlinian College, specifically researching the histories of the mystical arts. He was excommunicated from the order a few decades ago when it was discovered that he was pilfering various tomes from our archives and researching the darker arts. More recently, he has been charged with the theft of one of the order's artifacts from an esteemed member, an Oculus Zeteo." He noticed the expectant faces before him and sighed again before continuing. "The Oculus Zeteo is a device, round and a bit bigger than a fist in diameter with a flat top and bottom." He held up his hands and shaped the imaginary Oculus in front of them. "Imagine a ball of clay, with the upper and lower quarters cut off. That is what it would look like, but made of copper and brass." He adjusted himself and leaned forward slightly as he continued in a lowered tone. "The Oculus Zeteo is used to search for an object or person related to the object or person that it is attuned to." A slight smile perked his lips as his energy picked up. "For people, it looks for blood relatives only. But for items, however, it looks for others that have some relation, be they created as part of the same set, or created using the same basic components, like jewelry that has been created from the same hunk of ore. It will even seek out the pieces of an item if it has been broken." He raised a hand to bring about the final point and spoke in a hushed reverence. "It looks for that indelible mark left upon an item and its counterparts when created. Once tuned, it will show the relative distance and number of items that it can detect. The range covers most of the continent, and as you may guess, it could be quite useful if needed to find something."

Taryn looked unimpressed. "So, a magic compass. And why would you need our help?"

Morolinn's response took on a tone of subdued annoyance as he shrugged off the flippant observation. "The mage who took the artifact, Pan Gorak, is a dangerous individual. His involvement has been implicated in several... altercations over the years. He has found a way to thwart our attempts at scrying him, and we have been unable to find him for questioning. Fortunately, he cannot stop me from using other methods of tracking him down." He started to turn away, but paused as he looked back at Taryn to correct himself. "Or at least the Oculus that was taken."

Arden sat up and looked curiously at the mage. "Dangerous how? Surely if there was a crazed mage sacking villages we would've heard about it by now."

The mage shook his head. "Not in that sense, no. He is far more dangerous. He is a cold and calculating man twisted by the very dark arts he seeks to exploit."

"Hmm." Arden's interest faded as he leaned back. "How are we expected to find him?"

"Yes, you mentioned other methods?" She asked. "Why not use another compass to find the first? Wouldn't that be easier?"

The mage shifted uncomfortably in his seat as he briefly looked down before answering. "Indeed, that would be. But, the one he stole was mine and there were no others that were readily available." The lanky mage stood and brushed his legs off before stretching his arms. "Now if you'll pardon me, it's time for me to use those other methods before I go to sleep for the night."

Taryn watched their strange companion as he walked to a nearby tree and sat down, resting his back against the trunk as he crossed his legs and set his hands in his lap while humming to himself. Within moments, his eyes closed and he was lost within his rhythmic humming.

Arden cast an amused glance at his peer and nodded toward the humming mage. "This should prove quite interesting."

The apprentice raised her eyebrow and glanced at Hugh.

The ranger simply shrugged. "Some things, ya don't question. Mages are an enigma not easily explained. It's probably from the unnatural forces they tap inta." Hugh stood up and poked at the charred remains of the campfire, pushing the dying embers away from the hearthstones and into the middle of the camp's pit. "I think I'll be turnin' in. Good night." He nodded as he turned to head toward his sleeping roll.

Taryn turned from her companions and watched the dying embers pulse in the firepit, glowing their oranges and reds as they slowly consumed the last charred remnants of firewood. Her thoughts drifted as she enjoyed the heat before it faded in the chilled night air. She reflected on the conversation, and wondered what else this Pan Gorak had done to make him so reviled.

Arden's breath caught behind her, and drew her attention to the faint glow starting to emanate from where Morolinn rested. One of the mage's necklaces flickered with a blue light for an instant before dying out. The mage's eyes opened and drifted ahead, gradually floating to her as they reflected a powerful, yet distant echo of something unnatural and foreign, as if the mage not only looked at her, but peered into her and inspected her very soul. This sense of powerlessness left her raw and forced a shiver down her spine as she instinctively looked back to the fire's embers. She barely acknowledged the mage as he stood up and headed to his bedroll for the night.

The thought of a single person able to tap into such an unnamed power filled her with unease; even inasmuch as she was unfamiliar with the extent of those powers, she knew it was nothing to be trifled with just the same.

"By the god," her companion whispered reverently. "Did you

feel that?" His distant gaze echoed a fear that mirrored what she felt.

Taryn looked up and frowned as he steered his eyes away from hers, shying away nervously. She so desperately wanted to sit near him and hold him, to feel the reassurance and safety that he seemed to need as well. But knew that she could not, at least not until she was sure he felt the same.

Arden coughed and quickly moved to his own bedroll and wished Taryn a safe night. A shiver overcame him, forcing his body to shake for the briefest moment as he settled in and turned away to look out into the night.

Once morning struck, and both Taryn and Arden recovered from the strange experience, they settled into their normal routine. Though neither discussed it, all it took was a knowing glance between them to acknowledge the previous night's event.

As the day progressed, Morolinn kept his distance from the younger companions, which seemed to suit Arden just fine.

Taryn, on the other hand, overcame her reservations and decided to confront the mage.

"So, what was that, last night?" She asked as the group broke their midday meal.

The mage glanced at both apprentices before answering. "That was the farsight. It helps me focus in on specific details on those I seek."

Taryn shuddered. "That didn't feel like anything distant to me. It felt like my soul was exposed and left out for all to see." The feeling of raw helplessness edged into her words as the memory of being laid open swept her periphery. She hardened herself against the encroaching feelings and shuddered.

"I'm sorry." His head drooped apologetically. "It happens at times when I look for something specific." He glanced at Arden and back to Taryn. "Nearby energies can cast off these... shadows that can appear to mimic what I look for. No harm was intended, rest assured."

The apprentice watched the young man put on a brave face

as she talked with the mage, but saw past the bravado and saw a remnant of the fear she saw the night before. She smiled at Arden as she talked with the mage, comforted by the fact she was not alone in her depth of unease with what happened, and glad the power used was not done so maliciously.

CHAPTER 9

THE CENTRAL STRETCH OF THE Untarian mountains
loomed before the group. The four travelers journeyed
three days north of the Tramirian border in the Arturian
province and Morolinn was convinced they were getting closer
to the rogue sorcerer with every step.

The slope was not unlike any other stretch Taryn had seen
before. Its parched exterior rested gray in large swaths of rocky
terrain, marred only by the stray green of some shoot that dared
encroach upon the dry surface. The only difference was that the
break in the mountains they climbed bore weather-worn signs
of dwarven stone-smithing, which grew more commonplace the
higher they traveled.

As they worked their way up the mountainside, Hugh led
them up a narrow ravine until a ledge of stone came into view,
revealing a broad, flat plain which led to the broken face of the
mountain. Etched into the face itself rested a worn figure of
an armored dwarf standing roughly three men in height, his
legs flanking an entrance carved into the mountain's side. The
warrior held a hammer high above his head, where two alcoves
sat carved into the surface above the head of the hammer and

the warrior's hand, apparently where braziers would have rested at one point, long ago. The dwarf looked down upon the group, staring at them in a silently reproving gaze.

Hugh paused before the sight, admiring the stonework on his horse as he waited for the others to catch up. Once Morolinn stopped next to him, he turned and motioned to the dark entrance. "This the place?"

The mage looked at the entrance and narrowed his brow for a moment while he focused on it. "Aye, this is the place." He nodded.

Hugh dismounted and led his mount toward a thick patch of grass off the path. The others quickly followed suit and walked with him to the mountain's entrance.

"What do you think this place was?" Taryn stood in awe as Arden walked up next to her. The craftsmanship looked as if it stood on the mountainside for countless ages, and ignited a fascination for the dwarves who may have lived and worked here so long ago.

Morolinn stepped forward and put a hand on his chin as he examined the features carefully. "It looks to have been a dwarven ancestral shrine, long since abandoned. They are used as places of solitude and respect that their priests and elders can come to in order to reflect, study, or seek answers in the hope that their ancestors would share the wisdom gained over the ages."

"So, a burial crypt of sorts," she said with a hint of reverence. She was *not* looking forward to breaking the sanctity of the dead, especially when it looked like it had been left undisturbed for so long.

The mage shook his head. "Not at all, actually. Dwarves believe that the rock itself contains the very essence of their souls when they die. It is likely that the ancestors they sought to appease were buried within this range of mountains, but not here. When dwarves pass away, they are said to join their ancestral spirits within the mountains, so they have access to all of their clan's ancestry, assuming they are buried within the same range." He looked up, toward the warrior's hammer, and quoted a passage from some text read long ago. "'From the stone we are born; to the stone we will go. In the stone, with our family, we will never be alone.'"

Arden spoke up as he turned to the mage. "Why did the dwarves leave this place if it's so prized?"

The mage shook his head. "That is unclear. The best guess I would make is that their wars with the trolls north of the spine drew them away and further into the lands of their hated enemies." He shifted his weight as he turned to the apprentice, his eyes widened in pride. "In fact, when you hear their songs, you will—"

"Not ta intrude on yer respectful indulgence, but—" Hugh interjected.

Morolinn nodded immediately and contained his enthusiastic smile. "Of course, it's just rare to encounter such an unspoiled example of ancient dwarven culture out here along with such obvious interest." He motioned toward the apprentices. "I got lost in the moment." He turned to Hugh and readied himself. "Shall we?"

The ranger nodded and turned to the members of the small band as he pulled out his bow. "Now, as we go in, we have ta work as a team." He looked to Taryn. "Why don't ya stick with Morolinn while I take point and Arden guards our backs?"

Taryn started to agree and stopped. "No, that doesn't make sense." She frowned. "You wouldn't normally have a pallitine guard the flank, would you?"

"No, but yer not a pallitine."

"Not yet, but how else are we supposed to learn if we aren't given the chance to do what we're meant to?"

Arden stepped forward and watched the exchange. He looked like he wanted to say something, but thought better of it and kept quiet.

Hugh glanced between the two apprentices and frowned while he thought about it. "Fair 'nuff. Well then, what would ya suggest?"

Taryn nodded, bolstered by the faith Hugh placed in her. Although she felt comforted by the reassurance that they were not desecrating a crypt, she still held her reservations about running into the sorcerer Morolinn described in their journeys. "I'll take point." She looked at Arden. "You stick with Morolinn behind me, and Hugh will guard our flank. Since he has a bow, it makes sense that he can work better from a distance, and his experience will help us if we need to retreat."

The ranger looked at Taryn appreciatively. "Sounds like a plan. If we run inta trouble though, ya gotta listen to me no matter what. Agreed?"

She quickly nodded.

"Fair 'nuff." Hugh turned to the mage. "Is there anything ya need ta say 'fore we go in?"

Morolinn shook his head and chanted softly to himself. During the incantation, he touched his companions' shoulders and squeezed them as he finished his lyrical chant. "Just in case," he said quietly before heading toward the entrance.

Taryn's mind firmed itself in the present as she pulled a torch out from her pack. A well of confidence took grip within her and cleared the uneasiness she felt in her mind not moments ago. She felt odd with the sensation of this unnatural confidence as it took hold, but welcomed the fearlessness it brought. Once the torch was lit, she pulled out her sword and led her companions into the inner depths of the ancient shrine.

The dark, gray walls of the shrine they walked in were incredibly smooth, marking the precise craftsmanship dwarves were known for. The wide tunnel stretched out so three men could comfortably walk side by side, and rose a fair head taller than Morolinn, who was a tall man in his own right. The iron brackets spaced evenly along both sides of the hall had long since rusted from the elements, leaving the telltale shards of rusted iron filings and dust in the recesses and scattered along the floor. After a minute of careful but steady progress, the passage ended and broke out into a wide chamber whose walls arched up into a grand and vaulted ceiling. Two large columns spread up from the ground to support the stone above from either side of the entrance they walked through, each carved with care to represent what could only be interpreted as the ancestors Morolinn described earlier. Each representation was etched to emphasize one trait or another, whether it be one hammering a weapon in front of a burning forge, another hefting a hammer over her head while standing over a fallen foe, or yet another rallying a force as he stood speaking above a gathering, a hand outstretched to the people below.

Taryn's eyes drifted up the stone walls as she walked in and turned around to find a balcony about thirty feet up which appeared to lead out toward the outer walls. She was struck by the raw beauty of the room, the carvings, all of it. A part of her yearned to reach out to the past and spend even a day with these people to learn more about them. After several long moments of admiring the detailed work in the columns, she stopped herself as she recalled the reason they were there in the first place. She turned to Hugh, who, with Arden, was also caught off-guard by the ornate craftsmanship of the room they were in, as the mage was when she looked at him. She looked in the more immediate area and saw three passages leading away from the room, one on each of the opposing walls. She walked up to Hugh and spoke in a hushed voice. "There doesn't seem to be anything here, perhaps we should move in further to investigate?"

The ranger nodded and turned his gaze downward as he looked at the passages out. "Of course, I've never seen the likes of this before. This is simply..."

"Astounding." Morolinn interrupted as he walked up to them. "Just remember, there is a reason Pan Gorak would have come here. Being that this was likely used as a place of study, there may be things left here of some value. I pray whatever he came for was pilfered long ago." He peered at each of the openings and stepped toward the central hall leading forward. "If I'm right, this would have gone to a central foundry or smithy, as well as the common areas. Let us instead investigate the side corridors first, before continuing forward."

Taryn looked down the hall appreciatively. "Sounds good to me. Shall we continue on over here then?" she asked as she turned to the corridor to her right.

The corridor Taryn led the group through grew more shallow than the first, and forced Hugh to remove his cap since the ceiling allowed only the slightest room for his head. The iron brackets here, however, were in much better shape than the ones they saw at the entrance, being only partially rusted at the beginning, and showing less wear as they progressed. Eventually they came to another chamber, similar to the first with intricate carvings present along the side walls. In the far corners, two statues of dwarven warriors were carved from individual blocks of granite and struck a protective pose over the area. Two stone tables flanked the interior, each accompanied by stone blocks on either side used for seating. Anything of value that may have been placed on the tables were long since removed, leaving the room barren and devoid of anything of note.

When Morolinn was convinced there was nothing to be found in the room, Taryn led the way back and walked toward the other hall.

An identical chamber met the group as they progressed to the other side of the ruins. The members of the group each came in to examine the area and once again found nothing.

Not interested in spending more time searching another empty room, Taryn turned to join Arden who stood near the passage and began to head back out.

"Stop, Taryn," Hugh urged the young pallitine-in-training.

She turned to see him holding his hand in askance as he walked to the far end of the room, examining one of the statues.

"Unless the shadows're playing tricks on my eyes, I think I've seen somethin' here."

The mage rushed to Hugh and looked in the same spot. "I'm

not sure what you mean, I don't see anything."

Hugh stepped forward to better examine the statue, and looked behind it. "Aha, there we are."

"What is it?" Taryn asked, her heart raced from the discovery as she walked to the statue.

Hugh stepped back from behind the statue and pointed behind it. "There's a stairwell dug out from behind the statue here. It looks like it was meant ta hide in the shadow." He commented admiringly. He bowed slightly and smiled graciously at Taryn. "After ya, of course."

Taryn grinned back at the aging ranger and took the lead.

The ranger glanced back at Arden who still lingered by the passage. "Come now, lad. There's nothing here ta be worried for." He ribbed the other apprentice and waited for the last member of the small band to fall in before heading down the ancient stairs.

Once through the narrow opening, the stairwell opened up to fit two people side by side as it wound its way down to another chamber. As she stopped to look around, she found much of the same carvings in this rock. The drier and notably warmer air contrasted sharply with the more humid and colder air above. Cobwebs grew more prevalent down below the chamber, adding to the sense of abandonment that already permeated the shrine. She looked past the stairwell as she walked further into the room and saw a wooden door, slightly ajar with the barest hint of light flickering beyond. And then it struck her, the door was solid, and showed no signs of decay or deterioration.

Morolinn was the next to take note of the discovery.

They both turned to silently warn the others and pointed toward the mysterious door.

The ranger motioned for everyone to stay put as he stalked quietly toward the door and poked his head in the doorway. His face took on the look of earnest concentration as he listened to what lay beyond. A hand gracefully pressed against the ancient wood, opening the door before he continued his investigation within. After several heartbeats passed, he called out to them. "It's all right, come in."

What greeted Taryn's eyes as she walked through the doorway was as disorienting and awe-inspiring as the hall above. Along the far wall, flanked by two bookcases with several intact tomes held within, was a broad and thick table covered by two pestles and mortars of differing sizes, a number of crystalline jars filled with various powders, and some bottles whose contents had long since dissipated, leaving the caked remnants of some liquid they once held. Several candelabra were nestled into nooks along the wall, with nothing but remnants of wax melted long ago left in their grip. A central brazier was hoisted above the table and flickered faintly, illuminating the room with its gentle light, casting odd shadows along the web-covered walls as the flames danced behind the thick chains that held it up.

Morolinn stepped forward and adjusted his robes as he knelt in front of one of the bookcases, examining it carefully. After a minute, he cursed.

"What is it?" Hugh asked.

"I can't read a word here. This script is from a variant I am unfamiliar with," he answered ruefully. "What I can tell you, though," he continued while pointing along the bookcase, "is someone was here and disturbed these books. It looks like at least one was taken, but without someone to translate these surrounding texts, I am unable to determine what sort of book may have been taken."

"How are these books even standing? Shouldn't they be dust by now?" Taryn observed, quite unsure she could believe the sights in front of her.

"By all rights, yes, you would be correct," Morolinn agreed. "These, however, have been preserved by some rite to stand the test of time. They still rip, and can burn, and are likely a bit more brittle than they were ages ago, but if left alone, I suspect they would last another age or more. It is a preservation technique usually saved for the most unusual or valued of tomes.

Were these human, I would expect them to have a religious significance. Until these are translated, however, we cannot be sure what significance these will have, if any."

Hugh paced next to the table, frowning as he examined its contents. "What now?"

Arden shivered as he looked about the chamber. "Since he's come and gone, shouldn't we follow suit?"

Morolinn stood, crossed his arms, and drummed his fingers as he looked at the brazier burning above the table. After a moment, he spoke. "I agree. We should. I must meditate and see if I cannot find our quarry."

"We'll be outside." Hugh motioned for Taryn and Arden to follow him out of the chamber.

Once they were outside the room, they could hear the rhythmic chanting they had grown so familiar with in their time with the mage. Hugh headed up the stairs while Taryn walked slowly behind with her friend as she admired the abandoned shrine.

"Doesn't this spook you?" he asked, the look of distaste dominating his frown as they climbed the stairs.

Taryn smiled. "Not at all. Don't tell me ancient buildings bother you." She scoffed.

"No, of course not." He paused. "Not much anyways. It feels..." He glanced about uneasily. "Like something's not right. I need to get upstairs."

She laughed as it dawned on her what's been unsettling him. "You don't like being underground, do you?" A grin spread across her face as she glanced at him. The vulnerability he showed wore well on him, and further sparked her interest.

"Ugh." He complained. "Let's get upstairs."

"Don't worry." Taryn watched the ranger and paused. "I'll keep you safe." She smiled as she squeezed by Arden to lead the way up the stairs.

He gazed at her curiously as she walked by. His nervous fidgeting stopped as his mouth opened in response to her close proximity.

The feelings that had been sitting with her since she first saw him had finally emboldened her to action. She stepped on the first stair and pulled him to her and pressed her lips to his.

Arden's reaction was a gasp of surprise as he set his warm hands on her side and pressed her close.

His lips were firm, yet giving as she surrendered herself to the kiss, melting with him. She fell back against the cold stone of the stairwell and pulled him with her. And then it set in. They were kissing in a stairwell in ancient dwarven ruins. *Oh, gods. What am I doing?* She blushed furiously as she pulled away. The feelings that were fluttering around her gut made her feel warm, like this was meant to happen. "We'd better get up before Hugh wonders what happened to us."

He looked between her eyes and stepped back, nodding as he caught his breath. "You're right."

Even distracted with their discovered affections, the ancient stone carvings still impressed her as they left. The detailed and immaculate etchings of the various dwarven figures were impressive, she couldn't help but wonder what this place was like when it was actively used. Once they found their way to the passage outside, Hugh stood off, away from them and listened attentively to something they had both missed.

The ranger turned as they walked out, and held up a hand to caution silence. He quickly walked over to the apprentices with a concerned look. "I may be wrong, but I thought I heard something downhill from us. Stay here; I won't be long. Go inside, just in case."

"Sure." Arden agreed and turned to go inside. "You coming?" His smile held the same charm that drew her to him so long ago.

"Yes, yes. In a moment." She agreed as she watched the ranger pull his bow and loosely prepare an arrow, moving out of sight as he jogged ahead to scout the slope. Even with her heart soaring, she wanted to stay where she was, and keep an ear out for trouble. Her thoughts drifted to Arden's lips and that look in his eyes in the stairwell. She could not help but smile while she stepped back to examine the shrine's twenty-foot guardian carved into the mountain's side.

"Breathtaking, isn't it?" An amused voice called out from behind her.

Taryn jumped in surprise and turned around, immediately placing her hand on the hilt of her blade. She tugged on the weapon as he stepped forward and began to speak.

"Now, that isn't too nice. Drawing a weapon on a complete stranger. How rude!" the new arrival mocked with a smirk. He was dressed in colorful, but worn robes that looked as if they had not been washed in weeks. His gaunt frame held a strength and sureness beyond the scope of physical perception. The faint lines of a goatee and stubble rested below a curled mop of black hair and betrayed a slight hint of graying toward the front.

In response, she inched out her blade in warning as she adopted a readied stance.

The smile faded as he reprimanded the young woman. "I thought I said that wasn't nice." He muttered a phrase while flicking his wrist in a singly fluid maneuver. "There, that's much better, isn't it?" The playful smile returned and faded into a cruel grin as he approached Taryn.

Terror struck the apprentice as she realized she was unable to move. A breeze flitted across her skin, emphasizing her inability to react, to even shiver from the cold touch of the mountain air. Her eyes searched the area for any signs of Hugh, and instantly refocused on the man in front of her when she realized no one was coming.

"Ahh, yes. The realization that you are prone to my whims, and indeed, alone." He turned back to the slope and laughed to himself. "How easily some people are fooled by a simple incantation. Make someone think they hear voices in the mountains and watch them run off." He mused with satisfaction. "Let me introduce myself, I am—"

"Pan Gorak." She spat out. Pan's all-too-amused look was beginning to stir her ire enough to look him defiantly in the eyes.

His eyes grew wide for a moment before receding back into his self-assured amusement. "My, my. Aren't we the informed one? I'm afraid you have me at somewhat of a disadvantage, youngling. If time were not of the essence, I might bother to find out more about you, but no." He shook his head slowly. "I need information, and unfortunately for you, I am not here to play games." His countenance took on a sadistic anticipation as he produced his left hand and held it up before her as he whispered a quick incantation. The moment he finished, his hand was consumed by a blazing green flame.

The heat that poured out of Pan's hand pulsed and instantly made her sweat under her thick clothing. Still unable to move, she did the only thing she could do, talk. "What do you want?" Fear crept into her voice much louder than she wanted it to, for which she cursed herself.

"All I want to know, is why you are here. You know my name, so it seems likely that you are following me. Is that so?" He raised his eyebrows and rolled his fingers in front of her playfully.

"Go kiss the Abider's arse." She scowled, looking around for Hugh.

The sorcerer laughed. "Met him. Had tea. Nice try, however." He lessened the flames on his hand as he untied Taryn's cloak and let it slip to the ground. "Wouldn't want that damaged, would we? Now, shall we try for another answer?" He pried expectantly.

Taryn resolutely looked away, choking back a tear as fear began to harden in the pit of her stomach.

Pan sighed. "I thought as much; what a pity." He commanded the flames to rise on his hand and placed it firmly on Taryn's shoulder, soliciting an agonizing scream from his victim as the flames blazed through the links in Taryn's chain shirt and burned away her woven vest and shirt underneath, exposing the shoulder below. He watched the links grow red hot and listened for the sizzling of her skin as the steel mail seared her flesh before pulling his hand away.

The pain from the searing heat jolted her through the core.

The scream that tore from her throat echoed throughout the open plain in front of the shrine and down the rocky mountainside. Not only did she have to endure the torture itself, but the sheer inability to react physically frustrated her to the point of madness. Her lips quivered as the sobs lessened. She looked up at the sadistic man and was torn between the need to run away and hide, and the need to skewer him alive with her sword. Hate poured out from her, barely hidden by the pain and fear within.

The sorcerer looked upon his victim with a feigned compassion. "See? Now, if you only listened I wouldn't have done that. It truly *is* your fault, you know." He stepped back and took on a more serious tone. "Now, if you please. Why are you following me?"

Heavy footfalls resounded behind her and grew close as they left the confines of the shrine and slapped on the rocky ground.

"And now we have another," Pan observed as he turned away from Taryn and toward the shrine.

Relief washed over Taryn at the sound of the footsteps. "Arden, run! Get Morolinn!"

Within moments, Arden's cautious steps brought him into Taryn's line of sight. His eyes widened with fear when he saw Taryn's burned and blistering shoulder. "Pan!"

The sorcerer looked at the newcomer with a dulled glance. "Yes, yes. I'm here. Introduction made. Now, perhaps *you* would be so kind as to cooperate and let me know why you are following me?" He raised an eyebrow expectantly.

The apprentice bowed his head as he responded. "Of course, your eminence."

Taryn's heart sank. *What?*

"Pardon?" Pan took a double-take and looked at the young man. "Arden, is it? How is it that *you* know me?" He scoffed aloud. "Am I the only one left out in the cold here?"

Arden looked up. "In absolution's grace will all be revealed."

Pan's lips parted in joyful surprise. "How unexpected. A believer. Now, tell me. Why am I being followed?"

"Don't! You can't!" Taryn's lips quivered, her mind reeling from the shock of seeing the one person she let in and opened her heart to take so readily to this man who so quickly and willingly attacked her.

Arden looked uncomfortably at Taryn before answering. "The mage Morolinn is following you. Something about you taking a prized artifact, an Oculus, a compass of some sort. He's below, chanting some spell to find you this very moment."

"Interesting." He frowned appreciatively and pursed his lips in thought.

Tears streamed down Taryn's face. "How could you?" She could still feel the brush of his lips to hers, even now with the duplicity revealed to her.

Arden avoided her gaze. "I'm sorry; I truly am." He looked up to Pan. "Does she have to die?" His brow narrowed while the typically boisterous voice shook in concern.

"We all have our time to die; this happens to be hers," the sorcerer answered dismissively. "You don't think after seeing you speak freely with me, she would let you go without consequence, do you?"

Arden nervously looked at Taryn and lowered his head. "No, your eminence."

She choked on her sobs. The heart-wrenching pain of not only the betrayal, but also the casual discussion of her death, would have knocked her to her feet if she were not already firmly rooted in place.

"Good, at least you have *some* wit about you." Pan stopped and cocked his head thoughtfully until inspiration flowed across his brow. He turned his gaze back to Taryn with his all-too-eager grin. "So be it, there may be a way for you to live through this yet, young Arden. You *are* a true believer, are you not?"

"Of course."

"Excellent. Now take your blade from your sheath and run her through."

The apprentice spat in surprise. "Kill her?"

The sorcerer glanced at the younger man. "Tarry not, for I will do the job for you and bestow absolution on *you* as well."

"You... you can't. We... We're... The last two years... Why?" She pleaded between sobs.

Sorrow filled the apprentice's eyes as he pulled his sword from his sheath. He lifted the blade to where the point was aimed right above Taryn's waist. His lips moved, and whispered his apology. "I'm sorry."

"You..." Her sobs halted as she felt the tip of the blade flick up and lift the chain shirt and the padding underneath. The cold of the steel weapon pushed on her skin, resting there as Arden closed his eyes and braced the pommel with his palm, preparing to push through. Her pain and terror chilled as the finality of her life drew near. She looked up with burning hate. "You deserve every bit of hell that's coming."

Pan looked at her with a patronizing smile. "No, my dear. *You* are the one who will suffer its warm embrace this day."

"I think not." Hugh's voice called out from behind the sorcerer before the telltale swoosh of an arrow broke the light droning of the wind around them.

Both Arden and Pan turned, but only the younger man looked surprised at the sight of an arrow loosed and streaming through the air toward them.

The arrow sped straight for the sorcerer in its deadly aim. It bore down on him and flew within an arm span's distance when Pan flicked his wrist and pointed at the young man next to him.

Arden's eyes grew wide as the grip on his blade slackened and he dropped the sword. He fell to his knees, the arrow jutting out of his chest as he grabbed it. His lips parted in silent protest while his body slumped to the side.

Taryn's eyes crossed Pan's shoulder and focused on Hugh as the ranger came into view. He took aim with his bow and released another arrow.

Pan countered this next attack as easily as the first. "Ahh, yes. The ranger. Now *this* is exciting." His eyes grew brighter with glee as a new smile crossed his sadistic face. "You," he glanced sidelong at Taryn. "Don't move." He raised his hand and shot a blast of the green fire out at the ranger.

Hugh ducked quickly to the side, and easily escaped the attack, righting himself as he pulled another arrow from his quiver.

"And quick, too. Remarkable." The sorcerer's thrill of battle pushed his movements. He became more animated while watching Hugh fire another arrow at him, which was sidestepped with ease. "Let's see how well you deal with this." Pan mocked gleefully as he raised both of his hands and pushed them downward while muttering in some vile and foreign tongue.

Hugh shouted in distress as the ground broke beneath him, and his legs began to sink within the rocky earth, rooting him to the spot.

"Much better." He glowed with satisfaction. "Tell me something, ranger. How does it feel to know you are about to die?" He held his flaming hand out and prepared another volley of green flame.

The attack was interrupted by a separate cry as an arc of lightning flew out from the shrine's entrance and slammed into Pan Gorak, sending him tumbling several feet away.

Hugh spat on the ground and tugged at his legs. "I'll have ta tell ya when it happens." He chuckled with a heavy breath of relief as he looked at Morolinn who was now walking onto the field.

Taryn immediately stumbled over as she regained control of her body. The apprentice struggled to retain her balance and once she did so, gripped her burned shoulder which forced her knees to buckle from the agony. Pain tore down her arm as the freshly seared flesh cried out at her touch.

Arden's body lay just out of reach, staring blankly into the sky, and ushered in a new storm of emotions. The sound of the mage passing her snapped her back to the present. She braced herself to stand as she caught her breath and watched the battle.

The sorcerer stood quickly and brushed his legs off. "About time you showed up. Typical, you must be from the council." He shook his head with an exaggerated impatience. "Wait a moment," he said while narrowing his eyes, "I know you. I have your Oculus." He laughed. "You *really* need to keep better track of your belongings."

Hugh took advantage of the distraction and loosed another arrow. A stream of curses came spewing when it was easily deflected.

Pan raised an eyebrow in pity toward Hugh before turning back to Morolinn who was walking closer to the fray. "And now, we shall truly have some fun." He fired a blast of green fire toward the council mage.

Morolinn didn't miss a beat as he continued his advance, countering the fire with a blast of frost. He shot back another bolt of lightning, which Pan answered with a shield of blue force, and simply watched as the lightning arced uselessly around him.

Taryn gritted her teeth and ignored the pain in her shoulder as she stood on her feet and drew her blade.

The sorcerer glanced at his three opponents and bowed his head. "As much fun as this has been, I'm afraid that it is time for me to depart." He let out a sharp whistle and winked at Taryn before rushing down the slope.

Morolinn and Taryn both ran to see Pan Gorak mount a sleek mare and ride down the slope and away from the shrine.

"Dangerous is right." Hugh observed as Morolinn helped pull his legs out of the ground. "How are ya holding up?" He looked up at Taryn, and for the first time, noticed the exposed shoulder and burned flesh covering it.

Taryn looked at her shoulder and immediately regretted doing so. The rush of excitement crashed, and with it, her ability to withstand the agony that crept down her limb and chest. She was hit with the weight of the mail as it dug into her charred shoulder, and brought with it a new, deeper pain every time she moved. The burden of Arden's betrayal coupled with the pain, aching in counterpoint to the agony stemming from her shoulder. What little adrenaline that lingered evaporated and brought her turmoil to the forefront, forcing her down on her knees. Her eyelids fluttered while she looked up. Hugh's silhouette stood before her as she tried to focus. "Not well."

CHAPTER 10

THE GRAYED WALLS OF THE stable's worn wood stood out, matching the dull exterior of Guardians Keep even moreso than Taryn recalled. The trio trotted along the western side of the keep toward the aged building in silence. Taryn knew she should be glad to be home, but she couldn't shake the oppressive sense of loss that filled her since she felt the cold touch of Arden's blade a week earlier. She searched in her mind for any signs that he wasn't true, that he wasn't who he said he was and found none. His betrayal seemed so unreal, so unlike him, it was difficult for her to accept. She would not have believed it were it not for the sting of the blade that he was commanded to wield against her. She looked up the massive walls, and found them joyless. The overcast sky hung over the keep and shrouded the sun from view as it blanketed the area in a chill. Exhaustion clung to her limbs, sinking them with a leaden weight. The constant pain and suffering from her shoulder took its toll on her, and all she really wanted to do was have her bandage cleaned and go to bed and wish it all away.

Asher ran out from behind the stables, and watched Taryn as she was helped off her horse. He trotted over to her, looking up, his sad eyes not seeking the playful attention normally called for. He planted himself next to her and assumed a protective stance. His head snapped toward the keep when the rear door slammed open.

"What happened?" Thoman's voice bawled out in an excitement Taryn had rarely heard. She turned to see him marching straight to the trio, trailed closely behind by Pallitine Harrold.

"Where's Arden," the District Pallitine asked as he stared at the mage who accompanied his apprentice and childhood friend, "and who is this?"

Hugh stepped from his mount and looked to the District Pallitine with a somber look of regret. "Arden's dead. I'm afraid he wasn't everything he seemed."

"What do you mean?" He asked, bewildered. He glanced over to Taryn and saw old bandages plastered to her shoulder, covered only by the badly burned scraps of a shirt and her cloak. He looked down and noticed how she cradled her arm under the cloak. He rushed to her, his eyes wide with dismay. "How did this happen?" The question was left hanging for only a moment when he looked into Taryn's eyes with a concern that caught even her off-guard. "How are you?" The words held little meaning compared to the raw and vulnerable look that cradled itself in his gaze.

"I'm fine, I just need to rest." She winced as she tried to put on an air of confidence behind the words.

He nodded, and his manner took on a cold edge as his brow furrowed in rage. He turned to the ranger and stepped firmly toward the man. "I need to know who did this. Now." He commanded.

Hugh held a hand up in acquiescence. "I bet. The man's name is Pan Gorak; he's a rogue mage, which is why our friend here," he nodded toward Morolinn, "was with us. He enlisted my aid in finding him an' taking him down."

"And you took two apprentices with you." Thoman glowered.

Hugh pointed at Thoman. "Ya know how the trainin' works.

Don't start in on me." His offense quickly faded when he saw Thoman's concern behind the rage. His shoulders slumped as he sighed and lowered his hand. "I'm sorry fer what happened ta Taryn. I am. We weren't ready ta deal with such a deadly force; he caught us by surprise."

Thoman stepped back and nodded. "I know you did everything you could, but I still need to know who this Pan is."

Morolinn spoke up. "He is either a figurehead, or the leader of an old cult, the Absolutionists."

Pallitine Harrold chimed in. "And what do they have to do with this?"

"We don't know, really." He turned to the pallitine. "The Absolutionists have been around for centuries, insidious and lurking in the shadows, biding their time for their god to claim our world. They never expose themselves; this move is quite unlike them."

"Until now, you mean." Thoman added.

The mage glanced back to the District Pallitine. "Right. Anyways, when Pan attacked, Arden revealed himself as an Absolutionist and called him *your eminence,* which seems to confirm some suspicions the council had regarding his involvement in the cult." His eyes strayed toward Taryn as he went on. "After Pan tortured Taryn, Arden came out to investigate the commotion. This is when he saw Pan, and revealed his allegiance. Pan ordered Taryn's death and Hugh was able to stop him before the traitor could follow orders."

Thoman turned to the ranger. "By killing him."

"Not ta sound cold, but Pan killed him. I simply loosed the arrow." He shrugged.

The pallitine raised an eyebrow.

"Sorcery." Hugh spat on the ground. "In either case, she's still alive. That's what matters when the sun sets."

Taryn closed her arms around her and fought off memories the conversation was dragging up. While the men were talking, the only vision that filled her mind was watching Arden hold the blade to her gut as she stood there, held in place by unnatural forces and completely helpless. Her good arm slid down to cradle her stomach as she rocked gently back and forth from the pain wracking her shoulder. Tears silently beaded at the corner of her eyes as she looked away, silently begging the torture to stop. All sounds, including the soft whining coming from her self-appointed protector next to her, seemed muted as she focused on something other than her injury and the memories it brought.

Thoman, reacting to Asher's sympathetic whine, looked to his apprentice and saw the agony wearing on her. "Let's get her resting, we can continue this inside."

Several minutes later, Taryn thankfully slumped against the backboard of her bed while the apothecary came to tend to her wound. With Maddoc bunking upstairs in the pallitines' quarters, and Arden's few belongings being hauled off by Pallitine Harrold, the room seemed quiet. *At least I'll finally have a room to myself.*

Thoman and the others watched silently as the apothecary went about his business tending her shoulder.

The apothecary ignored Asher's dutiful hovering as the dog paced behind him, watching every move. "How in the divines did this happen?" the brown-haired elf asked as he removed the soiled bandage.

"Sorcerer's fire," Hugh answered.

The apothecary shook his head as he inspected the burned and dead flesh. "It's a wonder she isn't worse off. We'll need to cut the worst of the dead skin and watch it carefully as it heals."

Morolinn stepped toward Taryn's bed and looked over the man's shoulder. "I did what I could, but I'm afraid for all my knowledge, my skill in the healing arts is somewhat lacking. Fortunately Hugh has a good mind toward natural remedies."

"Indeed. She's lucky you both were there. I doubt the wound would be in such good shape were you not able to treat it." He frowned as he took a small set of iron tongs and gripped the charred skin while he produced a sharp blade. A low, rumbling growl called out from behind him, giving him pause.

Asher stood, tensed on all fours and glared at the man who was holding a knife to Taryn's shoulder.

"Can someone get this mutt out of here?" he pleaded.

"No." Taryn cut him off. "He stays with me." She patted the spot next to her on the other side of the bed.

The dog immediately trotted over to where she was patting and climbed up, setting his head in her lap as he eyed the frustrated man warily.

"Why don't you simply spell the injury away?" Thoman asked from over the apothecary's shoulder. "That should take care of the worst of it, right?"

The elf sighed and looked up at Thoman. "No, I cannot. There are consequences to everything we do."

His brow knit in anger. "She's in pain. *Do something!*"

A look of resignation covered the apothecary's face. "True, we could heal every injury that might happen. To everyone. But doing so has a toll. Eventually we would grow dependent on the magic, and not our own bodies to cure our injuries. And when the magic fades, what then? We've grown too dependent on the magic and are weaker for it. We must encourage our bodies to heal on their own. Only by doing this, can we ensure that our strength lives on."

"What kind of grief is that? Do something, man!"

"It's happened before. There's always a price to pay." He looked to Taryn, then back up to the pallitine looming over him and sighed. "Fine. I'll do what I can to ease her discomfort and bolster her body's natural ability to heal. Nothing more aside from the standard treatments."

Thoman shook his head, but backed down, mollified by the response.

The apothecary muttered his displeasure as he turned back to his patient. He chanted softly in a tongue that reminded Taryn of a babbling brook as he went back to his task at hand of carefully cutting the blackened flesh that still clung to Taryn's shoulder.

The familiar tingle of magic surrounded her, with only the vaguest difference in feel from the violent magic that pierced her body days before. Were it not for the exhaustion that hung down on her, she would have shied from the contact, and away from this unnatural force. The events that transpired previously, however, left little inspiration to fight.

Taryn stroked Asher's head, glad for the comfort the creature brought. She turned to watch the elf work and instantly regretted it. Nausea made her head swim, not from the sight, but from the sense that she knew this should have hurt more. The simple fact it didn't filled her with a thick sense of dread. She refused to watch the man and listened instead to the conversation that was resuming with a discussion of the mage.

"Why is the council so interested in this Pan?" Thoman asked the mage, pulling him into the conversation.

"He was once a promising member of the Irlinian College, but was excommunicated from the order when it was discovered that he dabbled in the dark arts and stole tomes from our inner vaults. He has proven himself to be a ruthless man who will stop at nothing to get what he wants."

"What is it he wants?"

"I only know rumors really." The mage looked unsure in his explanation. "It's been said that he seeks a bridge between life and death, though for what purpose I know not. Perhaps he has found a common goal with the Absolutionists, and their desire to cleanse the world for their god?" He shrugged.

Thoman sighed and looked back to Taryn. "No matter, if he chooses death as his tool to get what he wants, I would think he should be given that which he seems to freely dole out." He turned back to Hugh. "I'm sorry for reacting poorly earlier, I *do* know you would've avoided this if at all possible."

Hugh set his hand on his friend's shoulder. "Not ta worry. I understand. Truly, I do. What will ya do?"

Thoman frowned and narrowed his brow. "I still have a

contact within the Revenants. I'll send an inquiry out to see what they can find for me."

Hugh's eyebrow raised in surprise. "I thought they ran a bit dark for your tastes?"

"Dark times call for dark measures, my friend. And this certainly calls out for darker measures."

Hugh turned to watch the apothecary apply a salve to some new dressings and place them gingerly on Taryn's shoulder. "Can't argue with ya there."

Thoman embraced Hugh's shoulders and smiled weakly. "Go, get some food and rest. You've had a long journey. We can catch up once I've had a moment with my apprentice."

Taryn watched the others leave, relieved to have the chance to truly rest. Her eyes wearily watched Thoman sit on her bed, next to her.

"How are you doing? I mean, really doing?" His eyes held that look again, the one filled with an undeniable depth of concern.

She shook her head, not wanting to let go of her feelings, she held on to the despair and fear that clung to her heart. "I've been better."

He nodded. "I can appreciate that. I can't imagine what you must be feeling. To face such a ruthless foe, and have a close friend reveal his true colors so brutally."

Her jaw quivered as she failed to fight off the rush of emotion that filled her to bursting. "He was going to kill me. *Arden was going to kill me.*" She choked back a sob and went on. "The tip of his sword was here," she placed a hand over the point where the blade touched her skin. "And there was *nothing* I could do. I was stuck, frozen in place, and I felt it press into me. If it wasn't for Hugh I'd have been skewered and bleeding out on the ground." A reminder of the terror she felt swept into the turmoil, clouding her despair with fear. "There was *nothing* I could do."

Thoman frowned helplessly. "I'll bring this man to justice. I swear to you."

Taryn sniffled and nodded, breathing more slowly as she composed herself. "Good." She hardened her heart at the thought of Arden, and vowed to never let anyone in like that again. Never again would she let herself slide into a complacent trust, open to be betrayed at the basest level. *Never again.*

Thoman reached out and placed his hand on hers, and squeezed it. "Never should anyone have to suffer the unjust wrath of another. Not you, nor anyone else."

Something in his words struck a chord with her. The ring of truth behind the need to protect others pushed her to look past her immediate hurt and move on. Her breast burned with the revelation that she needed to pick up the sword in the defense of those who truly could not defend themselves. Having suffered this tragedy opened her eyes to what she thought she knew, and passively tried to embrace, but now having felt this firsthand she knew she needed to hunt these Absolutionists down and stop them from inflicting harm on anyone else. Her hand squeezed Thoman's in return as she stared forward with a newfound conviction and shook her head. "No, *we* will bring this man to justice. Him and anyone else who would stand in our way."

CHAPTER 11

TARYN STRETCHED HER ARMS OUT and basked in the sun, savoring its warmth. The land looked lively, brighter than it had in a while for her, and her spirits were lifted from being out of the keep after being tucked away while her shoulder healed for the past two months. She stretched the arm, and while the skin on her shoulder was still tight, most of the pain she suffered had faded as her wounds healed. Nothing had been heard other than the stray murmurings regarding the Absolutionists since she came back, though it was unclear if that was because no news had been received, or if Thoman simply had not told her. Either way, she was happy to be out and away from Brother Hendrick, and the countless studies he forced upon her during her convalescence.

Thoman brought them to a local widow's home, Mrs. Ofsteader, on the far side of Durston. They came to aid in some repairs to her well and to make sure she was doing all right. A recent storm knocked down several trees near her house, and it was the pallitines' duty to aid their neighbors in these times of need.

Taryn walked alongside her mentor as they moved past the

widow's old, worn farmhouse. She flexed her hands in her gloves, preparing for the day's work. As much as she might like riding about in her chain shirt and leather cuirass when touring with her mentor, there were times she preferred her rugged work clothes. They just felt right; they seemed to call back to her roots, or at least what she imagined her father's roots would be if she knew him. The moment she turned past the front porch, her eyes widened at the sight of the two fallen trees that were knocked down in the storm. "You weren't kidding when you said they were big," she said appreciatively while examining the damage.

The first, larger tree lay strewn across the rock wall separating the homestead from the garden Mrs. Ofsteader tended, knocking much of it over. The next tree fell across the stone well not far off, leaving it in disarray with barely enough room between the tree and the broken stone ring of the well to get water out from its depths. Large puddles of water were still standing, sprinkled on either side of the fallen wall, and from the feel of the damp, chill air they weren't likely to disappear anytime soon.

Thoman nodded as he inspected the damage. "That, I was not. Good thing we came prepared. I'll get the axes and we can get started." Within moments, the pallitine returned with two axes and offered one to Taryn.

"Go ahead and get started on the larger one by the wall. Just be careful. When I'm done cutting the well free I'll join you." He urged, "Don't rush things, take it slow."

"Will do." She took the axe, walked to the wall, and picked a reasonably dry spot on the other side to start working on the tree.

After a time spent swinging her axe, she looked at the progress made and grew annoyed that only a handful of the larger branches had been removed thus far. She looked over the fallen tree, looking for an easier way to remove it. Within a moment, she saw a break between the tree and the wall that she could slip one of the larger branches through and use it as a

126

lever to push the tree off. She looked over to Thoman and saw that his progress was also going slow. She knew he wouldn't be ready to help anytime soon, so she shrugged to herself and started in with her plan.

Within moments, she had the branch in place and began to push, rocking it back and forth to gain the momentum she needed to push the tree off the wall. The work crept by slowly as the tree refused to move no matter how much effort she put into it, until a supporting stone eventually slid out of place, freeing the tree's movement. She pressed on, and rocked the tree harder until it teetered right to the edge of the wall. Thrilled with the development, she pushed the branch until it wouldn't budge.

Time slowed as her lever snapped, flicking across one of the wall's capstones, and knocked it over the edge and toward her foot. She deftly released the branch and moved out of the stone's way, watching it splash on the water-soaked ground with a wet thud and slip deeper into the mud under its own weight. The ground immediately made a violent slurping sound as the ground opened up and water drained down under the wall. So loud was the noise, she didn't realize the tree she pushed had skidded its way back across the wall and was skipping over the edge. By the time she saw the danger, it was too late.

Taryn was knocked backward by the force of the tree as it struck her, sending her sprawling backward in the mud. The tree skidded back to rest where she first found it, stopping in the space where the capstone rested moments ago. Unfortunately for her, one of the larger stones in the wall had been jarred loose when the capstone was knocked off, and now that the tree skidded back, its weight was quickly pushing the stone off the wall and toward her. Before she had a chance to move, the stone slipped out and landed on her leg with a sickening crack.

Her surprise quickly turned into a scream of pain that echoed against the stone wall, drowning out the chittering of several waterlogged rats that began to swarm out from under the wall, escaping the torrential flooding of their nest as they ran over the young woman.

Thoman dropped his axe and ran to Taryn, kicking a rat out of the way as he reached his apprentice.

"Get it off!" Taryn yelled as she lay on her back struggling to sit up and look at her leg.

The pallitine's boots sank in the muck as he reached down and pulled the stone off from her leg.

She gripped her leg and rocked back and forth wishing for the life of her that the pain would end.

After fighting his legs free, Thoman knelt on the wet ground next to her. "I'm going to need to take a look at your leg, are you ready?"

She scowled and looked away. "Do it."

He pulled the pant leg up past her ankle and winced at what he saw.

Taryn gritted her teeth and grunted in pain at the touch of the cloth as it was pulled over her wound. "How bad is it?" she asked as she reflexively turned her head to look.

Blood was smeared over the wound, masking most of the damage, but from what she could tell, no bones were sticking out where they shouldn't, and her leg wasn't twisted as bad as it felt.

Thoman lightly wiped some blood away with his hand to get a better look at the wound. "It's not as bad as it could be, though you've got quite the gash here. I wouldn't be too surprised if your leg broke from the impact. That was quite the blow you've taken there."

"Oh, dear. Is she all right?" Mrs. Ofsteader called out from her porch as she stepped toward them, wrapped up in a woolen shawl.

Taryn rolled her eyes as she tried to move her leg and rocked back from the pain.

"No, ma'am, she is not. Could you fetch us some clean water and bandages? We need to get her cleaned up."

After several lengthy minutes, the widow returned and

hobbled toward the two figures bearing a pail and some fresh wrappings.

Once the wound was cleaned and the leg wrapped in a bandage, Taryn soon found that the pain was too much to try to stand. Eventually with Thoman's help she found her way inside and rested while her mentor finished cutting the tree off the well so the widow would once again have free access to her water.

After an insufferable amount of time, the two were back on their mounts and headed toward the keep.

Pain shot through Taryn's leg, keeping time with the rhythm of her mount's movement. Irritated, she reached down with her hand, adjusted her splint, and instantly regretted moving her leg.

"How are you doing?" Thoman asked as he glanced at his apprentice.

"Fine." She fumed. Not only did she have to suffer the injury, and the humiliation of letting her impatience get the better of her, but she also had to suffer through those half amused, half compassionate 'I told you so' looks.

He nodded as he surveyed the land ahead. "Good. We should be back at the keep before nightfall. I'll have the apothecary take a look at your leg when we arrive."

Taryn scowled at that last comment. *Gods, and I just got done seeing him for my shoulder.* Her shin throbbed when she didn't move it, and sharp, biting pain lit her nerves every time she did.

"You'll be doing much better once you can rest and have a warm meal in you. I promise," Thoman reassured her.

She grunted, unimpressed with the words. The pain reminded her of the reason she had to see the apothecary in the first place. "Have you heard anything about the Absolutionists?"

Thoman looked curiously at her. "Only rumors. There was

mention of them stretching their influence among the Saerin to the south, although I'm not sure how much faith to put in that one. Why do you ask?"

"I remember you speaking to Hugh about asking someone for help. A Revenant?"

"Ahh. No, I wasn't expecting anything meaningful immediately, but my contact *is* resourceful. We could still hear something yet."

"What *is* a Revenant?"

Thoman looked off in thought before answering. "They are a small group that deals with gathering information others may not necessarily want known. Because of the very nature of their trade, they tend to be a secretive lot."

"And how do you know them?"

Thoman sighed and looked toward Taryn with a heavy heart. "When I first earned my rank as a pallitine, I was full of a righteous fury that drove me to bring wrongdoers to justice, fanatically so. That fury and drive came from my father's murder, and from watching my mentor die before me. Both helped to push me into the man I am today. Now, it wasn't long after I earned my place among our brothers that I was contacted by a Revenant who had information about my father's killers."

"So, he's who you got in touch with."

"No," he smiled. "He's a complete bastard. And he's dead. I got in touch with his apprentice, an honorable man, and very skilled in his own right."

Taryn looked at Thoman with a new respect. For every new detail she learned about him, there seemed to be several other pieces lurking off, waiting to be discovered. As much as she wanted to delve further into the story, she knew how much it bothered him to speak of that part of his past.

"Any news about the wyrm? I haven't heard mention of it recently."

Thoman frowned and shook his head. "No. There have been more pressing concerns. Namely, the Absolutionists." He turned to his apprentice. "Your experience with Pan Gorak has opened my eyes to the threat they pose. So I've refocused my efforts on the more immediate threat. The wyrm isn't going anywhere. Once this has been taken care of, the search will resume."

Part of Taryn felt a twinge of guilt for taking her mentor away from the search that had meant so much to him. Even with that, however, she was glad that he did. It comforted her to know that she had someone watching her back.

Gradually, the pain from Taryn's leg steered her mind away from its normal riding lull as she was jostled on her saddle. In need of a distraction, she decided to ask a question that had been bothering her. "Hey, Thoman," she started, "I've noticed there aren't many women in the order. Why is that?"

Her mentor shot a curious look at her and shrugged. "Being the dangerous job it is, I would imagine there hasn't been much interest." He looked as if in thought for a second before shrugging again. "I honestly don't know. That's something I've never really paid attention to. There are no rules prohibiting such, but of course, you already know that."

She turned and looked at Thoman as she speculated. "Knowing how much my apprenticeship was questioned when you first taught me, I can see why, in hindsight, some would shy away from it."

"Why is that?"

"Well," Taryn looked off as she recalled the initial reactions of several pallitines when she was first apprenticed, "some of the senior pallitines, while supportive, held some skepticism when you first brought me to the keep. It's like they thought me only fit to work in the scullery, that I was too delicate to handle the training."

"Hmm." Thoman furrowed his brow. "I can see that." He looked at her in a noncommittal frown. "It makes no difference, you're completely capable."

Taryn nodded and met Thoman's gaze. "Sure, but having to deal with the attitude of expected failure I think can put some girls off."

"Sure, but by the same token, if being a pallitine is truly what someone wants, they need to steel up and work toward their goal, female or no. As pallitines, we see adversity from all sides, be it in the judgmental opinions of our peers, or in an opportunistic attack from some backstabbing scoundrel. We are looked up to for our honor and for protection, and consequently, have many demands made of us. To be worthy of those demands, and of the respect of those we choose to protect, we need to move past many things." He looked more meaningfully at his apprentice. "You've never had issue before, is there a reason for this line of questioning?"

"Me?" Taryn's eyebrows rose as she shook her head. "No, not at all. I'm used to jerks and abrasive men. It's the kind ones that throw me off." She smirked at Thoman. "It just occurred to me there are so many who would, and do, treat myself and other women differently. It makes me wonder why you haven't."

"That's easy." Thoman smiled. "If I would have treated you different, then you would have *been* different. Don't get me wrong, I don't see you the same as any other aspiring pallitine. Not at all. You have the sort of fire and determination that our order needs."

Taryn started to smile at the praise, but winced as her horse trotted around a divot in the road. She reached down to scratch her leg while listening to her mentor.

"Besides, you remind me a lot of myself at your age." Thoman glanced sidelong at his apprentice as he spoke. "I was full of anger and willfulness. Without someone teaching us to focus that energy, you and I both would've ended up much different than we are now." He looked out onto the horizon and continued in a more contemplative tone. "We all have our own trials to bear, and though the reasons for our trials have no semblance, the trials themselves are not so different if you think about it. We started off needing to find focus for our anger. We both needed a suitable place to grow into the people we wanted to be. The only difference here is that I was fortunate enough to find one that I could teach those very lessons to that I was hard pressed to learn early on." Thoman flashed a subtle smile as he made the next point. "And like me, you choose to ignore some of the lessons taught. Patience, for example. Perhaps waiting for the leg to mend can help in that endeavor?" He grinned mischievously.

"Ugh." Taryn rolled her eyes, fighting off her annoyance. "I'm suddenly less thrown off by you."

Thoman laughed, and grinned at the retort made at his expense.

CHAPTER 12

THE OFFICE, WHICH HAD GROWN far too familiar to Taryn as of late, was strewn about in the elf's own style of organized chaos. Jars containing various salves, herbs, and powders were stacked in some unlabeled mess along one set of shelves, with books adorning other shelves along with an assortment of various items, knick knacks, and tools that Taryn could only guess at their use.

"How is her leg?" Thoman asked anxiously from the doorway of the apothecary's office.

The apothecary lightly pressed his thumbs across the apprentice's shin and looked away as if in concentration. "Pardon the curtness, District Pallitine, but I must focus if you want me to properly answer that question."

Thoman muttered an apology and looked up at Taryn, the concern wearing heavily in his gaze.

Taryn fought against the urge to yell out in pain from the probing touch and tensed the entire time her leg was being manhandled by the overrated nursemaid. While she appreciated having Thoman around, she wished he couldn't see her like this, feeling so helpless. "Ow!" she belted out as the sadistic man who professed to be a healer pushed down directly onto the gash. *If my leg weren't hurt I'd kick you across the room,* she fumed to herself.

"Hrmph," the apothecary muttered, "it's broken, but fortunately, it doesn't feel like the bone shattered. No infection setting in that I can see." He stood up and smoothed his clothes while turning to Thoman. "She'll need to have her wound cleaned and dressed for a few days, and watch it. Look for any redness or swelling." He walked over to a cupboard and pulled out a glass jar filled with thick, broad leaves. He crumpled them into a small bowl and poured some water in, mixing it with a powder from a clay jar he had pulled out when she arrived. He scraped the mixture against the side of the bowl and nodded in satisfaction. He scooped a portion of the mixture onto a bandage and dressed the wound. His face softened while wrapping the leg and he handled the leg carefully to not hurt his patient more than necessary, much to Taryn's relief. Once the bandage was in place, he splinted the leg firmly so it wouldn't move.

He looked up at the apprentice. "How does that feel?"

"Like a dagger's lodged in my leg and I can't get it out."

The healer smiled compassionately and clasped his hands together. "It will feel like that for a while yet, I'm afraid." He sat on a stool next to Taryn. "Needless to say, you shouldn't be up and about. You'll need to rest for a couple days, then I want to take another look at that leg of yours."

"How long until she's recovered?" Thoman asked as he stepped in.

"A few weeks, perhaps five or six depending on how serious it is. Possibly longer if it's worse than it looks. The main thing is for her to rest until I see her next. If all goes well, she can resume her studies then. I'll be better able to judge at that point when she can resume any sort of activity." A gentle smile broke across his face as he turned to Taryn. "That means no fighting for a while, miss."

"Ugh, you're as bad as Thoman," Taryn complained. Her spirit sank at the thought of doing nothing until she healed. The very idea of not being able to freely go out and train made her sick to her stomach. *Even with the shoulder, I could train a bit. There has to be something.* She stubbornly refused to acknowledge her fate and motioned for her mentor to come over and help her stand.

"Oh! Here, you'll need this before you go. Just because I've put you in a splint doesn't mean you can walk on it." The healer quickly grabbed a crutch from the corner and handed it to the apprentice. "And I mean it, don't make me restrict you to your room." He paused, smiling warmly. "And next time you want to visit for a chat, please don't feel the need to injure yourself. You're getting into quite the bad habit here."

<hr/>

"You've hardly touched your stew. What's going on?" Thoman inquired before gnawing a chunk off his half-loaf of raveled bread.

Taryn circled her spoon in the bowl, staring through it as her thoughts drifted listlessly about. "I'm tired of doing nothing." She groaned.

"The apothecary thinks you've only a week or so left to heal before he'll let you walk about without the crutch."

"I know," she shifted her gaze blankly across the table in her mentor's direction, "I'm sick of having to rely on others. You have *no* idea."

Thoman leaned back in his chair and looked at Taryn. "Have you given much thought to what you'd like to do once vetted?"

"I would like to stay in Tramire, and do what I can to help our people. Like what you were doing when we met. Touring the area and such, routing bandits."

"I've been thinking." He shifted in his seat. "With the attack, and now this, that perhaps it might not be a bad idea to consider one of the less dangerous postings, a permanent station somewhere, assisting someone like Maddoc is doing at the temple?"

"What?" She couldn't believe what she was hearing. "Why would you say that? You know this is what I want."

"I'm just saying give it some thought. No one would blame you for wanting a safer post. You've had a rocky training."

"Hmph." She frowned. There was no way she was going to back down. It was bad enough she had to wait for her leg to mend, but to be stuck as an assistant somewhere while people needed help? Unthinkable. "I can't. Not a chance. If you're so worried about me staying safe, why don't you take more time training me to fight?"

"More than we do now?"

She glowered. "We don't now. That's the point. More than we did before my accident." An idea struck. "Or I can have one of the other pallitines train me to fight." Her eyebrows raised as she dared him to not take her seriously.

He sighed and looked at her. "As stubborn as iron. Agreed, I will do that. Just think about it. And only when your leg is better."

A minor commotion turned Taryn's attention away from Thoman and drew it to the open archway of the keep's dining hall. Standing in the entrance were two men, dressed in the garb of the Pallitine Council. They spoke quietly with Brother Geoffries who led them to the hall and was now pointing the two men toward the table they sat at.

Both Taryn and Thoman looked curiously at the two figures as they walked purposefully in their direction.

Taryn glanced curiously at her mentor and pushed her bowl aside as they came to their table. Both men were well built, and possessed the sturdy frames of most active pallitines, but the insignias worn on their breasts indicated the first man worked for the council itself, while the other represented of the Church of Orn.

"District Pallitine Thoman?" The leader asked. His rounded features looked out of place on his otherwise muscular build, distracting from the dull gaze which sat under the short-cropped brown hair he kept pushed back atop his head.

Immediately Thoman acknowledged the newcomer and stood for a moment to offer the men a seat. "Yes, how can I be of service?"

"Pardon our intrusion. I am Herald Joren from the council, and this," he tipped an open hand toward his slightly foppish companion, "is Counselor Vaino from the church. We have some urgent news to relate." He glanced meaningfully at Taryn before looking back at Thoman.

"Please sit. Anything that can be told to me can be said in front of my apprentice."

Joren gratefully accepted the offer and sat next to Taryn. "So be it." The other figure took up a seat at the broad table next to Thoman. Joren's countenance adopted a subtle hue of somber reverence as he started. "First off, before it is fully known, I wish to inform you of the passing of our beloved High Pallitine."

Thoman's face flashed with surprise as a deep-felt sadness sank in his expression. "How long ago? What happened?"

Taryn watched the discussion, and thoughts of the man brought the glimmering of loss creeping into her breast. Although she didn't know him well on a personal level, the few times he did spend a meal with her he treated her as an equal, as he did all who lived in the keep. He took a genuine interest in her and showed confidence in her ability to pass the Trials of Honor once she completed her training. This warm and considerate manner was held for all whom he considered under his care. She was one among the many whose lives he touched that would miss him.

"Four days ago. He conferred with the king and other officials in Torvina. The talks were over and he was preparing to come back to the keep, but died in his chambers sometime in the middle of the night."

"How did he die?" Thoman's brow furrowed at the news, showing concern.

"There was no foul play, rest assured." Vaino interjected, his demeanor reassuring. "There were no signs of forced entry, nor any markings on the body. It is assumed for one of his years that he was called into Orn's good graces posthaste."

Joren agreed. "As a beloved leader, he shall be remembered for his years of service to the people, and to Orn."

Thoman looked aside and breathed deeply for a moment. He turned back to the visitors. "My thanks for coming to me first. I shall make the appropriate arrangements for his return, and his memorial."

Vaino started to talk, but was gently interrupted by Joren as he raised his hand. "Those concerns have been addressed. The reason we have come is for another, related matter."

"Oh?"

Taryn's interest was piqued, and she shifted to the side to get a better look at the herald as he spoke, wincing at the dull ache in her leg as she moved.

Joren glanced at Taryn uncomfortably and focused on Thoman. "With his passing a vacancy has been left, and the names of the district pallitines were discussed in length by the council."

Thoman nodded and glanced between both visitors. "That makes sense. All are good choices, to be honest. That must have been a difficult decision. How can I assist?"

"In the discussions, your name was brought up more frequently than most."

Thoman blinked as if he distrusted what was said. "Surely there are more qualified parties? I have only held this office for a handful of years."

Joren shook his head. "There is no mistake. You were chosen. Once the memorial is over, your induction will happen the very next day."

Thoman looked uncertainly at the two men then back at Taryn.

A pit grew in Taryn's gut as uncertainty washed over her.

A thought immediately sprang up. *What will happen with me?* Thoman was the only man she fully trusted. In two years of apprenticeship, she had grown to think of him more as family than as a mentor. Was that all about to change?

"We will look immediately for a suitable match for your apprentice so that your new duties can be addressed without distraction," Joren added gingerly.

"No." Thoman objected. His tone firmed in resolve as he stressed the point. "Under no circumstances will I let my responsibility to my apprentice fall to another, new office or no."

A weight lifted from Taryn's shoulders as the fear of having a new mentor and adjusting to someone else washed away. She visibly relaxed into her seat, smiling as she sank down in relief.

Vaino's compassionate expression waned in light of his concerns. "It is highly unusual—"

"But not unheard of, my friend." Joren interjected as he raised a hand gently toward the counselor. He turned to both Taryn and Thoman. "The council had considered this turn of events and supports the decision." He turned to Taryn and looked upon her seriously. "As apprentice to the High Pallitine, you will be held to a higher level of expectation, and certain duties that would have gone to an assistant may fall to you. Do you understand this?"

Taryn was caught off guard with the question, but quickly regained her poise. She replied in no uncertain terms. "Of course. I will gladly do what is called of me." She winced internally as she realized that she was one step closer to being the thing she refused to be once she was vetted. An assistant.

The herald looked satisfied with the response and turned back to the soon-to-be High Pallitine. "For the next item of business, whose name shall I forward for recommendation to assume your current role?"

Without hesitation, Thoman responded. "Pallitine Alistair. He has the courage needed for duty, and the foresight not to make unwise decisions. The demands of the position will be greatly suited for him."

"Excellent, I shall forward the recommendation on. The funeral and memorial will be five days hence. The arrangements have already been made for the transportation and I will take care of the rest. The next day, the appointment will be formally recognized, and you will need to leave to visit the capital for the administrative reception in Torvina. You will be briefed on the breadth of your new duties and concerns now, so that when you are appointed you can assume your responsibilities right away. This briefing will take the full attention of your time before the reception. It would ill behoove you to speak with the court unprepared."

Thoman nodded and his brow furrowed in silence as he took everything in.

Joren leaned back and glanced at the wrappings on Taryn's leg. "I trust the injury will not prevent travel?" He looked expectantly at her.

"Not at all." Taryn shook her head, her stubbornness refusing to let her admit weakness.

"Good. You will be briefed on your new duties as well, starting on the morrow." He stood from the table and bowed slightly to both Taryn and Thoman. "It was indeed a pleasure to meet you, District Pallitine. And you, apprentice. I shall return for any unforeseen questions, or if you need assistance with other matters in the morning." He curtly turned about and left the hall as quickly as he came, followed closely by Counselor Vaino.

She looked upon her mentor, a mix of sadness and relief overlaid a curious anticipation as to what the coming days would unfold.

Thoman returned the glance. "An interesting day, to be sure." He smirked as a mischievous glint crept into his eyes. "I trust that this is a suitable relief for your boredom?"

Taryn smiled, nodding. "Don't forget our agreement. High Pallitine or not, you're still training me to fight. More than before."

"I haven't forgotten. Just take what time you can now to prepare yourself." Thoman smiled sadly at his apprentice. "I think we'll both need time to adapt to the coming changes. And to remember our departed friend." His tone softened as he sighed and looked back toward the hall's entrance. "That is a large shadow to fill, indeed."

CHAPTER 13

"THERE SHE IS!" BEA EMBRACED Taryn as she limped into the kitchen. "I've missed my helper. Now all I'm stuck with is this lunk." She jabbed a thumb at the thick-necked youth behind her, a new boy eager to learn the ways of the pallitines.

Taryn looked fondly about the kitchen, the place of so many memories. "Time seemed so much simpler when all I had to worry about was not burning the stew." The recollections forced her lips up in a half smile.

"How's your leg healing?"

"I've only a week left before I'm rid of this infernal thing." The apprentice groaned as she leaned on her crutch.

"How are you handling the changes? It's quite a bit different being apprenticed to the High Pallitine I'd wager."

Taryn nodded. "We'll be busy preparing for the appointment until the memorial. A lot of what I've learned so far is how to conduct myself and greet people in an official capacity." She smirked. "Most of it revolves around knowing when not to speak, when to show deference to my superiors, and which of the district pallitines to go to for specific needs, and so on."

"It may seem like a lot of nothin' you'll be doing, but you're doing Orn's work. Remember that. A lot of people depend on the High Pallitine, and supporting him will help a lot of people."

"I know. Trust me." Taryn shook her head. "I've never seen the keep's steward as much as I have since the news was spread around last night. Though, even with as much as he's around and looking over my shoulder, I think it'll be good to have him here until things settle down."

"Aye, Charles is a good man. Proper and straight-lined, but a good one to have by your side to be sure." Bea nodded approvingly.

A cough rang out from the kitchen's entrance. Taryn turned to find Maddoc standing there, waiting patiently.

"I think you've someone that wants a word with you." Bea squeezed Taryn farewell. "I'll talk with you again. Be well, young lady." Warmth filled the matron's smile.

"Thanks." Taryn smiled and returned the affection. She limped her way out of the kitchen and looked to her former dorm-mate. "It's been a while."

Maddoc walked toward the rear entrance and nodded. "It has. I've been meaning to see you since I heard of what happened between you and Arden. But..." He led on, fidgeting as if he were unsure what to say.

Taryn nodded. "I understand."

The older boy opened the door for her and followed her outside. Once they were on the terrace overlooking the fighting circle, he leaned on the rail and turned to Taryn. "I just wanted—"

"No, please. Let me start." Taryn interrupted. The guilt of how she treated Maddoc was weighing heavily on her conscience. "I let Arden mislead me and, consequently, haven't given you the benefit of the doubt you deserved. I wasn't fair to you, and I'm sorry for that."

He nodded. "It's in the past, truly. I can't imagine what it would feel like to have a friend do what he did to you. I'm sorry you went through that."

She smiled sadly. "Thanks. It's a shame I had to go through

146

this to realize you were right all along."

"No worries, at all. Truly. Were I in your shoes I might've done the same. It's not like I didn't deserve some of what I got. I wasn't exactly warm and welcoming when you first arrived."

Taryn shrugged. "Like you said, it's the past. If you can see fit to move on and forgive me, I could do no less."

He smiled and relaxed, something that Taryn hadn't really seen from him before. "Thank you." He seemed to enjoy the moment, and even breathed easier as he leaned into the wall.

"You've heard Thoman will be appointed High Pallitine?"

Maddoc nodded. "I did, how are you taking it? Will he still be able to mentor you?"

"Yes, he made sure of that before accepting the appointment."

"Good, I was worried for you."

She looked at him curiously. "Really? Why?"

Maddoc shifted uncomfortably on his feet. "Just because we haven't gotten along much—"

"Ever?" Taryn jabbed lightly.

He chuckled lightly and agreed. "Ever. That doesn't mean I don't think highly of you. You've shown loyalty, and convinced me Thoman knew what he was doing when he took you on." He paused as he looked in her eyes. "I'm glad we talked." He looked off to the training circle briefly in thought. "I wanted to make sure I had a chance to see how you were before I left."

"You're leaving?" Taryn's smile dropped. "What happened?"

Maddoc blushed slightly and turned back to her. "I passed my trials and I've accepted a position assisting the Tramirian representative in the Prime Temple of Orn."

"By the gods!" Taryn lit up. "I had no idea. Congratulations."

"Thanks." He stammered.

The happiness she felt with the news flashed briefly before a thought occurred to her. "Say, what all have you heard about what happened with Arden?"

His mood shifted as he looked curiously at Taryn. "That he was an... Absolutionist? And he tried to kill you. Why?"

"I need a favor from you." She looked up at the newly appointed pallitine. "I need to know if you hear anything about the Absolutionists, it doesn't matter how small, but any news you can dig up, or happen to hear. Anything you can find out would help."

"Of course, gladly."

"Thank you." Her smile again found its place with the assurance of a new source of help. "I appreciate it."

The dining hall was busy, people talked in their groups, both those speaking quietly that were affected by the loss as well as the groups discussing things in lighter spirits.

Through good times or in grief, we all have one thing in common. Hunger.

Taryn hobbled into the dining hall and found her mentor sitting with Pallitine Harrold, conversing over a couple pints of mead.

He waved her over, and she made her way to the table.

"Taryn, glad you could make it. Harrold, here, has been foolish enough to offer his services now that Maddoc has earned his rank."

Taryn nodded. "Oh?"

Pallitine Harrold graciously agreed. "Of course. How could I not offer my assistance to the one who will soon be our High Pallitine?"

"And the help is greatly appreciated, indeed." Thoman slapped his hand on the pallitine's shoulder in good spirits.

Harrold drank the last of his mead. "Then, by your leave, there are things I must attend." He stood and acknowledged Thoman. "I will see you after the appointment is confirmed." He turned to Taryn and bowed slightly. "And to you, Taryn, good night."

"He seems to be in good spirits," Taryn observed.

Thoman nodded. "He should be, his prized student has earned his rank, and with it Harrold has earned a bit of a respite."

She turned back to her mentor. "So, what will he be doing for you?"

"Mostly errand work and such when you are unavailable. Handling correspondence between myself and the District Pallitines on occasion. The dry work that I will need to warm up to, in spirit if not in practice."

Taryn frowned. Something seemed off. "A bit quick to be groveling to the man in charge, isn't it?"

Thoman's joviality diminished. "That's a dark outlook. I've known him for years; he's being a friend." He lifted a hand from his stein and pointed a finger at her. "Something you may not be comfortable with, but on occasion, people will do things for their comrades for no reason other than seeing a need. You'll learn this in time."

Taryn shrugged. "Perhaps you're right." She thought back on the man who was Maddoc's mentor, the man who displayed nothing but a kind and supportive manner to her since the start. *Perhaps Arden left a bigger mark on me than I realized.* She pushed the doubt from her mind and thought to the days ahead. "What's Torvina like?"

CHAPTER 14

THE WARM AUTUMN EXPANSE ABOVE greeted Taryn as she stepped out of the keep. She looked up into the cloudless sky, and for once, had no reservations for the time of year. This day marked her eighteenth year on this world, and if the last couple years were to be a sign of things to come, she welcomed it all, challenges and good times alike.

She stepped to the edge of the terrace and looked for her mentor. Earlier in the day, he came to her with a conspiratorial smirk on his face and asked her to meet him outside when her lessons were done. He was leaning on the fence next to the training circle and waited for her, arms crossed. Asher sat nearby, and looked up at Taryn when she came into view. He stood anxiously and looked from Thoman to her, and started for the stairs.

What is he up to? This isn't another one of his lessons wrapped in a blanket of mischief, I hope. She walked down the stairs, scratched Asher's back and walked to the circle.

"About time you showed up, I was starting to think you were lost," Thoman quipped.

"I'm here. What did you need me for?" She looked into the

training circle. "Are we sparring today?" *He's looking way too happy with himself for this to be good.*

He chuckled to himself and shook his head. "No, nothing like that. As you know, according to the laws of the land, there are certain rights and responsibilities one is allowed when grown into adulthood."

Slag it, he remembered. Taryn braced herself for the worst.

"One of those rights, is very much a responsibility." He paused and looked at his apprentice with a look of pride. "And that is the right to bear arms. In the time I've known you, you've grown from the fierce alleycat I first encountered into the strong woman you are now. You learned much in your time here, and have done far better than I hoped for. You've made me proud by embracing what it is to be a pallitine, in both spirit, and in action. Your studies and training rival my own at your age, and I had a much earlier start than you."

The words brought an uncomfortable pride she had no idea how to react to. *Oh gods, at least no one has to witness this.*

Thoman looked up to the terrace and smiled.

Taryn looked behind her and saw Bea and Pallitine Harrold leaning over the railing, listening. Her face flushed in embarrassment. "You honor me with your kindness, too much so, I'm sure," she said behind gritted teeth.

Her mentor beamed at her. "Not at all. Now, in accordance with a tradition started by my own mentor, I had something made for you." He turned behind him and picked up a long, rigid bundle wrapped in burlap.

Taryn's eyes widened. Her heart stopped. *Is that a handle poking out?* "For me?" She couldn't believe it.

"Yes, for you." Thoman held the bundle out for her.

Taryn took it, and as much as she wanted to gingerly unwrap the gift, she threw the burlap off the weapon and found a sword sheathed in rigid brown leather. Slowly, she pulled the weapon free and found a leather-wrapped hilt that led to a polished blade. *My gods.* "This is beautiful." She stammered as she gazed upon the blade, at a loss for the right words. The blade was a great example of sturdy Tramirian craftsmanship, half again as long as her arm and sharpened on both sides. A polished and shallow groove rested in the middle of the blade, extending halfway up the sword and gave it a simple, but dignified appeal.

Thoman's smile widened. "I'm glad you like it. It's yours. Happy birthday."

She sheathed the blade and rushed over to her mentor, squeezing him. "Thank you. This is... truly the most precious thing I've been given."

He looked into her eyes and placed a hand on her shoulder. "I'm proud to call you apprentice and am honored to give it to you. There is truly no one I'd rather give such a gift to. Now, if I remember correctly, I think Bea has made some sweetloaf to celebrate the occasion."

Taryn turned around and glanced up toward the other two, who were both happily looking on.

Bea nodded and waved her in. "C'mon up, dear. It's your day after all."

"Happy birthday," Pallitine Harrold chimed in before following Bea inside.

⌒ゑﷺⱻ⌒

Taryn marveled at the weapon as it lay on the table in its sheath. She looked around at Bea, her mentor, and Harrold as they sat in the empty dining hall. A sense of calm retrospection filled her as she thought of the past year, and what the next might hold.

"It won't be long before you'll go through the Trials of Honor and earn your own place in the ranks," Thoman predicted. "Perhaps even as soon as this time next year. You never know."

Taryn handed her plate to Bea, who was cleaning up the table now that the sweetloaf was gone. "The trials seem so far away. You really think it will happen that quickly?"

He shrugged. "Depends on the fates, I suppose. But I can see it happening."

Harrold agreed. "Maddoc was twenty when he passed. If there is need in the ranks, I don't see why you couldn't pass either. You've got more than enough talent, and at least as much drive as any of us have had."

"Trust me, dear. The time will come closer than you think." Bea reassured her as she poured wine for the group.

"High Pallitine," Charles, the keep's steward, interrupted as he walked into the dining hall. "There is a messenger here to see you."

Thoman excused himself and stood from the table. "I'll be right back."

Harrold swirled the wine around in his cup. "And what are your plans when you join our esteemed ranks?"

Taryn looked deep into her own wine before answering. "I'd like to ferret out the Absolutionists, for one. No one should feel like they have the right to walk around and extinguish anyone's light at the merest hint of a whim. I don't care what you believe in, this Pan Gorak and his cult need to be put down."

He nodded in appreciation. "I thought as much. Noble of you to put others first. Yet another reason why you are thought so highly of." He raised his cup in salute.

It's not just for others. The image of his cruel face leering in front of her still haunted her dreams. The very thought of him made her shoulder ache. She looked over to Bea. "And perhaps champion the cause of bakers everywhere, and the insufferable under-appreciation of their craft." She grinned.

"Oh, now. You well know what it takes; you've learned a bit in your time." Bea stopped mid-sip in her wine. "Not nearly enough to replace me, of course. That'd take you a dozen years or more, but you've learned enough." She winked.

Thoman walked back through the entrance of the dining hall. The jovial, relaxed expression he wore moments ago was lost in a wash of thought. He held a parchment in one hand and took his wine with the other as he sat.

"What's wrong?" Taryn asked.

"Things are not always as they seem," he answered as he looked up. He turned to each person gathered in turn before expanding on the statement. "My contact with the Revenants sent some troubling news."

Harrold leaned forward. "What is it?"

Thoman sat back in his chair, the weight of a troubled mind bearing down across his brow. "The Absolutionists know that I've been seeking them out."

"But how?" Taryn gasped.

A dark scowl formed before the answer. "We have a traitor in our midst."

Harrold's jaw fell open. "Who?" The question sounded hollow in light of the revelation.

Thoman shook his head. "I know not. I only know that word has been ferreted out of the keep and made its way back in. And with this news, an order has been intercepted to stop our querying, no matter the cost."

Taryn sat stunned, and looked amongst all who were gathered.

Bea glanced around the table. "I know most anyone here, and can't think of a single person who would perform this sort of treachery."

"Apparently these Absolutionists are far craftier than we would think." Harrold's eyes blinked slowly as he took in the stunning news. "I'm truly at a loss for words."

"This goes no further than those gathered at this table, for if this were let out, there is no telling what might happen. We would likely lose any chance of discovering which hole this rat is hiding in."

"Makes sense." Taryn agreed. "What are we to do in the meantime?"

"And what of Charles? Does he know?" Harrold asked.

"No, he does not. The letter was properly sealed when it arrived, and there was no sign of tampering. No one knows but us." He turned to Taryn. "As far as our next step goes, while we do not know the identity of the traitor, we know his contact."

The pallitine looked sharply upon the High Pallitine. "Who?"

"His name is Travin; he's the smithy's assistant in the village."

"Ahh, yes, over by the Boar's Snout." Harrold looked to the side for a moment in thought. He saw Taryn's raised brow. "I have free time like any other pallitine. I just happen to like a good drink or two. Or enough to convince me they're good." He smirked sidelong at the apprentice.

The High Pallitine looked into his cup and drank the last of it. "In any case, I think the best course of action would be for us three to confront him on tomorrow's eve." He stood from the table and set his cup down. "And remember, not a word to anyone."

Taryn stood outside the smithy, unimpressed. Sure, it looked different than either of the smithies she saw in Miresbough, but those differences were superficial. The building was in better condition, the sign above the door hung straight, and the area wasn't left in disarray. The smells of worked iron and the forge's fire were the same as what she recalled, however. She tried to ignore her growling stomach, but found it distracting. Thoman didn't want to waste time eating supper, since he figured the best to time to act was in the early evening, when the day was winding down in the village and most people would be eating their own. *Best to catch him when he's most comfortable.* Hrmph, *we'll see.* With any luck, things would end quickly and they would be back at the keep, eating dinner before it got too late. The sun was descending over the horizon, and she was anxious to get this over with and discover who the traitor was. "You sure this is the place? I imagined it to be a bit seedier."

Thoman nodded. "Sometimes the best place to hide is

in plain sight. Now, you know the plan, right? I want you to stay behind us, and look for any exits he may want to use and block them off if possible. Harrold and I will confront him. Do you understand?"

Taryn nodded.

"It looks like the plan is clear. Lead the way, Thoman." Pallitine Harrold inclined his head and tipped his hand toward the door.

"When we're out of the keep, it's High Pallitine." He flexed his shoulder and made sure his sword was properly belted.

Taryn felt uneasy about the thought of entering the smithy and questioning someone, not to mention being armed while doing so. Even with her uneasy feelings, she knew the risk of a fight and did not want to be caught unprepared.

"Of course. My apologies, High Pallitine."

"Good. Let's go." Thoman strode toward the entrance to the smithy and tested the latch. It was unlocked. He pushed the door open and entered the shop.

Hammers, tongs, fullers, and a variety of other pieces of smithing equipment were scattered along the shop tables, with iron rods, steel bars, and a variety of weapons, tools, and farming equipment in all states of disrepair.

A young man entered the shop from the back room. He stood a hair taller than Taryn, and about as athletic. His light hair lay flat against his head, pulled back by a thin leather cord. A look of recognition filled his eyes as he wiped his hands on a dirty rag. "Hello, Pallitines. How can I help you?"

Harrold was the first to speak. "Are you the assistant, Travin?"

Confusion spread across Travin's face as he looked from Harrold to Thoman and back. "Yes, I am. What's this about?"

"We need to speak with you about your friends, the Absolutionists."

Taryn looked for an easy way to cut off his access to the back room, but found none. He was too near the door, and the shop was too cramped to do anything but make sure he didn't run past them. *Hrmph. Good thing I'm here.*

The young man's eyes widened with fright. "No, you don't understand. I—"

Thoman held a hand up and spoke in a calming voice. "Don't panic, son. We only want to talk."

"What's all this commotion about?" The smith came out from the forge attached to the shop. He was a burly man of ample size, both in his arms, and around his waist. "Oh, High Pallitine. What can we do ya for?"

"I'm in need of Travin's assistance. We believe he is in possession of some information that could be of use to the keep."

The smith glanced questioningly toward the young man. "Him?" He sounded doubtful. "By all means. Travin, help our friends out." The smith turned toward his assistant and waited.

The young man's hands started to shake. "Look, if I could just explain. Wait here, I have something." He ducked through the door leading to the back room.

"Taryn, circle around the back and make sure he doesn't escape." Thoman ordered as the two pallitines pushed for the door leading out of the shop.

Taryn rushed out, and as she circled the building, a commotion was heard of steel clashing on steel. Another door slammed open and the sound of fighting broke out. As she turned the far corner of the building, she found Harrold standing over the still form of the assistant's body, a long knife rested on the ground barely out of reach. Horrified regret sank in. "What did you do?"

Thoman walked up next to Harrold from behind, frustration accenting each step. "I told you not to rush him."

Harrold turned on the High Pallitine. "He pulled a knife on me. Was I supposed to fall on it?"

The High Pallitine glared at his subordinate. "Of course not, but you're trained. He wasn't. Disarm him." He walked to the doorway and slammed his fist in the wall. He glanced back at the pallitine who stood there, and the sword he still gripped. "You know better than this!"

Taryn had seen the High Pallitine this angry only once before, and she wasn't sure if this time wasn't worse.

The smith walked out cautiously and gasped when he saw the body. "My gods, you didn't have to kill him!"

Thoman motioned for Harrold to sheathe his sword. "There was little choice. He pulled a knife and threatened us."

The burly man looked at Harrold and scoffed angrily. "You fought a man with barely enough hair on his chin to be called so, with a sword when he wielded a pittance of a knife?"

"I had no choice," the pallitine spat out between gritted teeth. He took a breath, shook his head and looked up, the pain and sorrow evident in his eyes. "All we wanted to do was speak with him, truly. We never intended for this to happen."

"A lot of good talking will do now." He spat on the ground. "You." He pointed at Pallitine Harrold, eyes filling with hate. "I want you gone. Now."

Thoman turned to Harrold. "Go up to the keep and see that a detail comes down here to help deal with this." He turned back toward the smith, sorrow heavy in his actions. "I am sorry for the loss. The keep will help in any way we can, rest assured. But I must know, has Travin acted strangely as of late? Have you seen him speaking with any travelers, any strangers, anyone out of the ordinary?"

"What? Aside from you lot?" He glared in response. "No, I'm not his keeper. Just been trainin' the boy." He took in a deep breath and composed himself as realization of the loss started to settle in. "By the gods he had a bright future ahead o' him."

"This should not have happened. You have my sincerest condolences. We shall, of course, pay for any damages and my men will assist with anything you need until you find another assistant." He watched the smith as he stared at the young man's corpse in front of them. After a moment, he set a hand on the man's shoulder. "I truly am sorry. I'll be back in the morning to see how you're faring."

The large man's cheeks were flushed red as he acknowledged

the comment, but Taryn couldn't tell if it was from anger, sorrow, or a mixture of both. Reluctantly, she left with Thoman to head back toward the keep.

"What were you thinking?" Thoman cursed at Harrold. "This is a mistake an acolyte would make, not a seasoned man." He shoved a finger in the pallitine's direction. "You've much work ahead to heal these wounds. *If* they can be healed." He brought a gloved hand up to his face and breathed slowly as he tried to calm himself. "These are *our* people. If they can't trust us, then we've failed."

Harrold's eyes widened painfully as he looked down and shook his head. "You're right. That should never have happened."

"And what of the traitor? We *needed* that information. Now our hand is tipped, and any chance of finding out who is responsible has been pissed in the wind."

Taryn was still tense from the confrontation. *The traitor will get away and we'll be no closer to finding him. Worse yet, the Absolutionists want us dead.*

The pallitine spoke up. "Not necessarily. Perhaps if we made it seem like he talked before he died, then our traitor may just trip himself up."

Thoman grunted, unconvinced.

"Look, none of us have eaten. I'm going to the kitchen. Bea was kind enough to set out some bowls of stew before she went to bed."

Finally, I'm starving.

Thoman nodded and followed the pallitine.

Taryn replayed the events in her mind, looking for something that might've been done or said differently to prevent this, but nothing came to mind.

The kitchen was empty, save for the three that walked in.

Two bowls were dished up and set on the large table. Thoman took a bowl and set it near him and he motioned for Harrold to take the other. "I still can't believe it. How are we supposed to convince everyone that he spoke before you killed him?"

Taryn went over to the pot and scooped herself a bowl and started eating as she listened halfheartedly. Someone, maybe even someone near, was a traitor and they were no closer to finding them.

"We just say it happened. Keep it simple." He shrugged. The pallitine played with the stew and pushed the spoon around thoughtfully. "You know, if we casually mention it to the detail when they come back, word would spread in no time I'm sure."

"Bah, perhaps." The High Pallitine considered. "It should be you out there with the detail you know. If it weren't thoughtless I'd have you out there doing the assistant's work until he found another." He gritted his teeth in frustration. "I'm too angry to eat. I'm going to bed. Put my bowl in the slop pile for the dog. And don't forget to mention this ruse to the detail when they get back. We'll see how it pans out."

Harrold pushed the spoon around and looked at his bowl. "I'm not hungry either." He looked at Taryn with none of the amusement from the night before. "At least someone's got an appetite." He took both bowls and dumped them in the scrap bucket and picked it up to put out for Asher to eat.

Taryn still didn't know how to react. She saw men beaten for a variety of reasons in the slums of Miresbough, and on the odd night, one would've died. Tonight's events brought her back to those times. *The difference there, is Travin died in the pursuit of justice, he would've lived if he cooperated. That's on him. The stakes are higher, and these are dark times.* Anger burned inside for the pallitine's foolish mistake. She desperately wanted to blame him for killing the assistant before they could get some information. She would have been thrilled if they managed to get anything, but that was not how things played out. Deep inside, she realized that in order to come out ahead, they needed to look forward and plan for the worst.

Taryn walked outside and stretched her arms. She looked forward to her time in the practice ring; it was one of those few moments when she could let loose and push the worries away while she cleared her mind. The events from the night before hung over her, casting a pale shadow of gloom, and she really needed to clear her thoughts to focus on the problem ahead — the traitor.

Saul, the stable boy, wailed out of sight from where she stood at the stairs, breaking the relative calm of the morning air.

Her pulse raced as she ran toward the stable boy and found Saul standing at the side of the building, looking past the corner to where she couldn't see. "What's wrong?"

The boy turned, tears in his eyes and he looked up to Taryn, lips quivering. "He's dead!"

Time slowed for Taryn and she looked around for any signs of danger. "Who's dead, boy? Out with it." Her heart pounded, the unknown teased her mind with dire possibilities.

He sniffled and ran up to her and buried his head in her arms. "Asher's dead," he sniffled. "He died after I poured out last night's slop for him to eat."

She looked down and found the bucket from the night before resting on its side, the contents strewn in their usual spot on the side of the stable. Alarm struck. *That could've been us.*

Taryn looked down to the boy and squeezed him. "Stay here. Don't move, understand?"

He nodded and steered himself toward his chair in the nearest stall.

She hastened her pace to the keep and found Thoman as he was leaving the building.

"Good, I found you." His face was somber, as it was last night, and it contained the same urgent manner as it had immediately after the incident. His eyes narrowed as they danced between her own. "What happened?"

"Asher's dead. Poisoned from the stew last night."

Thoman's face blanched. "That explains the note."

Her heart plummeted. She braced herself for the worst. "What note?"

"Come, sit." He led the way back into the keep and headed for the kitchen where Bea's helpers were preparing the next meal. "Please, leave us," he ordered.

Both of the helpers were slow to leave, avoiding eye contact as they left in a wake of grief. When the room was cleared, and the kitchen's door was closed, Taryn looked around. "Where's Bea?" She regretted asking the question even as the words left her mouth. Thoman's sorrow said it all.

"She was found in her room when one of her helpers came to see why she wasn't helping with breakfast."

"What happened?" Cold regret slapped her in the face. *I've been so busy, I didn't mean to stop spending time with her, and now she's gone.*

"She poisoned herself sometime last night. A note was found next to her asking for forgiveness."

Her gut sank. She refused to the believe the news that her friend, her confidant, was dead. "That can't be!" Taryn told Thoman. "Why would she do it? She couldn't have."

"I don't know. But with Asher dead, the evidence is hanging rather heavily in front of us." He shook his head and looked down. "If Harrold and I had eaten our stew—" He left the thought unfinished.

The starkness of the loss crept in. She held her arms tightly around herself. *This can't be happening.*

The whole night didn't sit well with her, and now to be faced with this seemed unbearable. All she saw were images of Harrold standing over the assistant's body and the sight of the bucket tipped over, knowing that Asher lay dead just out of sight. She looked up at Thoman. "I know who the traitor is."

Thoman's vacant gaze focused on her as he straightened up. "Who is it?"

"I know that he's your friend, and that he's done nothing but help us, but it doesn't make sense. Travin, Asher dying, and now Bea's suicide. It *has* to be him. It's Harrold."

"And why do you say that? Have you seen something?" He asked, concerned.

She shook her head. "I just *know it.* Nothing else makes sense. Why else would he go out of his way to kill the one person who knew who the traitor was?"

"That was an unavoidable accident. You know this. You were there. Had he cooperated, Travin would be alive today."

"And what about Bea? She *hated* writing. Thought it a waste of time. Why change now to confess her wrongs? It doesn't make sense."

"I can't start accusing trusted friends based on hearsay, Taryn. You know this. It is our duty to look at situations, even in times like these, objectively. I know this loss has struck you painfully hard, but you can't use your pain and a flash of doubt to falsely accuse someone." He sighed and looked out the window thoughtfully. "I won't rule him out, but I've known him a long time. I can't imagine anyone being truer than he. I'll watch him, and have him close. If there is any doubt, I'll know it."

She stood, exasperated at the wall of disbelief she faced and pointed past the door out. "But I *know* it. He can't be trusted."

"Enough," her mentor commanded. "I will not stand idly by while you accuse someone, much less one of the few people who supported my decision to keep you on as an apprentice when *many* of the district pallitines and such argued with me against keeping you on. He even went so far as to promise to take you on had I opted to forgo your training."

Taryn stepped back. "What?"

Thoman nodded. "Your apprenticeship was never in doubt,

don't take me wrong. But once I was appointed and word let out that I refused to let you go, there were few who supported my position as strongly as he. Do not forget that."

Taryn felt a sense of shame sweep through her for thinking the worst of someone who had always had her back, even when she had no clue. If Harrold didn't do this, then someone else surely must have. Her shame quickly turned back to the anger and desperation she felt moments ago.

Pallitine Harrold opened the door and poked his head into the kitchen. "There you are. The arrangements have been made." He looked at Taryn and frowned. "I see she heard."

Thoman looked up at the newcomer. "Aye, she did."

He walked from the entrance and knelt to look in Taryn's eyes. "I'm sorry for the loss. I know she meant the world to you." He looked down and sighed before standing. He turned to the High Pallitine, his own sadness filtering through his otherwise stoic gaze. "That is not how I pictured this ending. How could she do this?"

"She didn't," Taryn growled. "I can't believe it."

Thoman shook his head. "I can't believe that she would do something like this either. It's so unlike her."

"As unlike her to be an absolutionist? Sometimes people, as much as we might want to put our faith in them, disappoint us when we least expect it."

Isn't that the truth.

Thoman nodded reluctantly. "Perhaps. But I refuse to let it mar my memory of her. She will get the funeral she deserves."

"You always were a true and kind friend to all around us." Harrold smiled approvingly. "So be it. Let us honor her memory and hope this tragic time is behind us."

CHAPTER 15

Prime Temple of Orn,
Near the City of Ghendt

A CHILL BREEZE WAFTED GENTLY OVER the stone walkway between the communal building where all who worked at the temple dined and were housed, and the Prime Temple itself. The well-maintained courtyard behind the expansive building lay empty at this hour, a stark contrast to the coming bustle of errand boys and young priests who would eagerly discuss the philosophical details of their various classes taught throughout the day.

The High Seeker looked fondly over the gardens. The light, soothing scent coming from the sea of yellows, blues and violets from the living tapestry before him brought a sense of calm he'd never quite appreciated in his youth. He took in the stillness and warmth such beauty always brought before the day intruded too far into his reflections.

When standing, the man was as tall as most. If not for the elegant attire he wore, he would look nondescript if judged solely by appearance. However, even alone in the garden, Erik commanded an aura of respect, as if he expected the air itself to bend to his will. His graying hair rested about his ears, roughly brushed back to give some semblance of organization to the wild locks.

He pulled his robes close to ward off the chill of the morning air before taking another sip of his tea. He stroked his neatly cropped beard and recalled memories of his time as a young priest, teaching even younger brothers and sisters of Orn's lessons. He thought of the times before that in Millstown, the days when he first left the seminary, and his best friend, to work in the service of Orn.

Morning clouds clustered above, darkening the sky and masking the waking dawn as thunder cracked through the sky off in the distance.

The sudden rumbling broke the High Seeker's fond reverie of the past and urged him to take a last drink of his chaff tea. Once he was ready for the day ahead, he pulled his thin form up from the stone bench he rested on and steered his thoughts toward the day ahead. He turned to proceed to his office high in the temple behind him and gazed upon the holy symbol of Orn as he drew closer to the marble pedestal that it stood upon. He touched the image lightly and paused, offering a prayer to request peace and enlightenment for the coming day. A frigid sense of loss was his only reply.

⁓ꝫ⚜Ꞓ⁓

A light rap on the office's door broke the High Seeker from his studies.

"Yes, come in."

The ornately carved oaken doors to his study parted to reveal a meekly dressed scribe scurrying in with a barely subdued excitement brimming from his eyes.

"My lord." The scribe stammered as he rushed to the High Seeker's desk.

The High Seeker tried to hide his irritation. "Yes, yes, out with it, Haenre. What is it?"

Reverently, the scribe opened his satchel and pulled out a carefully folded parchment bearing the holy seal of the Church of Orn upon it. Haenre handed the document to the High Seeker, eagerly waiting for news as to what the contents within held.

Gingerly, the High Seeker took the document and broke the seal. As the parchment unfolded, he pulled out a second page tucked within the first, scrawled in a hasty script.

My lord Seeker,

It is with both great excitement and great sadness that I spread news of our victory today. After many months of searching the mountains of Unt, we have found our quarry. We've tracked the beast and found that it resides in a pit thought by our men to be entered only through a vent spewing the most noxious of fumes. As the fates would have it, one of our men found a crack in the southern foothills that leads to the lair of the beast. The tunnels go on and split in many directions, but by following the stench of sulfur that leads from the inner reaches of the earth to where it flows out of the mountain, the lair can be found. I've enclosed a map of the mountains where the lair resides, and a sketch of the tunnels that need to be taken to find the beast. Unfortunately, this discovery has not come without cost. Two of our number were lost in the initial discovery as they ventured too far within the lair itself while unbeknownst to them they were being watched. Arren and Kurt fell before any had time to react. Knowing this, it is likely that the beast is aware of our presence now and shall try to make quick our demise. I pray to him who metes out Justice and Mercy that this message reaches you.

In Orn's name, blessings upon us all.
His Servant, Brother Normand Tremue

Once he read the last word, the High Seeker leaned back in his chair and brought a hand up to stroke his beard as he pondered the implications of this news and worried over the coincidence of his morning's experience. He looked up at the scribe. "Is there any word to the number of survivors?"

Haenre responded quickly, anticipating the question. "One, High Seeker, out of the original five. Bryn, the tracker, was the sole survivor. He arrived not long ago and has been shown to his quarters."

The High Seeker nodded in acknowledgment. "It's a shame to have lost so many to such a foul creature." He looked to the heavens and prayed for their warm welcome above. *Let his will be done.* His eyes darted back toward the eagerly awaiting scribe and requested the presence of High Pallitine Thoman as he issued detailed orders for the preparation of the High Pallitine's arrival. He was unsure whether he should be relieved the search was over or if he should be more worried for the fate of his childhood friend, the man who had sworn to kill the vile beast. The High Seeker paused in contemplation before finally ushering the scribe off to fulfill his duties.

One last thought struck the High Seeker as the scribe turned to depart. "Wait a moment, Haenre. Before we prepare for the High Pallitine's arrival, I would first like you to contact an old friend, a skilled Artificer in Irline..."

CHAPTER 16

Guardians Keep

THE SOUND OF STEEL CLASHING upon steel echoed throughout the morning air in the side yard of the keep as swords swung in their glorious arcs.

"You'll have to do better than that, I'm afraid, Taryn." The pallitine teased his younger, raven-haired protégé. "Here, when I parry your blade, notice that I'm trying to force it down to create an opening for my own sword. Do you see it?"

The pallitine's student wiped the sweat off her brow and nodded in acknowledgment.

"When I do that, turn your blade against mine like so, and move your shield up while bracing for my strike. By doing so, you can better prepare for my next opening when I swing."

A glimmer of inspiration shot in his student's eyes as if finally understanding the last hour's teachings. In the next round of strikes she skillfully parried his sword and struck him soundly in his armored shoulder.

"Excellent! Your intuition is serving you well." The pallitine praised her while rubbing his arm. "That is enough for now. Go put the swords away and prepare yourself for your studies. I'm sure Brother Arlow wouldn't appreciate it if I kept you longer than necessary."

Taryn rolled her eyes at the mention of her tutor's name and nodded in acquiescence. "Of course, High Pallitine." She said in her affectionately sarcastic tone.

"That isn't the way to show our beloved leader respect." Pallitine Harrold teased Taryn with a grin. He faced Thoman and nodded his greeting. "Your gear is ready, as requested."

Taryn looked at her mentor questioningly. "Gear? Where are you going?"

"*He* has managed to squeeze in some free time to tour the countryside and help our neighboring villages." He shook his head and frowned.

She turned to the pallitine. "This surprises you?"

"No, I simply don't like him going out alone. I'd hate to hear that *they* have caught wind of our Thoman acting more like a servant than a leader. It could provoke them knowing he was out alone."

The High Pallitine coughed and drew their attention. "I appreciate the concern, but this isn't my first time out."

Harrold narrowed his eyes, and agreed. "Of course not. Just be careful."

Taryn smirked. "If anyone can watch out for themselves, it's him."

Thoman watched the two head back to the keep and smiled, thankful for those close to him. With the day's training complete, he unclasped the straps that held his practice armor in place. In the years since he became a pallitine, he never believed he could meet someone who reminded him so much of himself at that age who could also be so *different* from how he was at that same age.

After he removed his armor, Thoman visited the trough next to the training circle to wash the sweat from his tall, muscular form and to make himself more presentable before heading out for the day. After he dried himself, the pallitine opted against shaving his day-old stubble as he replaced the rough woolen towel on a nearby post and firmly brushed his fingers through his shoulder-length graying brown hair. He took a moment to reflect on the past. It had been over a year since Bea's passing, and no other signs of the Absolutionists's infiltration had cropped up. Life continued peacefully, with little news about the cult aside from the stray rumor here and there. Once he deemed himself ready, he grabbed his shirt and ambled toward the keep, enjoying the warm spring air.

Past the stables, a robed figure with a pale complexion, sharp features, and short, matted brown hair walked up to greet him.

The man spoke in a hesitant, but formal manner. "High Pallitine Thoman?" He paused until Thoman nodded in affirmation. "I am Brother Wilehem, come on behalf of Father Koric. He is requesting your presence for his coming service three days hence to say a few words on the virtues of Diligence and Truth as it would help accentuate his sermon. It need not be overly elaborate, just enough to show our congregation the importance of these topics."

Thoman paused and turned to look at the brother as he waited patiently for a reply. After a brief internal debate, his sense of duty won over his distaste of speaking in public. He nodded firmly and agreed to the request. "Of course. Anything in the service of Orn. I shall prepare something suitable, but will need to leave shortly after as my duties will pull me away in *his* service."

"I shall tell the Father immediately." Brother Wilehem relaxed and smiled in gratitude. "Thank you for your services. May *he* bless and guide us always."

The brother bowed slightly and, having accomplished his task, turned to hurriedly walk past the keep's gardens toward the village's chapel.

Within the hour, suited in his rugged and worn suit of mail, High Pallitine Thoman placed his foot in the stirrup and mounted his proud, black and white painted stallion. With a firm but gentle prod he headed out to tour the surrounding villages and provide aid for those in need.

CHAPTER 17

EARLY EVENING CAME MORE QUICKLY than expected as Thoman arrived at Guardians Keep. A stable boy ran up to greet him as he wearily rode up to the stables. Thoman slid off his mount thankful for the help, gathered his gear, and bade the boy to take care of his horse.

Taryn walked up to him and took the gear from Thoman's hands as he entered the keep. "How'd the tour go?"

Grateful to stow the gear into his student's care, he paused before venturing farther into the keep. "Let's just say it was not what I was expecting." He smiled wearily at Taryn before turning to head toward the stairs. "Once I've had a warm meal and a good night's rest, I'll be more ready to discuss the past couple of days. Ask Charles to have dinner sent up to my office once the gear is stowed, if you would."

Taryn narrowed her eyes in curiosity as Thoman walked off, then turned to shuffle away with the gear.

Once he was seated at his desk, Thoman began steering his mind to the discussion on the virtues of truth that he was expected to give the next day. He was not looking forward to the task at hand, but it, like many other things, must be done.

A slight rap came on his open door, distracting the High Pallitine. Thoman's stomach growled in anticipation when he saw that the keep's steward, Charles was seeking audience.

"Sir? A courier came for you earlier today with what he purported to be urgent news."

His hopes were quickly dashed when he discovered Charles was not here to bring him his dinner. "Then where is his message?" Thoman replied with a hint of irritation.

"He refused to give it to any but you, High Pallitine. He waits in the library for your ear. Shall I send him up?"

Thoman agreed immediately. "Yes, if it's so important he should wait so long, then by all means."

The steward bowed his head in acquiescence, turned, and walked briskly out of the office. Moments later, a young man, clad in the simple finery of one serving the church, appeared at his doorway.

"Please, come in and be seated." He motioned to one of the chairs near his desk. "I understand there is some urgent news you wish to share?" Thoman asked his guest.

The young courier nodded and sat in the chair offered. "Yes, my lord. There is an urgent request for your presence in Ghendt. The High Seeker himself is asking for you personally."

Thoman scrutinized the messenger's face. "Would you know why I am being summoned?"

"No, m'lord, I would not. I know only that your presence is required."

The pallitine accepted the response, and thanked the courier before instructing Charles to make sure the young man was fed, to prepare a bed in the servant's quarters for him, and to come back for further instruction.

Thoman felt a twinge of guilty relief for no longer needing to speak in front of the congregation in light of the High Seeker's urgent request. He pulled out a piece of parchment from his desk and wrote instructions for Pallitine Harrold to follow for the coming weeks, including the discussion for the sermon the next day as well as the normal duties that would need his attention. When Charles returned from showing the courier where he would be for the evening, Thoman instructed him to have Taryn ready to leave with him at first light and to ensure the orders would be immediately delivered to Pallitine Harrold to prepare him for the service in the morning.

Thoman smiled to himself, picturing the chagrin his note would bring the pallitine, because much like him, Harrold disliked speaking in public. He relaxed, knowing his duties would be properly taken care of, and stared out the window curious about what the coming days would unfold.

⚛

A look of awe and respect swept over Taryn's face as she rode with her mentor toward the Prime Temple of Orn. Never before had she beheld such a grand building with so many people milling about. The temple in Tramire paled in comparison; she traveled there a handful of times during her training, but it was nothing compared to the majesty that now presented itself to her. She counted seven spires circling the building, and rising from within was a central tower, meant to house the grand chapel and the High Seeker's offices above. A three-story building housed the student and servant quarters and rested to one side of the temple. On the opposite side resided an identical building also utilitarian in nature, housing a library, offices, and several places of study. She had heard tales of the intricately carved stonework with its fine details of the heavens and the gods within, but any imaginings she may have had paled in comparison to the beauty of the temple itself. Even from this distance, the sunstone accents could be seen glistening in the light, sparkling against their onyx backdrops, casting the white charstone temple in the faintest of iridescent silhouettes. If ever an immortal would choose a place to call home, this would surely be it.

She turned to Thoman, and saw him smiling as he watched her amazement at the beauty before them.

"Taryn, let's take a moment before we're swept away by the fuss of our arrival. Look at the spires around the temple. Do you know what they represent?"

The young woman quickly responded as she recalled the lessons her tutors at the keep taught her. "Yes, aren't they meant to symbolize the seven Paragons of Orn?"

Thoman smiled approvingly and explained further. "They are. But the Paragons each have a specific trait they were chosen for. The first and best among them is Garamemnon, chosen for his insight and wisdom. It's also said he, more so than any other, is like a brother to Orn. Next we have Kelal and Brayce, the twin paragons of Truth and Justice. Then there's Dianna, chosen for her fierceness in battle, Brion for his unending compassion, Terinelle for her charm and influence, and finally Ellyiandre for her dedicated works. At each of the spires, were one to look, the base has been worked to display the likeness of each paragon and the virtues they represent."

Taryn interrupted before Thoman could continue. "I've read the stories of Garamemnon, and even the twins, but outside of those I don't know much of the other paragons. Were they truly mortal like us before being elevated to paragonhood?"

The pallitine nodded as they traveled forward. "That's what the scriptures tell us, but who knows? They're said to have lived so long ago, they *could* very well be stories, ideals meant to guide us to act in the best interest of our fellow man. Either way, they continue to inspire us and give us pause to think of how we act and lead our lives."

Thoman turned his attentions to some activity farther along the path where a priest and several servants gathered along the temple's grounds and watched them approach. "It appears we must continue this discussion another time. We're rapidly approaching the temple and from the looks of the commotion, our arrival has been noticed."

Taryn rode next to the High Pallitine and watched in amusement as the gathering fussed over Thoman when they stopped. Once they dismounted and handed the reins to one of the servants, the priest greeted Thoman formally with an aide following close behind.

"Welcome to the Prime Temple, High Pallitine. It is a privilege to have one of your station here. I am sure you are tired from such a long journey." The priest welcomed him with a practiced formality. "Please come in and refresh yourselves. Our services are at your disposal. The High Seeker is aware of your arrival and wishes for you to be cared for. He is currently indisposed, but will send for you when available. You have been assigned an aide, Nicia, to see to your needs. If there is anything you require, she will make it happen."

The priest motioned to his side and presented a humbly dressed aide who promptly curtsied and reiterated her ability to assist them during their stay at the temple. The priest promptly ushered them into the foyer and instructed Nicia to take them to their rooms so they could rest from their journey.

Taryn smiled to herself as she watched Thoman graciously accept the hospitality with a finely practiced patience, knowing he would have preferred to forego the formalities and be led inside.

The apprentice followed as Nicia led the way up an elegantly carved stairwell and down a hall to a wing of the temple intended for honored guests. Nicia showed them where their rooms were, as well as where she would be during their stay in case they needed anything. Once she was sure their needs were met, she bade them farewell, bowing slightly as she left.

～ɜ※ɛ～

Taryn walked into her room and was struck by the luxurious simplicity of the accommodations. The bed was far nicer than the straw and wool padding she slept on in the keep. She ran her hand across the bedding and savored the soft warmth of the fine sheets as she pressed down on the feathered padding of the mattress.

Beyond the bed resided a simple desk with an inkwell, an assortment of quills, and next to it a bookstand containing a book, likely a copy of the Holy Scripture, she figured. The windows overlooked a well-manicured courtyard in the back, surrounding a central fountain. Within the area, many people milled about or partook in simple discussions amongst themselves. After a moment of taking in the view, she admired the tapestries and other details of the room. *I just might have to rough it.*

She found a beautiful cream dress of finely spun cotton laid out next to her bed, intended for her to wear as she accompanied Thoman to meet the High Seeker. Taryn admired the cloth's gold accented green embroidery which complemented its curves. For a moment after she put on the gown, she felt as if she had been adopted into the ranks of the privileged. While awkward and completely foreign to her, a part of her welcomed the change. Still struck by the novelty, she admired the dress in the mirror one last time before walking into the hall to find that she was the first out of their rooms.

Taryn knew it might be a while until her mentor chose to come out, so she gladly took the opportunity to explore the hallway and admire the various tapestries, statuettes, and paintings that decorated the walls.

She smiled to herself as she thought about how her sister would react to this abundance of opulence. *Serra would die at the chance to hawk even one of these items.* And then it struck her. She had been so wrapped up in her training, that it had been at least two years since she thought of her. *I can't believe I haven't seen her in almost five years.* She sighed as she strained to recall what her sister looked like. Taryn felt the pangs of her absence as she realized her predominant memory was the image of her sister's bruised face the night she left.

In an effort to distract herself, she turned back to the art surrounding her. She saw figures upon figures she did not recognize, many of them bearing religious significance no doubt, but unknown nonetheless. One tapestry in particular caught her eye that depicted a familiar scene where Orn came to Garamemnon and recognized him for his wisdom before elevating him to become his prime paragon.

She moved on to the stairwell and looked over the first floor. An air of subdued curiosity hung over the area, hidden in the the occasional masked glance or whispered question. Taryn looked around at the grandeur of the building and from this vantage on the stairwell balcony, saw how dwarfed she was by the temple's looming presence and turned from the stairwell. A part of her felt like an intruder in such a refined place and needed something to ground her, a familiar presence, so she headed back toward their rooms and waited for Thoman to come out so they could dine before it was time to meet with the High Seeker.

~}※{~

After the meal, Thoman and Taryn were ushered upstairs to the Antechamber of the High Seeker's office. Taryn's nervousness must have amused Thoman; a glint in his eye preceded a calming smile as he leaned in to her and spoke quietly.

"This is your first visit to the temple, so listen carefully. The first thing to remember is to be still, respectful, and not to speak unless spoken to. Stay slightly behind me and follow my lead in all things." He paused briefly to stress the next point, and let a smirk slip. "The second thing is, if the High Seeker offers you a cup of chaff tea, do *not* take a cup. It tastes like cow urine and the only reason the High Seeker drinks it is for medicinal reasons. He takes a perverse joy in watching others force themselves to drink it out of politeness."

Taryn cocked her head to the side and squinted quizzically at the High Pallitine. She was about to question the last comment when the double doors before them parted to reveal one of the High Seeker's aides.

The aide ushered them into the grand office and presented the guests. "Your Holiness, High Pallitine Thoman of the Provincial House Tramire presents himself as per your request." He then inclined his head in a slight bow before he turned and closed the doors behind him as he left.

Thoman walked through the open doors and glanced back to his apprentice, watching her before he turned back to the High Seeker.

Taryn stood awestruck by the gilded craftsmanship that lay before her. She glanced past the various tapestries and statuettes praising their god and paragons and turned to where Thoman was focused.

Dwarfed behind a broad, ornately decorated desk, sat a middle-aged man bearing a warm and comforting smile. He dressed in the finest linens worthy of a man of his station and commanded an air of respect one could not help but acknowledge. The High Seeker quietly stood to move out from behind his desk and walked toward his guests with a subtle limp. He smiled with a warm enthusiasm as he extended a hand to the pallitine. "Thoman! Sorry for the wait, I haven't been myself of late. It has been *far* too long since last we spoke. I so missed our discussions. How are you?"

Thoman embraced the offered hand in his and shook it, glad to see his friend. He quickly changed his manner as he remembered protocol and uttered in a respectful tone, "I am doing well Your Grace. It is good to be back in *his* house. How are you doing?" He looked him over with concern.

The High Seeker chided Thoman, "My friend, there is no need for formality here. I will survive, my condition is nothing new as you well know." He motioned an open hand toward the other side of the room. "Please, take a seat and let us reacquaint ourselves." He moved purposefully to a table near an open balcony and sat down, motioning his guests to sit with him. "Now that we are all seated, would either of you like some chaff tea?" the High Seeker asked hopefully.

Respectfully, both of his guests shook their heads no while thanking him for the offer.

He nodded with an exaggerated sullenness and asked, "Who is this young woman with you? Training another knight I see?" Their host looked over the tall, athletic young woman before him and smiled knowingly at her.

Thoman acknowledged his friend. "Yes, Erik, Taryn has trained with me a few years and I daresay shows the same promise I had at her age. When the time comes for the Trials of Honor, I expect her to come out a fully vetted pallitine."

Erik nodded. "I see. That is encouraging news. I should expect Pallitines Patrick or Mathias of House Tramire to be stepping down in the next season or two if I know Orn's will." He paused as a faint smile crept along his face. "That would be fortuitous, indeed," he added with a wink.

After pouring himself a cup of chaff tea, he offered some water to his guests who gratefully accepted the offering. The High Seeker looked at the High Pallitine in a mildly reproving gaze. "You spend too much time away from the temple. Though I respect your commitment to the people, I shall never understand why you do not take a more active role within the temple itself, as befits one of your stature. Surely your services earned you that much."

Taryn sat back and watched the exchange, wondering what else she didn't know about Thoman as she watched him speaking casually with the church's leader. She still had a hard time accepting that she was sitting in the High Seeker's office. The confidence he exuded was inspiring, especially when he looked so casual sitting there discussing things as any other man would. An easy smile played across his face, his demeanor adding a genuine and kind wrinkle to the confidence. She looked back at

Thoman and wondered, *How are we even here? What else haven't you told me?*

Her mentor looked toward the balcony in silence before turning to the High Seeker in response. "My stance hasn't changed from the last time you've asked. It's still very much my belief that my services better benefit our people when I am out in the lands, helping them, than when confined in the walls of comfort. For even a divine and well-intended role here, while secluded, can diminish the ability to connect with people and serve them as they need. I feel more accomplished when helping others directly. I'm sure you understand."

Erik nodded. "Of course I do. It can do no harm to ask in the hopes one day you'll reconsider."

Thoman looked the High Seeker in the eyes and asked shrewdly, "I appreciate the pleasantries, but there must be a reason I was summoned here?"

Erik nodded regretfully as he let a soft sigh escape his lips. "Yes, there is. I recall what happened shortly before you were vetted. You confronted a horrific beast with Hadrian and two other pallitines all those years ago." His expression softened with compassion as he continued, "It was then that he died while you fought it off."

Taryn straightened herself up in her seat at that last mention and carefully watched her mentor, refusing to breathe as she watched things develop.

Anger flared across Thoman's face. The pallitine nodded and scowled with distaste. "Yes, I can still smell the sulfuric stench streaming from its breath."

The High Seeker placed his hand on Thoman's as he continued. "And you remember the promise I made as a young priest, to aid you as best as I could in your vow to slay this creature?"

Again the pallitine nodded, his attention now fully fixated on his friend's every word.

Erik pulled his hand back as he leaned into his chair. "I have recently learned where the beast resides. We lost some good men in the search, but it has been found."

Thoman blinked as his eyes flicked to the side and looked across the floor in thought. A renewed excitement flowed through his eyes as vigor returned to his movements. He tensed his fists before composing himself and gazed steadfastly into his friend's eyes. "Where?"

"The lair resides outside the empire's reaches. It falls within Saerinian territory in a southern ravine along the Untarian Mountains, not far from the west coast."

The High Pallitine gripped his arm rests in frustration. "I cannot. Not now, with Taryn's training and our hunt for the Absolutionists. We need to focus on righting those wrongs that lie near, and tangible. They *must* take priority over a vengeance sworn so long ago."

"I see. I *can* gather other men to see this through, but I know you, Thoman. I know how this will eat at you until you see it done. Know this: the beast is no distant memory, it came back, and as we speak the beast terrorizes the southern villages. We tracked the wyrm through its trail of carnage in the Untarian Mountains to where it now resides." The seeker pursed his lips in thought. "Tell me, what news have you of the Absolutionists? Perhaps there is a way I can aid you in this endeavor."

The pallitine's shoulders tensed as his frustration was egged on. "Since our brush with the traitor last year, the trail has gone cold. Even my contacts have found nothing as of late. Only some rumors of their wretched claws stretching south into Saerinian Territory."

"Then, perhaps I can assist you while you rid the world of this evil. I will find what I can about this group, and when you return I will share everything I've found. This way, your time is still spent doing good, and you will have yet another ally in this new fight as well. What say you?"

Thoman's frustration broke with a hint of a smile. "When do we leave?"

Erik nodded as if he expected the question. "Preparations have already begun and the journey starts in a month. You will need to prepare a replacement to cover your duties during the absence. This should also give you ample time to prepare yourselves for the journey."

"You knew I was going to accept." He snorted.

"We've been friends for a long time, Thoman. I suggest you begin your preparations as best you can, starting tomorrow. Until then, let us talk of lighter things."

Caught off guard by the weight of the news, Taryn sat back and watched her mentor as he reminisced of old times, and discussed newer concerns with his old friend.

CHAPTER 18

TARYN RETURNED TO THE TEMPLE's library, eager to finish her studies to help her prepare for the confrontation. She walked into the grand hall and found comfort in the tall, cathedral-like ceiling and wide, open space. This room, unlike the rest of the temple, was decorated in the most simple of furnishings. The dark wood of the padded chairs and tables matched the muted tones of the rugs to provide a peaceful, quiet place to conduct one's studies. Taryn found the last of the few tomes on wyrms available in the library and chose a secluded spot in the far corner near a window overlooking the gardens.

She settled into a plush, comfortable leather seat and opened the book. Although no one urged her, she felt duty-bound to learn as much as she could about the beast they were hunting. During her time here, she took every opportunity to speak to Thoman as well as some of the temple's scholars about the creature and its kind to glean as much information as she could to help in the coming hunt. She quickly became engrossed in the large book, trying to distinguish usable facts from the legends and myths that surrounded the beasts. So engrossed was she, that Taryn failed to notice a new arrival who looked out of place as he walked through the library's grand entrance and into the library itself.

The aging, fair-haired figure stood near the entrance, dressed in his well-used leather trimmed green tunic and faded riding cloak. He quietly moved to one of the younger priests and whispered a request. The priest pointed in the far corner, toward the chair where Taryn sat reading. The new arrival walked nonchalantly to the corner and moved behind her to read over her shoulder.

"Ya *do* realize it takes a special sort of crazy ta willin'ly go after such a beast? Especially since this one has a history of dispatchin' pallitines and *real* warriors alike." The new arrival leaned in to get a better view of the book.

Taryn fidgeted in annoyance and shifted to her side as she tried to stay focused on her studies. "You know, some would say it would be an honorable act to follow one's path and do their duty to protect the world from such a beast."

The tall man smirked to himself and continued, "And there are those who would say only the foolish would willin'ly pursue danger."

Taryn paused at the comment and strained her grip on the book as she closed it. The audacity of the stranger to interrupt her and start in on this over something that was obviously no one's business but her own really grated on her nerves. She slapped the tome down on the table next to her before she turned to start in on him, "Look, with all due respect, *sir,* I don't give a goat's..." The sight of her old friend Hugh standing behind the chair caught her completely off guard. She sat there gawking, unable to finish her thought. "Hugh!" she spouted as she jumped up to hug him. "When did you get here?"

Hugh laughed as he returned Taryn's embrace. "I got here earlier this afternoon. I asked that ya not be told so I could surprise ya two." The ranger stepped back and looked past Taryn into the gardens outside with an exaggerated scrutiny. "Speakin' of which, where's yer dotterin' mentor? Not lost in the weeds outside I hope."

She immediately broke out in a grin. "No, he's busy with the preparations and making sure our supplies are in order. This is quite the journey planned." Taryn paused as memories filtered in to the last time when she was away with Hugh. She placed a hand on her collarbone, and rubbed the scar that rested under her dress. "I haven't traveled for that long since…"

Hugh's gaze softened. "This trip will be much different. No crazed mages need huntin'. Only large beasts with sharp teeth and huge claws, I promise," he said winking, subduing her uneasiness with a smile. "'Sides, with critters like that, Thoman needs us. Someone's gotta keep our pallitine out of trouble, right?"

Taryn nodded, relaxing with the reassurance, and changed the subject. "Now that you're here, *old man*, why don't you tell me what *you* know of the beast?"

Thoman walked briskly to the ornate set of double doors where he was summoned. As he arrived at Erik's office, he found Haenre standing in front of the double doors bearing his typically impatient manner as he opened the doors and announced Thoman's presence. Concern over the sudden request for his presence hastened his steps as he walked in. "Erik, I trust all is well?"

"Ah, yes. Thank you for coming so quickly, my friend," the High Seeker said while he stood from behind his desk. "All is well here. I simply wanted to see how the final preparations are coming along, now that the hour is near."

Relief washed through his posture and was coupled with a slight annoyance as he answered. "The final members of our company arrived today and are yet to be briefed on our need. Otherwise, your staff has been of the utmost help in fetching what supplies we require and in the preparations themselves. You have left little room for want or need during this time and it is much appreciated."

The High Seeker bore a secretive smile as he looked meaningfully at the pallitine. "I am glad to hear that. There is one last thing you need, however. This arrived for you earlier today."

He signaled Haenre, who presented a long and narrow wooden case. Erik placed the case upon his desk and reverently opened it to reveal what seemed to be a sword bound in fine cloth, nestled within the padding inside. He unwrapped the weapon to reveal a broadsword resting in a scabbard of hardened leather. The darkened scabbard was decorated with only one simple silver band by the hilt of the sword, and another by the bottom of the scabbard as it circled the gray steel base that skirted the tip of the blade within. He gingerly drew the sword from the scabbard to reveal a beautiful blade whose surface was marred only by the etchings of runes that ran along the center of the sword from the hilt to the midpoint of the blade itself. The hilt met the steel blade in a cross-guard of brushed silver alloy, the top of which was adorned with a simple round image of a dragon rearing its head. The grip was bound in finely wrapped black leather, and the pommel was a round stone fitted with an onyx centerpiece. The High Seeker held out the gift, and presented the broadsword to the High Pallitine.

"This blade has the distinction of once being wielded by an honorable knight of the first pallitine order. I have had it reclaimed and brought to a master weaponsmith who repaired any cracks or signs of wear it once had and sharpened its edge as if it were new. From there, I requested a friend in the Council of Magi to strengthen the sword with enchantments, and I, myself, have blessed this blade with the Light of Orn. If ever there was a weapon worthy of an honorable knight pursuing an honorable quest, this is the blade and you are the man. Here, take it with my blessings. Orn's Razor is yours."

Touched by having such an honor bestowed on him, Thoman

accepted the sword with a ginger reverence. He held the blade up and gazed upon the weapon with a profound respect. "Erik, I know not what to say. This is indeed a gift of renown. I... thank you." He then stretched his arm, tested the weight of the sword, and swung it sharply away from the table. "The weight is sufficient, the balance perfect, and the swing natural. Never before have I beheld such a beauteous weapon," the pallitine continued as he sheathed the weapon. "I shall strive to use this in the spirit in which it was gifted."

The High Seeker embraced Thoman's shoulders solemnly. "I am only doing this to ensure the success of one of my dearest friends in his hour of need. I truly did mean it when I swore to help you in this endeavor." A concerned smile crept across his face as he locked his gaze with Thoman's. "Now, by Orn's will, shall you find your destiny." He turned to move behind his desk and sat down. "I'm sure there are many things that require your attention before you leave. I shall see you on the morrow for the commencement."

Thoman thanked him again as he bade the High Seeker farewell and, still taken aback from the gift, left the chamber to continue his work.

～∃※Ɛ～

Once the scabbard was properly belted, Thoman rested his hand on the pommel of his new blade and walked back to the stables where the gear was stowed for their journey the next day. After he inspected the supplies and made sure that all was as it should be, he set forth to gather his companions in the back gardens to brief them before the next day's journey.

With the last of the companions gathered outside, Thoman urged the nine figures to sit on the stone benches surrounding the southern side of the central fountain. He paused to reflect on his time here, and the importance of what he needed to address before he proceeded. "I thank each of you for coming here and answering my call. Not all of you know what it is I require of you, yet you came all the same. And for that I'm grateful." Thoman's eyes widened briefly as he realized not everyone present knew one another, and proceeded with the introductions. "First off, let me introduce everyone present."

He drew his hand first toward the graying fair-haired ranger. "On the far left we have Hugh. He is a veteran amongst the Tramirian Rangers, and longtime friend. Never has one had a truer companion, nor a better tracker at his side. Sitting next to him, my apprentice, Taryn. She is as skilled as I was at her age and shows even more promise."

Next, Thoman singled out a solitary man standing behind the group, dressed in a fine suit of ceremonial armor under an unblemished tabard that proudly bore the symbol of the Arturian branch of pallitines. He held a plumed helm at his side which set his normally confined thick locks of long, wavy brown hair and tanned skin free to feel the midday sun. "The pallitine standing proudly in the rear is Bartholomew. His reputation as a skilled combatant is only bested by his proven sense of honor. He may be newly appointed, but his earnestness in his duties reflects nothing but a true Arturian pallitine in all regards."

The pallitine looked abashed by the introduction and bowed slightly to Thoman. "Methinks thou dost speak too highly of me, High Pallitine. Regardless of thine opinions, however, I am but here to serve. In Orn's name always."

Next to be introduced was another pallitine, this time dressed in armor showing much greater wear and obvious signs of abuse. "Pallitine Derren sitting in front of him hails from my homeland of Tramire. I had the honor of riding with him several times as he was trained by District Pallitine Alistair. A dependable man of few words, if there ever was one."

Next to Pallitine Derren sat a recent arrival. The High Pallitine looked at his trusted friend and the pallitine who was his rock in the trying times since he took his current position and called him out. "Another of my pallitine brethren, Pallitine Harrold, who also hails from Guardians Keep."

Thoman turned next to a slight woman bearing an ageless, simple beauty. The sparsely decorated robes she wore held loosely about her shoulders and gradually tapered down to two belts which circled her waist, each lined with an array of pouches of varying sizes. Her faintly pointed ears and sharpened features marked her mixed heritage. She turned to each member of the group with an inquisitive glance and soft smile bearing her greeting to all. "And here we have Illyandra; sage, herbalist, and alchemist. She often succeeds when brute force cannot. She is skilled with the mystical arts, but it is her mind that is her greatest asset. We have journeyed for a time in my early career, and I would not be here today if not for her."

She spoke with a barely muted excitement. "Please, call me Illya. I am quite thrilled to be amongst such reputable company and cannot wait to get to know each of you in our travels."

Thoman nodded at the last person in the group. "Last and certainly not least, we have Bryn. He guided the original expedition to where we are headed. He is a skilled tracker and a master mountaineer in his own right and with him, two of his trusted allies, Cirrus and Errol, Arturian Swordsmen, and no strangers to battle."

With each of the companions formally introduced, he continued. "Now, some of you know why your presence has been requested. But for those of you who do not, allow me to apprise you of our goal. There is a beast, a land wyrm of sizable proportion that I swore to slay many years ago. It is this beast that slew my friend and mentor, Pallitine Hadrian. This same creature has ravaged many villages in its southward trek through the Untarian Mountains. Its lair has recently been uncovered and it is this beast we are to set out for to slay. Each of you has been summoned for your skills and talents, all of which will be of use to us." Thoman's brow furrowed as he paused to stress the next point. "I will not lie to you. This journey is fraught with danger, and will end in a bloody conflict from which some of us may not escape. That being said, this beast *must* be slain. It has spent far too many years devouring the innocent and destroying farmland. We must stop it, and now that we know where it resides, we will do so. I understand this could very well be the most danger you have ever placed yourselves in, but I asked you to join me for your skills, loyalty, and sense of honor. If there is any doubt you can aid in this journey, please, tell me so. There will be no shame and I shall be indebted to you just the same for answering my call."

Taryn and Hugh stood with conviction brimming from their eyes.

"My friend, I would follow ya ta the ends of the earth for a just cause. My bow is yers." Hugh swore while embracing Thoman's hand in his.

"You know full well my loyalty is yours to command. Never has one had the fortune to have a noble soul such as yours to guide them." Taryn voiced immediately after.

One by one the other members of the gathering swore their aid to the cause, firmly sealing them as a group.

～ぅ༚ᘎ～

Thoman looked up at the sun from his room as the first light broke the night with streaks of orange and red streaming across the morning sky. Nervous tension laced his preparations as the prospect of revenge drew nigh. Eager to start the lengthy journey, he barely had the stomach to finish his breakfast, preferring instead to pack some dried fruit, meat, and bread to eat while they rode. Thoman rested his hand on the window's sill as his thoughts drifted to his mentor. His heart filled with affection as he thought of all Hadrian had taught him before he passed. The moment he thought of his mentor's death, his gut steeled into a cold knot as memory of the beast's attack brought forth much of the pain and bitterness he thought had passed with the years. Inasmuch as he might miss his time here in the temple, he looked forward to completing the vow taken so many years ago, eagerly embracing the hatred and wrath he felt as he reflected on that solitary day. *Finally, I will exact my revenge.*

The High Pallitine stepped out of the temple. He was dressed in his riding armor, and composed himself while he fought to control his stronger emotions as he moved purposefully down to the courtyard in front of the temple to where the rest of his group waited. The High Seeker walked out as Thoman greeted the group, and was followed by a handful of priests.

"Friends," The High Seeker started once everyone's attention was focused on him. "It is with solemn gratitude that I thank you for your courage and your sacrifices in this coming journey. I prepared and blessed a gift for each of you, a pendant bearing the symbol of Orn. May it protect you and bless your journeys. That is, with the exception of you, Illyandra. I had a separate pendant crafted for you, a symbol worthy of Orn's sister in spirit Oriah, the World-Mother. May it guide you and protect you always."

With the introduction made, the gathered priests moved forward and presented each of the group with their appropriate gifts before moving behind the High Seeker. Once the priests were in their positions, the High Seeker started the chant of protection, followed quietly by his accompanying priests. Once finished, he continued to speak on the importance of the task at hand and went on to glorify the will of Orn, and the importance he must have in their lives.

Thoman fought off a wave of annoyance as the need to start the journey stirred within him while he braced himself for what he expected to be a lengthy ceremony.

The members of the group each fidgeted as the gathering stood there and listened to the High Seeker. After several minutes of listening, Hugh leaned in to Thoman and whispered. "How long-winded is the Seeker, anyways?"

The pallitine hid his amused smile and turned slightly to whisper back. "This is nothing. You should've known him in his youth. He truly did not know when to stop speaking at times, I swear." He chuckled softly. "I felt sorry for his congregations when he grew to be in charge of his first chapel. *Those* sermons would purge even the most devout soul of any form of consciousness, surely. It took the intervention of the area's Arch-Priest to teach him the value of brevity in his services."

Late afternoon passed by the time the band traveled out of Ghendt's territorial boundaries and set into their journey. When safely out of earshot of the others, Taryn steered her mount to ride next to Thoman.

"Yes, Taryn? What is on your mind?" the pallitine inquired.

The pallitine-in-training smiled sheepishly as she asked, "You know Bartholomew, right?"

"I know of him, but until now I've not had the chance to meet him face to face," he acknowledged.

"Why does he speak like that? All the 'thees' and 'thous', doesn't it seem a bit pretentious?"

"I've met others like that. I would simply take it to be how Bartholomew is. The speech is typically spoken in ceremonies and celebrations out of respect of their forefather's language. While uncommon, there are some Arturians, particularly amongst knights, pallitines, and those of station, who have such a strong tie to their ancestry that they use the ceremonial speech in their day-to-day communications. Much like he has," Thoman explained.

Taryn urged her horse on and pondered the explanation as they continued to ride.

"Tell me about yourself, Derren," Illya urged the pallitine while they dismounted to set up camp for the night.

The pallitine narrowed his eyes briefly as he turned to look at the sage, curious as to her intentions. "There's not much to tell, truth be told. I've lived my life in Tramire doing Orn's work. What is it you would like to know?"

"Oh, anything really. I'm always interested in learning about my companions, especially when they differ so much from me." She shrugged. "Start with your life. Why do you do what you do?"

Derren pondered the question for a moment as he rested a hand on his mount's back. "I became a pallitine because of the number of misdeeds that take place in this world. My parents were poor and, consequently, were looked down upon and treated like filth. My father was a simple cobbler, but could never afford the materials he needed to make the shoes his talents would have allowed. My mother was very supportive of him and worked in the fields when she was able. As she grew older her joints grew too painful to move. Since they couldn't afford any of the local apothecary's remedies, she went without and could not work. My family got by, don't get me wrong. But if only the world was more compassionate, and less unscrupulous, we wouldn't have suffered as many hardships as we did." He found the totality of his answer and gazed directly into Illya's bright-green eyes. "I do what I do to right the wrongs around us and bring what little compassion I can to this world that would not otherwise be present."

Illya impulsively released the reins of her mount and skipped over to Derren to hug him. She looked at his confused expression and beamed forth. "You truly *are* selfless. And *that* is why I like pallitines so much. With few exceptions, you have one noble trait or another that drives you to do what you do. Far different than most types of people, too." Her cheeks flushed and she shied away, averting her gaze away from Derren's, and moved back to take the reins of her horse. "Sorry if I made you uncomfortable, I... tend to act before I think. Especially when I see something I like." She quickly looked up at Derren before turning to tie her mount to a nearby tree and whistled while she made her way toward the others.

Derren stood and recovered himself, not sure of what to make of his companion.

Bartholomew walked up to him and chuckled lightly while he clapped his hand on Derren's shoulder. "Methinks this one couldst be trouble, my friend." He winked slyly and moved on to join the others.

The group set up camp and drew a fire large enough for them to sit comfortably around and ate a simple meal of rations and venison.

After dinner, Bartholomew turned to the group's leader. "High Pallitine, do not most dragon-kind live near The Spine? What would such a beast be doing so far from its home?"

Thoman gazed thoughtfully into the fire for a moment before answering. "I don't know why it's strayed so far from where they hail. Perhaps Illya can answer this question better than I can?"

"Oh, dragon-kind, what an interesting topic!" Illya's excitement streamed out as she started to go on about the creatures. "Actually Bartholomew, yes, dragons do hail from The Spine. Those mountains are said to be the birthplace of all dragons and their kin. But, the wyrm we're hunting isn't technically a full-blooded dragon, you see. It could be considered a cousin to their full-blooded brethren. Wyrms tend to be wingless, grounded variants that don't grow nearly as large as full-blooded dragons are able. While they may not be as mobile, they tend to be more agile. Their scaly hides grow about as thick as the hide of their cousins and most of them retain some form of fire-breath. They are oft compared to oversized salamanders, of course being much more dangerous than the smaller creatures. But, to get back to the question, The Spine is merely where the dragons are said to originate from. Like anything, they can migrate when the situation is right. My guess is this one, or its progenitor, must have moved from The Spine. Perhaps there was too much competition for food?" She shrugged as she turned back to the fire.

"And this wyrm we hunt, doth it breathe fire?"

Thoman gazed into his cup and nodded. "Yes, I have seen it breathe a solid stream of fire several yards out, burning all the flames touch. It looked more like it spat out the stream, rather than breathe it out, however."

Illya's eyes beamed with joy as she jumped in. "Quite! Most wyrms aren't as innately connected to magic as their cousins, but they've formed similar measures by ingesting sulfur and some metals, such as iron. They hold special glands in protected sacks immediately under their jaw that hold secretions made from these components that when squeezed, are ignited within their mouths and either spat, or breathed out to burn their victims. They then eat those unfortunate enough to be killed, and the meat serves to nourish the beast while the charred remains serve to fuel the breath itself."

Bartholomew turned to Illya, bearing an amused expression. "Ha! Methinks thou hast quite an infatuation with the beasts from thine exuberance, Lady Illyandra."

Illya's cheeks flushed in response to the ribbing. "They *are* majestic creatures. How could one *not* appreciate the beauty of their design? Of course they must be put down, but still. One *has* to respect their beauty!"

Derren looked thoughtfully at Bryn. "Didn't you face the beast as well? What can you tell us about it?"

The mountaineer shook his head and replied. "No, I was with the group that found its lair, but I didn't actually face the beast. If I had, I doubt I'd be here now. I was with Brother Tremue while the others were searching out the tunnels. By the time Pallitine Gerard made it out from the catacombs, we lost two members of our group. The brother sent me ahead since I had the best chance of returning with a message without being caught by the beast. Out of an original party of one brother, three fighting men, and myself, I was the only one to survive."

The other members of the party listened intently, each nodding as they reflected upon the tale.

"What *I* can tell you about the wyrm is the same as I've told Taryn," Thoman added. "The creature is large and quick. We must spread out, otherwise it will try to catch us all with its breath. It has a tail it uses to dangerous advantage. It can lash out to knock you down before you'll even realize you're in danger. Never have I seen something so huge move so sure and quick. I was incredibly lucky to have fought it off." He pulled out a pendant made from the horn he knocked off the beast all those many years ago and held it thoughtfully. "When we do face the wyrm, it would be best if we flanked it from all sides and if faced with a chance to strike, do *not* hesitate. Strike with all your might. This creature is covered in thick scales, so you *will* need to strike hard. I suggest trying to go under the scales and skewering it with your blades if possible. Hugh." The High Pallitine turned to his old friend. "You'll need to be sure and find any open gaps in the creature's armor and fill them with your arrows. If you see any weakness in its armor it's your job to let the front line know about it. I thought I saw the scales grow softer along its underbelly, but I can't be sure."

Illya nodded, affirming his observation. "Yes, it has been observed both in dragons, and their kind that the underbellies are covered in smaller, softer scales. Another place to look would be the underside of their necks, but the areas around the glands which fuel their breath will be heavily protected and not easily pierced."

Bryn spoke up. "Are we all to go with you to confront this wyrm? As you well know, I am skilled as are my men." He turned to the sage. "And how is your magic in a fight? Are you able to assist?" he asked with a raised eyebrow.

Illya shook her head emphatically. "Me? Oh heavens, no. My skills rest mostly within the realm of nature. I know much about plants, making potions and salves, understanding animals, and am able to communicate with some creatures on a primal level. I might be able to grace you with some protective wards, but that's all really, not much use in a direct fight."

Thoman looked at Bryn. "I appreciate the offer, Bryn, and I recognize your talents. But no, you and Illya will not be joining the fight. Your job is to make sure we make it there, and to help us get around any unforeseen obstacles we might face in the mountains. Illya's task is to lend us her knowledge, help anticipate anything I might not have foreseen, and to aid us if we get injured. The rest of us are here to fight the wyrm. I'm hoping with the seven of us engaging the beast directly and Hugh hitting the vulnerable areas from a distance that we can dispatch it without too many injuries."

Derren looked at the two bladesmen and couldn't hold his concerns back any longer. "Bryn, are you sure we can count on these two in the heat of battle? It's rare to meet a hired sword that will stick it through a tough fight."

Bryn snorted in irritation. "Yes, I'm sure. These men are bound to me and will fight to the end if necessary. They've more honor than most pallitines I've met, rest assured."

Both Cirrus and Errol grunted their approval. "Don't doubt our steel. We'll be there. Just don't blink when the beast dies from our blades." Errol smirked.

Darren continued to watch them and kept his reservations to himself. If the High Pallitine trusted this Bryn, then he could only show the same trust in turn.

***

Derren sat atop his horse and watched Illya bask in the warmth of the morning sun as the group broke camp. He admired her ability to maintain a genuine excitement about her travels though she was obviously a well-traveled individual. She turned to him and smiled as she urged her mount forward to ride next to him.

"Good morning to you, Illya." He greeted her as she drew close. His face broke in a warm smile while he surveyed the land.

He lost himself in the warm summer blues above and fresh scent of pine drifting along the gentle breeze. Even with such pleasant distractions, the curiosity he faced won out over the rhythm of their travels. "If you don't mind, you mentioned something last night that intrigued me."

"Oh? And what would that be?"

"You mentioned you can communicate with creatures? How exactly does that work? Can you tell what they say?"

Illya chuckled softly. "No, it's nothing like that." She looked to the side for a moment before responding. "The way I speak with them tends to be basic. I communicate using feelings and urges. Likewise, I can read the emotional states and needs when I focus on the creature. When I form a closer bond, I can even relate basic ideas and receive the same from them. I suppose you could call it empathic in nature."

Intrigued, he turned to face his companion. "And how does one learn this, or must one be born with these talents?"

"Oh, this is something my mother did as well, so I suppose I inherited it from her. She has always had a strong talent in dealing with animals, like she could relate to them as you and I would with each other."

"Interesting. Can you use it now, on your horse, for example?"

Illya stroked the mane of her horse gently. "It's not a *trick* to use at my whim. But I do try to bond with any creatures I am going to be spending time with. My horse especially. It makes guiding much easier if you work with your mount. That is why I don't use a bridle, only a simple halter for when I need to tie him up. What I *can* tell you is *your* horse is quite happy with you, but she would very much like her mane brushed, to be allowed to run more, and be given more apples."

Derren laughed, enjoying the response. "Is that what she said?"

"Well no, but isn't that what *every* horse wants?" She smiled coyly at the pallitine, teasing him. "Besides, I *told* you I can't talk directly with them. You *really* need to listen better, I think."

Derren grinned at the sage, and noticed for the first time how the sunlight caught her luminous eyes. "Perhaps you're right."

CHAPTER 19

"WHOA, LET'S STOP A MOMENT." Bryn signaled the others as he slowed to a halt, gazing at a ragged wolf slumped on the road several yards away. "Hugh, what do you make of this?" the guide asked as he watched the beast raise its head and cough up some blood.

Hugh trotted up alongside his companion and looked at the wolf. The ranger's rough face creased with concern for the sight before him. "It's the beast plague." He dismounted and unslung his bow before walking to where the beast lay on the road. As he moved closer, the wolf pawed the ground as it tried to pull itself toward the ranger. Hugh slowed his approach and pulled an arrow from his quiver and nocked it, watching the beast closely as he moved in.

Taryn sat from her mount and watched. The sight of this wolf brought her back to the first time when she saw a creature struck by the plague. She shivered from the memory of the creature attacking her, and trying to bite her even as it lay on top of her, dying. She nudged her mount forward and looked at the beast. Patches of fur were gone, replaced by swaths of broken skin, barely clotted with a murky crust. Dark, fetid blood still dripped from its teeth as thick saliva mixed with the crimson fluid and trickled onto the dirt road. Milky streaks ran through both dark eyes, clouding its vision as the pained creature snapped laboriously in Hugh's direction. With as much effort as it took when the wolf moved to attack, it could barely muster a wheeze without coughing up more of the sickly colored ooze that crept out of the wolf's veins.

Illya slid off her mount and patted the equine reassuringly before moving up to join Hugh to take a closer look. Her brow sank in sadness as she inspected the suffering creature.

The ranger paused as he watched the beast labor its way toward him. His stance firmed with resolve and he pulled the bowstring back and let an arrow fly, putting the beast out of its misery.

The gathering looked on, engrossed in a morbid fascination while the ranger approached the corpse and examined it. He turned to the group and motioned for the sage to join him.

Illya's brow furrowed as she leaned in to inspect the corpse. She sighed compassionately while she examined the sores, looking for something to explain the affliction. She picked up a nearby stick and, careful to not touch the body, lifted a back leg to inspect an injury the beast had suffered. The sage frowned and pointed vaguely toward the wounds. "It was no wonder the wolf went mad. Pain from the agitated sores and injuries must have driven it over the edge."

Hugh stepped to the side and watched the sage, his gaze wrought with concern. "What do ya see?"

She pushed her pained compassion aside and looked up at the ranger. "I honestly don't know. I've only seen a handful of the afflicted before, and none while alive or near enough as this one. It looks as if the beast suffered some infection; the wounds along its body bear the typical signs, just worse. Aside from the festering sores, there is another recent injury the wolf suffered, but it appears as if it was healing normally. It looks to be a bite on its rear leg, but bears none of the ill signs the other wounds do. Perhaps it's nothing," Illya's voice grew with concern. "With it coughing up so much blood I would be quite reluctant to move the body, much less touch the poor creature for fear of spreading the sickness. Oh, how it must have suffered." She tilted her head as her eyes narrowed in afterthought. "But perhaps there *is* something I can do."

Illya's hand drifted up to her neck. Her fingers found a worn leathery necklace and pulled it out from the mess of cords and chains she wore to reveal a small green crystal hanging on the end. She held the shard in one hand and carefully moved closer to the corpse. Her other hand hovered over the body as she lowered her head and chanted softly. Light, melodic tones flowed from her mouth and felt as if they could color the air as she stood there hunched over the wolf's body, focusing on it.

Taryn pulled on the reins and urged her mount to step back slowly as she felt the forces of magic coalesce in the air. Having suffered its touch so intimately, she was keenly aware of the signs to look for.

The sage's eyelids drooped as she focused on the still body of the wolf. The crystal Illya gripped pulsed to life as her concentration deepened. A full minute passed until she stopped chanting, causing the light within the small crystal to flutter out. She slowly stood and shook her head while recovering from the effort.

"What? What is it?" The ranger asked, concern weighing heavily in his rugged voice.

Illya stood there, breathing slowly as she looked vacantly ahead. "It's... strange. Dark. Definitely an illness, but not one found in nature." She continued speaking as she pieced the clues together. "It's almost as if some curse has found a means of transference through a disease and affected this creature. That is the only way I can explain what I saw. Whatever this is, we need to burn the body. We cannot risk spreading this plague."

"So, we don't know what this is?"

"I'm afraid not. I've heard stories, much like you have I'm

sure, but I've never been fortunate enough to be able to study one so near life."

Hugh motioned the others that everything was all right.

Bryn, Cirrus, and Errol immediately set out to gather wood for the fire. The trio each came walking back to the road with an armful of wood and placed their bundles carefully on the corpse.

A sharp yelp shot through the air as Hugh approached the pyre, stopping him in his tracks. The noise came from farther down the road, but didn't seem far.

Cirrus and Errol immediately pulled their swords and gazed to where the noise came from.

Hugh called out to Thoman and unslung the bow from his shoulder. "We'll be right back, stick with the mounts and be ready for anythin'," the ranger warned before heading out.

Thoman looked to Taryn and commanded her to do the same. "I don't know what's going on, but listen. I don't need you risking yourself unnecessarily. Stay put."

Illya nervously thumbed the crystal as she watched the two men cautiously rush down to the source of the noise and walk past a tightly knit copse of trees.

Taryn watched the men leave and refused to stand idly by. She pulled her own blade and followed while motioning the others to stay behind.

The two men immediately stopped in their tracks and held their weapons high as they both readied themselves for combat. A low growl echoed from somewhere past the trees, followed quickly by a chorus of growls.

Taryn caught up with the men and found the growls were coming from three more wolves, each struck with the same illness which felled the first, but none seemed as near to death.

"I thought I told you to stay back," Thoman muttered.

"It sounded like you needed help. And from the look of things, I was right."

He rolled his shoulders, loosening them. "Since you're here, might as well join in the fun. Call the others and prepare to fight."

Taryn backed up and called out for help, then readied her blade.

Hugh nocked an arrow and sent it flying into the lead wolf, dropping it as the arrow penetrated its skull.

Thoman raised his blade and stepped in front of Hugh, bracing himself for the charging beasts.

The wolves' baying broke through the air and called the others to action. Harrold, Bartholomew, and Derren ran ahead to assist their comrades, drawing their blades as they drew closer while Bryn and the bladesmen stayed with Illya.

The first of the remaining wolves leapt at Thoman, nearly knocking the pallitine over as he deflected the beast while bashing it with the flat of his blade. The second wolf took advantage of the opening and finished what its companion started, knocking the aging pallitine over and gripped his armored forearm viciously in its maw.

"Thoman!" Taryn ran for her mentor, and slashed at the beast with her sword, cutting open the creature's matted flesh with ease, and little noticeable effect.

Hugh drew another arrow and released it at the wolf that now pinned Thoman to the ground.

The first wolf regained its footing and joined its companion in attacking the downed pallitine. It tore at the pallitine's sword arm, pinning it within its jaws as it looked for an opening on the otherwise well-armored man.

Taryn moved over and kicked the first wolf off Thoman's arm. It landed with a whine and scrambled up, glaring at the sword she waved between them.

Desperately, Hugh pulled another arrow and sank it into the other wolf's ribcage, jarring it so the beast released its grip on the High Pallitine and slowly turned to the archer. Its eyes glowered in hate as the wolf coughed up a stream of the darkened blood.

Thoman knelt as he started to get up, attracting the attention of the first wolf who charged him.

The wolf looked from Thoman's unarmored head to the blade that danced before it. The beast growled as it leapt for the exposed flesh, and dodged the blade as it swung wildly by.

The High Pallitine bashed the charging beast in its skull with his armored fist, deflecting the wolf's attack as it plowed into the ground before him. He quickly used his sword to brace himself, stood, and prepared to strike.

That pause was all the time Taryn needed to plunge her sword straight down the beast's back and into the ground below.

The creature turned back to the pallitine as the blade struck the earth, and resumed its charge. The rabid beast growled as the weapon slid into its body and refused to back down. It pushed forward, forcing the sword back through its body, tearing it apart as the wolf stubbornly tried to bite the pallitine until it collapsed in a twitching heap.

Derren was the first of the pallitines to catch up to the battle right as the last wolf leapt at its prey. He swung his blade at the beast's head, knocking it back to the ground in a sudden heap.

Bartholomew caught up and ran to the other side of the creature. He skewered the struggling wolf, planting it firmly to the ground with his blade.

An arrow announced the wolf's final moments as it plunged into its skull, ending the battle as quickly as it started.

Taryn moved to help Thoman up and looked around cautiously. "It looks like this is more dangerous than we thought." She wiped her blade on the matted fur of the wolf, scraping the sickly blood off.

The pallitine nodded in agreement. "So it would seem. I pray this is the extent of our problems. These beasts seem to shrug off blows they normally would fall to."

"By his sword, those beasts are mad. Ne'er before hath mine eyes witnessed such ferocity!" Bartholomew chimed in as he cleaned his blade.

As Bryn and the others caught up with the group, another set of growls echoed throughout the air.

"Ash and bones, more beasts? When will this end?" Muttered Bryn.

The group proceeded carefully down the road until they saw two bears stood grappling, locked in deadly combat as each ripped the other with its claws. As they drew closer, it became clear only one of the bears was diseased and the other was fighting for its life.

Hugh drew an arrow and let it fly, sinking it into the flank of the sickly beast. The bears continued their struggle, unaware or uncaring of the new arrivals. Hugh soon loosed another arrow, this time hitting the beast in its shoulder, causing it to pause mid-attack.

The other bear took advantage of the distraction and embraced the aggressor's head within its paws and twisted it, snapping the neck with a sharp crack.

Now satisfied that its foe was no longer a problem, the beast settled on all fours and eyed the group as it slowly walked toward them.

Hugh nocked an arrow and eyed the bear, bracing himself for another attack. As the animal approached, he raised his bow and took aim at the battered creature's head.

Illya stepped forward and tilted her head as she stared at the creature. She gently placed a hand on Hugh's arm and reassured him. "That is no bear, friend Hugh. Please, wait a moment if you would," Illya urged as she stepped forward.

When Hugh lowered his bow, the bear stopped in its tracks and looked at the party, examining its members carefully.

Illya stepped boldly toward the creature and held a hand out in greeting. "Hello, friend druid."

The bear cocked its head at the half-elf and began to blur. Slowly the animal changed before them. The rough, coarse fur covering the bear began to recede, replaced by a set of roughly cut brown leather pants and a torn, bloodstained tunic. Taking the creature's place was now a man stooped over and sitting on his legs.

The figure stood to greet the strangers. Now on his feet, he towered over the slight frame of the sage who greeted him. The hardy druid wore his long, dark hair tied behind him in a tail that ended between his shoulder blades. His hairless face, much like his hands, was touched in parts with a light mixture of dirt and blood. His countenance gave the initial impression of some gentleman who chose to live in the wild, picking fights with stray animals for the sport of it.

He looked upon Illya with a piercing gaze. He carefully stepped forward, addressing Illya. "Hello," As he drew closer an intrigued expression crossed his face, "sister?"

"Me? Oh, no. I'm not gifted by Oriah." Illya giggled. "My mother was, but not me. I have only a minor talent, nothing like her."

The druid smirked and inclined his head in apology. "Of course not. My mistake." He nodded toward Thoman and continued. "Interesting company you keep."

Illya smiled broadly. "This is my friend Thoman. He is a pallitine."

He regarded Thoman with a sly grin. "Ahh, but he is no mere pallitine. I've heard mention of a High Pallitine by that name, isn't that so?" he asked expectantly.

Illya cocked her head and looked questioningly at the new arrival. "Well, yes if you must ask. What is your business here? Are you investigating the animals and the plague they carry? Why is it driving them mad?"

Thoman stepped forward, concern crossing his brow. "Yes, what are you doing here, and how is it that you know of me?"

The druid smiled playfully. "There are only so many pallitines bearing your name, or am I mistaken?" He looked Thoman over thoughtfully. The barest hint of regret flashed across the druid's face as he suffered a realization. He bowed his head while addressing Thoman. "I forget my manners, High Pallitine. My name is Greve, and as my..." he paused to nod in Illya's direction, "*little sister* guessed, I am searching for what is corrupting these fine beasts. The corruption has spread much in the past months and slowly gains ground." Greve's face turned sour as he thought of the corruption and the damage left in its wake. "I fear if left unchecked, the balance of life could be overturned, and I seek to prevent that from happening."

"But what of Graevenholt? Does the council send others to seek this out?" Illya asked, concern creasing her brow.

Greve spat harshly on the ground. "Pah! The council moves with wit slower than a sleeping obraki." The agitation within the druid grew as he continued. "I tried warning them, but all they do is sit and argue over what's been found. I doubt they've stopped bickering since I left them two seasons past."

"What do you think is happening here?" Thoman inquired, trying to grasp the severity of the situation at hand.

The druid composed himself and turned to the High Pallitine. "Honestly, I am at a loss as to what caused this. All I know is that once bitten, animals grow agitated to the point of spreading violence upon any not in their immediate herd. I've seen strange things since I've been looking: a mastiff taken down by several rats, cows laying waste to a farm's yard, and other bizarre attacks. You've witnessed the victim of a wolf attack when it made no sense. Wolves don't attack men when there is an abundance of easier prey to be had." Greve looked upon Thoman with a confused frustration. "It makes no sense at all. None of this does."

"The thought doth occur to me that a resemblance exists between such a sickness and one of men turning rabid with Lycanthropy when being attacked by were-wolves, wouldst this be similar?" Bartholomew offered to the druid.

Greve's face twisted in disgust. "No, that is an altogether different blight. This is something else."

Harrold stepped forward. "How do we know to even trust him? He's a druid. Let him be on his way so we can be on ours."

Illya turned on the pallitine and stepped forward. "My mother was a druid. Does that make me any less trustworthy?"

She waited a heartbeat and interrupted Harrold's stuttered response. "No, it does not. Do you have a problem with elves as well? Simply because one is not human does not mean we aren't to be trusted. If I were you, I would take your prejudices and lodge them elsewhere, or I may forget my place." She glared, daring the pallitine to say another word.

Greve laughed. "Well said, little sister."

Bryn looked at the receding sun and turned to Thoman. "Whatever's happening here, we still have work to do. The other body needs to be burned, and it appears we have more bodies to burn as well."

The druid stepped forward to interrupt. "Seeking to contain the infection? Don't bother, it dies within minutes of the victim. Anything that eats of their flesh will feel nothing worse than a stomach ache." He frowned slightly as he placed a hand on his midsection. "I should know. The real challenge is to stop them before they attack more creatures and spread this any further. Fortunately, most creatures don't survive the assaults, but the few that do live move on to infect others."

Thoman raised an eyebrow and frowned. "Why eat something so sickly?"

Greve simply shrugged and grinned mischievously at Thoman. "Why do bears eat anything? Hunger. Besides, aside from the curse the victims are unusually healthy. Once you get past the bitterness from the tainted blood, and the otherwise grotesque exterior, it's actually not much different from normal fare."

Sounds of disgust ruffled through the group at the last comment.

"Be that as it may," Thoman added, "we have a camp to set up. Our appetites aren't as forgiving, and the area may prove too dangerous to travel in the dark."

"Of course." Greve nodded. "I trust it will be no issue were I to join your camp this night?"

"By all means. All I ask is if you choose to indulge in your unique tastes, do so outside of the camp."

Greve feigned sincerity and tilted his head. "Certainly, I wouldn't want to offend any of your more delicate sensibilities."

~~~※~~~

"Tell me, little sister, why is it you travel with these folk?" Greve asked as he poked a stick into the firepit, stirring some hot coals under the burning wood.

Illya turned from her hushed conversation with Derren to address the druid and smiled. "Thoman, Derren, and the rest? We have been quested to slay a wyrm that has terrorized villages, ravaged innocents, and needs to be put down."

Greve cocked his head as he looked at her. "And you support the slaughter of such a great beast?"

Illya shook her head. "Typically, no. I would not. *This* wyrm, however, has a lengthy history of encroaching upon civilized lands and slaughtering many and disappearing for years at a time. That, and this is the creature that slew Thoman's mentor, Pallitine Hadrian. It wasn't until recently that its lair was found. And now we are off to slay it."

The druid perked up at the mention of the pallitine. "I see. How long have you traveled with Thoman?"

"We've only recently begun this journey. But I've known him since he was but a boy starting the road to being a man."

"And you knew him when he went to Graevenholt when he was a boy?" he pressed, hiding his interest in idle conversation.

Illya paused and turned to face the druid. "Yes, I did. How did you know?" Interest sparked her gaze.

Greve shrugged. "There are only so many pallitines named Hadrian who have been in Graevenholt, and even fewer who traveled with an apprentice. Much less a half-elven druid. You know stories stick. Especially from *that* time." He looked across the campfire at the High Pallitine. "Where do your journeys take you next? You don't seem to be traveling up to the Spine."

Bryn, Harrold, and the rest broke from their conversations and listened, now that the conversation steered toward a more interesting topic.

Thoman took a sip from his waterskin and spoke. "No, we aren't. The beast has made his lair down in the Untarian Mountains, inside Saerinian territory."

"Interesting to be laired so far from the Spine," Greve mused.

The sage turned back to Greve. "Where is your search taking you? You are following the curse, are you not?" She asked.

Greve inclined his head to Illya as he answered. "Yes, little sister. The trail I follow leads me north, I believe toward the Van Wordian Mountains, or perhaps somewhere between. It meanders erratically, making it hard to follow, but that's the general pattern I've gleaned from its current course."

"How hast thou come across this plague to begin with, Greve?" Bartholomew asked.

"For years there have been beasts that've cropped up showing the same sickness, but within the last few seasons it's grown in frequency. Enough to concern the council, but not enough to stir them to action." He shifted his weight as he addressed the pallitine and calmed the frustration that boiled within. "I took it upon myself to deal with the infected beasts and found a trail of creatures, both dead and infected that showed the same signs we've seen near Graevenholt, and followed them. Within a few months I was lucky enough to find a pack of wolves near River's Bend and dispatched them. From there the path grew cold as it twisted south. I managed to pick it back up and have followed it as it finally turned north, and believe I am closing in upon the trail to its source."

"Good. Then I wish you the best of luck as we part ways in the morning," Thoman added.

The exuberant pallitine's eyes glowed with conviction. "Aye, may your hunt prove fruitful, druid. I wish Orn to guide thine hand when smiting the source of this evil. Had I not already been preordained to follow mine current path, I would gladly help thee with thine," Bartholomew offered apologetically.

Greve smirked in amusement at the proclamation. "I believe you, pallitine." His smile dimmed in the firelight as he acknowledged the younger man. "Who knows? Perhaps you shall yet have the chance."

CHAPTER 20

TARYN RODE UP ALONGSIDE HER mentor and stopped where he had been sitting atop the ridge overlooking the valley below them.

"We're close now aren't we?" she asked.

Thoman swept his gaze across the valley, scrutinizing the land before them. "That we are. This valley marks the beginning of Saerinian Territory." He pointed vaguely toward the east. "If we were to head back to Guardians Keep, it would take us two days travel to give you reference."

"I had no idea the border traveled this far north." Her concern peaked, not liking the sound of their violent southern neighbor seeming so close to their home.

"It matters little. The border moves seasonally. Sometimes we provide a show of arms in the area. Other times, they do. Neither side has a vested interest in the valley aside from the fact that it provides a buffer between us." He shrugged.

Thoman urged his horse aside and addressed the group. "Let's set up camp, behind the ridge here. Tomorrow we'll enter the valley."

A chorus of tired voices agreed. Everyone looked more than

eager to take a break from riding, even if it was still a few hours before sunset.

In the time they traveled together, the routine became automatic. Bryn, Cirrus, Errol, and Bartholomew would set up the three tents and spread out the sleeping rolls, while Illya and Derren set up the firepit in preparation for the evening meal. Hugh, Thoman, and Taryn would unload the supplies from the horses and would then move out to scout the area and hunt for the night's meal.

The sun started to mark its downward march as it touched the tips of the Untarian Mountains in the west when the three made their way back from a successful hunt with several quail eggs, three quails, and a wild turkey. Illya gathered some wild mushrooms and leeks and had already started preparing them for dinner.

Once their repast was finished, and the group had all but finished eating, everyone settled back and grew more sociable as they relaxed.

"Bryn, being the most traveled amongst us, what can you tell us of the Saerinian Territory?" Thoman asked over the firepit as night settled on the camp.

"Not much that hasn't already been discussed in our preparations." Bryn shrugged as he tore a chunk of roast quail off the leg he held. "The borders here tend to fluctuate with the seasons, so it's hard to say where or when we'll see any Saerin bands. It's best to keep our campfires infrequent and short to stay hidden as much as possible until we get to the foothills nearing the mountains where it will be easier to hide our presence."

"Pah, let them come. We shall best them in the heat of battle," Bartholomew chimed in, confidence brimming with each word.

Thoman narrowed his eyes to the young pallitine. "This is one battle we don't wish to face too early in our journey."

Harrold grunted. "Not that they don't deserve it."

"Aye, lad. Ya don't want ta go pokin' a nest o' hornets like that one, trust me." Hugh grinned at Bartholomew.

"Not if the stories of their barbaric strength and brutal nature are to be believed. Especially since they've grown more organized in the last several seasons," Derren added.

Bryn snorted in agreement.

"Why do you think that is, Thoman?" Derren asked.

The High Pallitine shook his head as he stared into the flames. "I've only heard rumors to that effect. Rumors I don't wish to believe, but if the Saerin are truly banding together we may have no choice but to pay attention to our southern border." His gaze shifted to Derren. "It was suggested that the Absolutionist movement has taken root within the Saerin chieftains and they are all falling under its sway. Regardless if that is or is not the truth, the territories are still fractured enough to not warrant much thought, just something to watch."

"Until something gels them together under a single cause, such as a perceived weakness, affront, or whatever their holy men can envision," Bryn snarled. "In any event, we should only need to travel for three days within their territory before being far enough in the foothills to be of much concern, and then it's another day before we're where we need to be."

Taryn sat and watched the interactions in silence and turned to Illya. "What do you make of this?" Her eyes betrayed an uneasiness about the topic being discussed.

"Which part?" Illya inquired as she moved to face the apprentice pallitine.

"Everything," she shrugged. "Leaving Arturian land, the Absolutionists, the Saerin clans. All of it."

Illya pondered the question, only briefly glancing toward the men as they continued their discourse on strategies for travel. "I have faith we will get through the territory fine. Bryn has traveled the area before and will take us through it with little difficulty, I'm sure."

The sage leaned back on an elbow and continued. "Regarding the Saerin clans, I can't claim to have personal experience with them, but with any luck we won't have to worry about them. If we do, then perhaps we shall be fortunate enough to not need to fight. They tend to be a superstitious lot, and from growing up in Graevenholt, there are many stories of the Old Wars where bands would turn in fear from a handful of Oriah's gifted simply because they changed in front of them. Apparently they think us demons or somesuch?" She laughed softly as she played with a braided leather bracelet she wore. "I honestly don't know."

The lilt of the half-elf's laugh helped to ease the seriousness of Taryn's mood.

Illya sat up and her smile faded as she scooted in closer to Taryn to stress the next point. "The Absolutionists, however, are a much more serious thing to consider in my opinion. Especially if they are banding the Saerin clans together."

Taryn narrowed her eyes as she asked the question that festered in her mind since the topic was raised. "I've had the misfortune of running into them before. What do you know of them?"

Illya squeezed Taryn's hand. "I've heard. From what I know of them, they are clever, troublesome, and insidious. The cult has been around for generations upon generations, and their population is unknown, but seems to rise and fall like anything else. Until the last decade or so, it was thought that the cult had all but died. They are men, women, people from all walks who believe in the darker path to reach the supposed light of their mission's end. Their strength draws from their fanaticism, their ability to brainwash the most stalwart of people. They believe it is Orn's will to absolve the world of its sins. And that means, quite literally, killing all of the non-believers. By purging the world of all contrary belief, they are preparing for Orn's return. All sins will be washed away and thus the world will be absolved and ready for the pure of heart to thrive and live the glorious life promised to them."

Taryn backed away, scowling in distaste. "That's much more than I've heard yet. It sounds more like the Abider's work than Orn's."

Illya nodded, agreeing. "Those are my thoughts as well. But because their faith aligns with some of Orn's philosophies, and in parts, Oriah's, it enables them to convert many of the more weak-willed individuals to their cause."

"Such as the Saerin."

"Well," Illya looked doubtful as she replied, "*they* have a history of rejecting all faiths since they look to their ancestors and beliefs for guidance. I've only read a smattering of scrolls regarding their culture, but they seem to be a proud, if not misguided, people strongly tied to their traditions. To fall in line with the Absolutionists is unusual indeed. Something quite convincing or out of the ordinary must have happened to get them to follow a cause that runs contradictory to their heritage."

"How do you know so much about the Absolutionists?"

"Theological history at the college in Irline. I have somewhat of a vested interest in the subject."

"Oh? You don't strike me as the religious type."

"I'm not, at least beyond my love for Mother Oriah." She touched the earth they rested on and smiled.

Taryn mulled over what was discussed, wondering how far-reaching the threat truly was. A subdued cough interrupted her thoughts.

The two women turned to find Derren standing, waiting politely for a moment to interrupt. "Illya, you mentioned earlier that you wanted to show me how to find that one herb. Is this a good time?" he asked, feigning innocence with the request.

"Oh yes, dear me. I nearly forgot," she exclaimed. "Forgive me, Taryn, but I've prior commitments that need tending. You understand?" Her eyes pleaded as she stood to join Derren.

Taryn chuckled lightly and casually waved her hand toward the darkness surrounding them. "Of course, this seems like the perfect time to go out foraging for herbs," she stressed in the sincerest tone she could muster.

As soon as the couple was out of earshot, Bartholomew burst

out laughing. "Looking for herbs, indeed! Methinks they'll find more than herbs in *those* trees." He nudged Cirrus and pointed to where the couple left. "Mayhaps we should allow them their own tent for the eve? That swiving scoundrel." He laughed and shoved another hunk of roast quail in his mouth.

Taryn couldn't help but smile, as she took a bit of joy in knowing things weren't going in quite the same direction as the Arturite implied.

"You know, in all my travels, I've never met anyone who's lived in Irline and willingly came back," Derren commented as he held a branch back for Illya to walk past.

"Oh, it is a glorious place, but far too removed from what I love to truly keep me away. I enjoy my time there, but between my homes in Eorlin and Graevenholt I'm quite happy where I am."

"Then it's your fondness of nature, friends, and family that keep you here?"

"Indeed." She agreed as they walked to a secluded section of the ridge that overlooked the valley.

"Well then, I'm glad for that, and glad to do what I can to help it continue," he quipped ingratiatingly.

Illya laughed with an affected reservation. "A charming smile *and* a clever tongue. I just might need to be careful around you." She paused once the peak of the ridge was reached and drew her breath slowly as she took in the view.

Before them, a blanket of forest rested in the valley below, highlighted by the half-moon as its sparse light accented the scenery. In the distance the mountains lined the western horizon as the valley merged with the plains to the east.

"It will never be as easy as it is now, you know."

"What?" Derren asked, as he slid an arm across her shoulder, enjoying the view with her.

She angled her face to look at him. "This. Our journey. Us."
She slid her arm around his waist and continued. "It's easy to
fall in the embrace of another when one faces the prospect of
hard times. It's much harder when the urgency is over."

His eyes flashed with concern. "What do you mean? I pray
you aren't implying my affections are opportune?"

She smiled, comforted by his uncertainty. "Oh, heavens no.
What I mean is that when this is done, our lives will resume
where they were. You will pick up your sword and parade it
around the countryside, and I will be back in the world of books
and herbs and traveling. Let us enjoy what we have now and
not place too much importance upon where we are when we
get back."

Derren smiled and squeezed her close. "Oh, that I was
planning on. Though, I daresay I will not give up so easily when
this is done, if you'll have me of course."

"Well then," she smiled slyly into his eyes, "perhaps you'll
have to convince me."

⁓ӠӜϾ⁓

Taryn looked through the woods to the open field approaching
them. She was glad to be well past the halfway point through
the valley and grew eager to finish this stretch of the journey.
She welcomed the sun as it broke through the thinning trees,
and saw the forest begin to disappear the further west they rode
as they neared the foothills. The group agreed to stay within the
cover of the trees for as long as they could before they veered
too far off course.

"Are those riders up ahead?" Illya asked, as she placed a hand
up to her eyes, blocking the stray shafts of sunlight that broke
through the canopy.

"Where?" Bryn slowed his mount, and gazed through the

break in the trees to where the forest gave way to an open field.

The half-elf rode up and pointed to a spot farther along the field past the forest to a band of riders heading away from the group.

Bryn spat on the ground. "I knew these last two days were too easy. Let's be careful and hope there aren't more." He turned his mount and trotted to the High Pallitine. "We need to go around the field. There are riders up ahead, and from the looks of them, it's a Saerin hunting party."

"Good idea," Thoman agreed. "The field would leave us open, far too likely to be spotted were we to try and head to the mountains now." He turned and found that Hugh had leapt off his horse and was kneeling on the ground.

The ranger touched the earth and looked around the trampled covering and frowned. Hugh stood and walked to Bryn and Thoman with a worried look in his eyes. "I'm not sure how many were here, but this area has been well traveled in the last few days. I see tracks from a couple o' different sources, both men walkin' as well as horses. Whatever we decide, we must travel cautiously, ready ta run if needed."

Bartholomew snorted in contempt. "Orn will guide our blades, mine friends."

"If it comes to that, he will," Derren agreed. "But for now, discretion would seem the wiser course of action."

"As much as I'd hate to admit it, he's right," Harrold agreed. "Best to focus on our task now and wait to cut a swath of Saerin blood in our journey back home."

Flushed with nervous energy from the discovery, Taryn's eyes flicked about the area. She turned to look behind the group and found that they weren't alone. Two riders were trotting in their direction back from where they came. "Abider's luck." She frowned. "We're being followed, Thoman."

Each member of the party turned and watched the newcomers anxiously. As out in the open as the group was, there was little chance they had not been seen.

Taryn reached behind her and down to where her scabbard was belted on her saddlebag. "There's only two of them. We could dispatch them without much trouble."

Thoman glanced at her. "Don't follow Bartholomew's lead. Not every situation needs to be met with bloodshed. Let's see what they have to say."

She moved her hand from the scabbard, though she disliked feeling so helpless in an unknown situation.

The men were dressed in a strange mix of the rough furs common with Saerin hunters, and finer, more colorful rags underneath. They were well armed, but neither rider had drawn a weapon, though they rested in easy reach.

"Hrm." Bryn grunted. "Possibly traders or mercenaries. Always hard to tell out here. Either way, it'll cost us." He turned to Thoman. "You brought the tolls I suggested?"

Thoman nodded.

"Good. We might need 'em."

Taryn nudged her mount to Thoman's side and stayed a step behind as he hailed the riders. She nervously flexed her hand, ready to draw her blade. Even with Bryn's meager assurances, she found it hard to relax this far in Saerin land. She looked to the others and found comfort in the fact they were doing the same.

As the riders approached, one took the lead while the other hung back and kept a hand on an ornate horn, carved from what looked to be a bone of some beast, hollowed out and etched with designs Taryn could not see.

The lead rider stopped and raised an open hand outward and spoke with a thick Saerin accent. "Hail, outlanders." His mouth opened to reveal dark and discolored teeth hidden in the depths of his overgrown beard. His eyes, while seeming friendly, held a cold edge that implied a keen sense for survival.

"Hail," Thoman replied, offering the same gesture in greeting.

The speaker took a formal posture and ingratiated himself to the group. "I am Tchor, and my companion here is Gravk.

With whom do I have the pleasure of parlaying?"

Thoman held Tchor's gaze confidently. "I am Thoman, leader of this group. How can I be of service?"

The rider's countenance eased, showing his approval of the response. "You're a far ways from home, Thoman, and at such an unfortunate time," he observed in amusement.

"We are, but why is that unfortunate?" Thoman pried conversationally.

Tchor swept his hand toward the field behind the group. "Surely you've seen the hunters out in force. I'm quite surprised you have not had any chance encounters. It would be a shame indeed if that were to happen, would it not?" he stated in an exaggerated and agreeable manner.

Out of the corner of her eye, Taryn saw Bartholomew scowl as he gripped the handle of his sword and inched it out of the scabbard.

Cirrus and Errol glanced to Bryn who subtly shook his head.

Hugh nudged his horse next to Bartholomew's, and placed a hand on his arm.

The speaker looked on in amusement and continued. "Yes, of course it would."

"What would you suggest to help us in our travels to keep us from notice, if you were inclined to do so?"

"Ahh, yes. *If* I were the generous sort to be so inclined, I would suggest wearing the furs the hunters themselves wear. At least the five of you," Tchor vaguely pointed toward the pallitines, "if not the rest. You stick out like a sick mare, bloated with the stench of outlanders. This way you see," he grinned in anticipation, "you may be overlooked as another band of hunters."

"And where would we get such a set of furs?" Thoman prodded. His words sounded forced under the threat of the implied extortion.

"Well, *if* I had a few fur cloaks to spare and *if* I were so inclined, my dry throat would be sated by no less than the amount of wine that could be purchased by a pouch filled with your northern coin," He suggested.

Thoman glanced at Bryn, who inclined his head almost imperceptibly. Thoman nodded. "Agreed, one pouch of coin for your generous donation of the fur cloaks."

The rider behind him coughed conspicuously.

"Ah, my companion here is quite thirsty as well. Shall we make it two?"

Taryn saw her mentor twitch with annoyance as he agreed.

"Fine, two bags. But that is all we can spare for the cloaks. We did not come prepared to trade properly. I'm sure you understand." He agreed between gritted teeth.

"Of course, my friend. I can appreciate that," the rider said smoothly.

Thoman motioned for Taryn to reach within his saddlebags and pull out the two pouches of coin agreed upon. Once he had them in his hand, he tossed them over.

Once the exchange was made, and the pallitines had their cloaks, the group started to head toward the field.

"Oh, you weren't intending to run out into the fields on *this* day I hope? As I said, the hunters move in force and have traveled throughout this forest. It would sadden me if something were to happen to you, so quickly after we've made our trade," he voiced in genuine concern.

Thoman turned toward the man and his companion, his patience for bartering wearing thin. "What would our new friend suggest? It would seem to me that the safest route would be back to where we came."

"Yes, that is, of course, always a safe option. But I don't think that's what you want. Otherwise why would you be here?" He shrugged. "No, *if* I were so inclined, I *might* be convinced to share our camp with you. It is not unusual for freerunners such as myself to travel with foreigners. Until the morrow, when most of the hunters would have left."

Thoman turned once more to Bryn, who had been studying the riders carefully during the negotiations. Again, he nodded.

"And what would it take to make this an agreeable arrangement?" Thoman glowered.

"My friend, since we are already acquainted, I will open my camp and accommodations to you for merely another pouch to cover the cost of food and drink for all. More than fair, no?"

"Agreed. But I would like some information in exchange for this arrangement, and our coin."

"Ha! Agreed." Tchor spurred his mount closer to the group, his hand outstretched for Thoman's. "I knew you were a shrewd man." His smile grew broad and genuine as he shook the High Pallitine's hand.

Once the pallitines were properly dressed in their furs, the group was off. Within the hour, they arrived in a small clearing nestled in a thicker part of the forest. A large, beige tent was set up on one side of the camp across from a ring of stones circling several pieces of charred wood. The rest of the clearing sloped gently to where the underbrush met with the trees.

"There." Tchor directed Taryn. "You may set your tents on this side of the camp and be sure to remove any markings of your homeland. Otherwise, I cannot guarantee your safety. That is fair, no?" He turned to Illya next. "And for you, my elven beauty. Fetch some wood for the fire. Us men have things to discuss."

Derren stepped away from his mount once it was properly tied to a nearby tree and rushed to Illya's side. "Allow me." He tersely acknowledged the host as he walked with Illya to find some wood for the fire.

Tchor's hands lifted in a shrug. "Is she his? I meant no disrespect, of course. Pah, come here, my friend." He clapped his hand on Thoman's shoulder and led him to a stump near the firepit.

Gravk came up to Taryn apologetically. "You must forgive my friend. He can be somewhat boisterous when he hosts. He has the chance to visit with such interesting company so rarely. I can help with the tents if you wish." He bore a lighter complexion, suggesting a distant ancestry might have been shared with the northerners. His hair, while still unkempt, was straighter and brushed off to the back and his beard was closer cropped than Tchor's.

Taryn bit back her distaste for the man and was relieved when Bartholomew walked over and dropped the tents on the ground before her. "My thanks, but my friend can help." She reached down to unroll the nearest tent while Bartholomew started setting up the other.

"Of course, of course, I understand." He backed away as he looked between both pallitines and inclined his head. "I shall head out then to hunt for dinner. It seems we have a few mouths to feed."

Taryn's head perked up from the bundle of tarps and cords. "Oh? Great. Take Hugh with you. He's an avid hunter as well."

"As you wish. Which one of you is he, if you do not mind?"

Taryn laughed to herself. "My apologies. He's the tall one in leathers with the graying hair."

Bartholomew warily watched Gravk walk away as he picked one edge of the tarp up and directed Taryn to gather the wooden poles that fell from inside the folds. "What dost thou thinkest of our hosts? Though they be opportune, they strike me as genuine once let in."

Taryn bobbed her head in reluctant agreement. "It would certainly seem that way. Let's just hope their loyalties aren't put to the test. I fear we rest on the longer end of that blade."

The pallitine's eyebrows raised at Taryn's insightful comment. "T'would appear to be wisdom in thine words indeed."

"So, my friend, what is it that you wish to know?" Tchor inquired as he offered a wooden mug filled with wine to Thoman.

Thoman graciously accepted the drink and held it purposefully. "Namely, I'm concerned about the hunting parties you referred to."

Tchor lifted a hand in response. "I expected as much. What I can tell you is this. There is a gathering out east of a great force. I know not what it is for, but the forces are gathered by those who wish to unite our clans and abolish the old ways." His eyes turned darker as he continued. "I distrust what is happening with the clans *and* their leaders. It never bodes well for those, such as myself, who drift on the edge and travel from clan to clan trading what we can for tools and information."

"My apologies. I'm unfamiliar with your old ways, but if what you describe has to do with the Absolutionists, then we may have similar problems with them," the High Pallitine observed. He scowled as he took a quick pull of the bitter wine.

"Ha, that there is Long Barrel wine, made from bitter root and berries. Never go anywhere without it." He inclined his head slyly and held up his mug before taking a long drink. "Truth be had, Thoman, there's trouble stirring in the hills." His countenance shifted as his tone took on a more serious note. "Our ancestors have been moaning in their graves and no one's the wiser. I don't know what it is, but it's out east. It's all out east. Or at least it was until their prophet made some comment over some holy relic lost in the mountains."

"Holy relic?"

Tchor took another drink of wine, and closed his eyes as he savored it. "Yes," he said as he opened his eyes, "some relic supposedly lost to the ages of legend until of late when it was prophesied in some madman's vision. The thing is, no one's found it!" He pointed firmly to the southwest. "They've amassed a large force to scour the mountains for this relic and no one knows what it is, or where to look." Tchor's face twisted in a sneer.

Thoman's face sunk as the blood rushed out. "How sizeable of a force are we discussing here?"

"Two, three hundred. I have long stopped trying to count. More are coming and they should be leaving in a matter of days, but they gather to the south toward the Untarian mountains."

Thoman welcomed the bitter burning of the wine as he took another drink. "That does not bode well. I fear our journeys –"

"No. Do not tell me anything you do not wish relayed to others." Tchor brusquely interrupted. "It keeps things much friendlier that way," he said with a wink. "That is my policy, and it should be yours. Do not be too trusting out here, outlander."

Thoman looked at Tchor with a newfound respect and agreed. "So be it. When do you believe it will be safe for us to travel?"

"Depends on where you go. Southern travel is recommended against, but if you must, travel the long way around, suggested paths would be east for a day and then south, going where you must. If that is not the direction you seek, head straight west to the mountains from here and stick to the foothills until you reach your desired path. It, too, may take longer, but either way you'll be safer."

"My thanks. That does indeed help."

"Not a problem my friend. Now it is my turn. Tell me tales of your lands, how is the empire these days?" Tchor grinned as he took another drink of wine and listened.

❦

"That is not necessary, truly." Tchor's voice called out from the other side of the camp. The exasperation present in his voice snapped Taryn's eyes open as she saw the first glimmer of daylight had already struck her tent. She looked about and found that Bartholomew and Derren were likewise waking and she saw Thoman kneeling by the flap of their tent peering out.

"What's happening?" She asked quietly as she sidled up to Thoman.

He glanced sidelong at her and responded. "It would seem a couple of scouts are interrogating our gracious host as to why we are here. He seems to be losing ground in credibility as one of the scouts already poked his head in our tent earlier."

Taryn looked at the oversized symbol of the Arturite pallitines emblazoned on Bartholomew's tabard, and worried that it was seen.

After a few tense minutes, Thoman visibly relaxed.

"Good, they're leaving."

Taryn realized she was holding her breath and sighed in relief.

The loud slapping of their host's boots preceded Tchor's head before it poked through their tent's flap. "My friends, you must go. Scouts have been here, but I fear from the pittance of a bribe taken they are on to you. You must leave now."

He immediately darted to the other tents and advised them of the same.

Once the urgency of their situation set in, it took only moments for everyone to pitch in and disassemble the camp.

Taryn gathered her equipment with the practiced discipline her training afforded and hurried to where the horses were waiting. "What was that bit about the scouts taking too small of a bribe, Bryn?" Taryn asked as she was tying her saddlebags onto her mount.

Bryn folded the canvas of their tents into a larger tarp and secured it in place as he replied. "Some customs dictate that if one plans on reneging on an agreement, they cannot take more than what is polite to accept. Apparently, that is what happened here."

Taryn looked past the camp and stood for a moment as the implication sunk in. "So, in a way, they paid for a tip-off that they would be raided before it happened?"

Bryn nodded. "That's one way to look at it; others look at it as a professional courtesy. One of the upsides of a deceitful society that's held by a strict sense of honor."

Tchor's typically confident gaze was awash in worry as he rushed to the group. "Are you ready? You must hurry," he insisted.

Thoman walked over to him and took his hand. "Again, I

thank you my friend. Best of luck to you."

"And to you. Now go!" The trader insisted.

"Where to?" Bryn asked as he mounted his horse.

He spurred his mount on and once the group was well outside of earshot, Thoman turned around with his answer. "West."

CHAPTER 21

D ARKNESS SWELLED IN THE FOOTHILLS, drowning what little light was left as the sun crept over the mountains looming over the group.

Taryn looked about the land around them. If it were not for the fact that she knew better, she would think they were up in Tramire, barely more than a day away from the keep she called home. But she did know better, and the simple fact that they were deep into Saerinian land kept her focused and on task.

Thoman urged his mount over to Bryn's and conversed with him. After a moment, the two had agreed and Thoman declared the gully they found themselves in a fit place to set up camp for the night.

The sun had all but disappeared behind the mountains when the camp was established and a meager fire started.

"How far?" Derren asked as he watched the flames flicker in the firepit.

Bryn looked south and shrugged. "About a half-day's journey from here."

One by one, the group trudged to their bedrolls once dinner was finished. Being so near the end had changed the group. The lightheartedness they carried in the start of their travels was nowhere to be seen. The journey was wearing on each of the members, especially from the hard ride they had the day before, constantly keeping an eye over their shoulder for any signs of pursuit, of which there were none.

Taryn yawned, tired, and yearned for the comfort of her bedroll. She stayed up longer than she should have, considering she was to take the second watch after Derren.

She bade the lone pallitine good night and ducked into her tent and slid thankfully into her bedroll, and blissfully ignored Thoman's light snoring and the shifting of Illya's restless legs.

Her eyes shot open at the tapping against her leg.

"Hey, wake up. It's your turn for watch."

Taryn's mouth opened in a yawn. "Already? I *just* went to bed."

Derren chuckled. "You've been asleep for quite a while. I'll let you wake up, but don't be too long."

A loud snap from a twig breaking broke the silence of the camp.

Taryn froze, and was instantly awake. "Did—"

Derren nodded and motioned that he would head out to investigate as he drew his sword.

The apprentice scrambled out of her bedroll and belted her own. Once her boots were on, she started for the flap outside when a commotion was started.

"Taryn, get everyone up *now!*" Derren's voice called out from the other side of the camp.

Instantly, she nudged Illya as she made her way to Thoman, whose eyes opened from the shout.

"I think there's trouble, let's go."

He nodded and motioned for her to go out and help Derren.

Taryn leapt out of the tent and saw three men circling the pallitine, who was barely able to fend off their blows. Already, she could see a slash along his back and one down the length of his shield arm. A glance to her side confirmed that he never had the chance to pick it up.

She raised her sword and charged the nearest foe, a man dressed in furs. Obviously Saerinian.

"Unbelievers, the prophet said you would be here." He sneered in his thick Saerinian accent as he blocked her attack.

Thoman charged out of his tent, followed quickly by Illya who ran to the other tents. He ran up to Derren and struck one of the men flanking him, forcing him to cry out.

Taryn cursed being caught outside her armor, and countered a weakly timed feint.

"Absolution will have you all." The man's eyes lit as he pressed forward and attacked her with a barrage of hurried, but strong blows.

Out of the corner of her eyes, she saw the tent flaps open and bodies come out, but her focus was centered completely on the man fighting her. It was all she could do to stand her ground. The man had obviously seen a lot of combat and countered her blows expertly. In the back of her mind, Taryn wasn't sure if she should feel good about being evenly matched with a seasoned warrior, or concerned that she needed to focus more on her training. She narrowed her gaze and pushed her attack as realization suggested survival would dictate the latter.

Derren cried out in pain somewhere behind her and she could hear the voices of Bartholomew and Thoman as they coordinated their attacks. Other voices were also heard, Hugh's shouting for someone to duck, and two others she was too busy to place.

Her attacker's eyes went wide as he saw her distraction and he pressed ahead, parrying her sword down as he grabbed her tunic with his left hand and pushed her over.

She fell off balanced and smacked her head on the ground.

From her blurred vantage, she caught the sight of the man looming over her and his grin all but declaring her defeat.

She blinked and heard a quick whistle followed by a telltale thud. She looked back and saw the man grasping an arrow stuck in his chest and stumbling back.

"I told ya ta duck." Hugh growled from behind her.

She rolled over and looked across the camp. "I couldn't tell who you were talking to, sorry."

"No worries. Fallin' was just as good," he retorted as he pulled her up.

The pain in the back of her head throbbed, but lessened as she looked around. The battle was all but over. Two of the hunters were already down, and the third was fighting too hard to be taken alive.

"Where's Bryn and Cirrus?" Her eyes widened as she took stock of everyone present.

"Right here." Bryn called out from behind her. "There were three others who were skirting the other side of the camp we dispatched." He shoved his thumb behind him and smirked at Errol. "He even managed to get one."

Taryn looked at two curved, short blades that hung loosely from the scout's belt and curiously back to the man himself.

"You took out two of them?" Harrold asked as he cleaned his blade on the body of a hunter. "How did you manage that?"

Cirrus cleaned his own sword, a classic Arturian longblade, and nodded to the pallitine. "That he did. Let's just say he's a good man to know."

Harrold looked at the muscular warrior who stood before him and incredulously back to the lean scout. "Hmph."

Taryn walked to Derren, who was being fussed over by Illya. Blood stained his armor, liberally covering his arms and face. Concern for her comrade quickened her pace until she was close enough to see that his wounds, while many, appeared to be shallow.

The sage began chanting as she gingerly placed her hands on

240

the wounds while the veil of magic surrounded her.

The feel of the power, while different from what she experienced with Pan, still made Taryn shiver. She stepped back and watched the pallitine carefully. "How are you doing?"

"Better, now that she's here." He coughed and nodded toward the sage.

The pallitine's wounds began to close, and within a few moments, he was fully healed.

I suppose there are uses for it. Taryn fought off a shiver that ran down her spine as the chanting stopped.

"Have we figured out how they found us?" Bryn asked as he stepped toward Thoman.

"No, we have not."

"The man I fought was speaking of absolution before he died," Taryn offered.

"The rumors are true." Thoman cursed. "And now they know we're here."

Bryn shrugged. "Not necessarily. This could have been a scouting party."

"With six members? Methinks that's a bit much to scout with," Bartholomew countered.

Thoman paced. "The Arturian is right. They're on to us. We need to go."

"What?" Taryn spat out. She looked at the congregation of tired and battered faces. "We've taken care of the enemy. We can't stand another attack if we run off without the proper rest. How are we supposed to defend ourselves if faced again, much less attack the beast if we lack the strength to properly do so?"

Derren stood with Illya's help. "We will do what we must. It is the duty of all pallitines to persevere."

"I don't expect you to understand, not having witnessed it firsthand," Thoman replied. "But if we're stopped now, then this accursed creature will *never* be stopped. He will continue on ravaging villages, and killing countless innocents."

She pulled Thoman away from the group and once they were

out of earshot, she spoke in earnest. "Look, I understand how important this is. I know how many lives are at stake, but we must think to our safety first. We must take care of ourselves first. And we must consider how *they* knew to find us here."

"Are you suggesting they were led here? By who, one of us?"

"No!" Her voice trailed while deep down she knew this to be a truth. "Yes, I do. Look at the evidence. They sent a group specifically to kill us. How can I not?" She glanced at the group, then turned away.

"Then what would you have me do? Let it roam the countryside, slaughtering whomever it encounters with no thought to their lives while we interrogate every member of our party?"

"Of course not. I'm just worried. I haven't seen you this obsessed with a hunt *ever*. I know this means a lot to you, but you've got to stay focused." Her shoulders drooped slightly as she sighed. "I know how much Hadrian meant to you, but you can't let the past dictate your actions. You will betray your *very cause* if you can't let it go. You can't let your need to avenge Hadrian blind you to the facts right in front of you."

Anger filled the High Pallitine's gaze as his voiced raised with his temper. "I *am* focused! What do you think I've been focused on for the last twenty years? That creature slew my mentor, my friend. I…" Spittle shot from his mouth as the rage he felt thickened his tongue with hate and fouled his words. He stepped threateningly close to Taryn and leaned in to her. "You have *no* idea what it's like. To be helpless as you sit there, and watch the one person who cared for you die, to have the stink from his charred flesh sicken you, and to know as he lay there dying, that it was all *your* fault." Regret instantly flashed across his face as he turned, and burned shame into his tensed and snarled features.

Thoman shrugged off Hugh's hand as the ranger approached and reached out for the High Pallitine's shoulder. He glanced back to his apprentice. "Look, I'm sorry for the outburst, but believe *this* if you believe anything." His intense gaze flicked between her eyes, daring her to ignore him. "There is *nothing* I want more than to watch this creature be put to a stop before it hurts *anyone else*." He turned his back on her and moved away. "And if you can't believe that, then there is nothing left for you here."

Taryn stepped back and looked at each of her companions. The looks that met her each told their own story, some in agreement with her, some not. The one thing they all shared was doubt and an echo of the distrust that she carried with her throughout her life. Her own words echoed back to her. *She needed to let go of the past.* She knew then, that however right she was, the distrust she clung to for so long would do more than hurt herself. It would create a rift in the group. To openly question the group's leader would divide them, and prevent them from gaining the cohesion needed to fight such a beast as what they were destined to face.

She knew then that in order for this group to be successful and help rid the world of the evil they were sworn to destroy, she had to swallow her pride and fear, and place her faith wholly into the one person who proved time and again to be the one rock of loyalty and trust that she clung to more than any other.

"You're right," She stammered.

Thoman stopped and turned toward her.

She looked apologetically at the group before turning back to her mentor. *I need to stop looking for betrayal at every turn. This stops now.* She pulled in her resolve and stepped toward her mentor. The time for words and empty promises was over. She needed to prove where her heart truly rested, and the only way she knew to do that was to stop talking and embrace it. "All of it. Everything you've told me all along. You're right. I am here, and have your back in everything you do." She looked around at the group. She swallowed the lump of regret that began to form in the back of her throat. "I'm sorry. I'm so sorry. I never meant to hurt you. You're the closest thing—"

"Shh." He whispered as he pulled her in for a warm embrace. "I know, Taryn, I know."

He sighed and cast a glance at each of the assembled members. "Perhaps it isn't unthinkable to realize that my alleycat has grown, and may well be right about being targeted." He nodded and turned to her. "Which is precisely *why* we must go."

Chapter 22

THE GROUP SLOWED AS BRYN signaled they were coming close to the breach in the mountains that would lead to the beast's lair. The half-day's journey they traveled felt like an eternity as they watched their backs, waiting for an impending pursuit that never came. Now assured that they had arrived safely, each member of the party dismounted to survey their immediate surroundings. The morning sun rose over the eastern stretch of the forest and warmed their tired bodies.

Thoman directed Cirrus and Errol to join Hugh in the morning hunt for breakfast, so they could be fed before they journeyed toward their final destination.

Thoman and Taryn checked their gear carefully, and packed only what was needed to bring into the depths of the mountain before them. Once he made sure everything was in order, the pallitine walked over to speak with Bryn. The guide went over the map with him, describing the path they would take, and reminded him the journey to the lair would take a couple hours or more inside the earth itself. Thoman knew this; he had studied the maps for the last several weeks. On a journey of such import, he cared little for leaving things to chance and wanted to make sure Bryn was as prepared as he.

He ordered the two pallitines and Hugh to load up their backpacks with supplies and food, and prepare for as much as they could without being over-burdened. Next, he instructed Illya and Bryn to seek shelter, care for the horses, and make camp, while reminding them that if the party did not return within a day to head out and tell the High Seeker of their failure.

Thoman's thoughts drifted to Pallitine Hadrian, and how his life brought him to this point. Anger boiled beneath the surface as the thought of the beast who took his mentor and friend came to the forefront of his mind. He had tried throughout this journey to suppress the rage that he had clung to for all this time, but now that he was this near his goal, he found it hard to suppress. The pallitine looked around to survey the surroundings. His gaze flicked up to the sky and drifted between clouds as he focused on these last few moments before their descent, not really sure whether to believe that the time had finally come.

Thoman made sure everyone had eaten and was ready before he started. "Taryn," the High Pallitine said, as he pulled his squire aside and addressed her directly, "we are about to enter the mountain's innards and face the accursed beast. Do you know what this means?"

Taryn nodded. *This is the moment I've been preparing for since we left Guardians Keep. Of course I know what it means.* She turned her gaze up to Thoman's and listened to the advice he gave, careful to not betray the annoyance at the repeated words since she knew the importance of this mission.

"Good, there are many untold dangers that may lurk at every turn when we're in there. You *must* be careful and keep your eyes open always. Vigilance is key. Remember, it's during these times that you must never show uncertainty to our adversaries, expected or no. Never must they sense any hesitation for they would surely take advantage of it. Always keep them guessing, even if you've no clue what course of action needs to be taken."

Thoman addressed the companions and paused as if collecting his thoughts before speaking. "Each of you has been chosen specifically for your loyalty and bravery. *This* is the time when we must act. *This* is the time when glory must be had. *This* is the place where we will find success." The pallitine looked at each of the party, one after the other, directly in the eyes. "When we brave these depths, remember I have full confidence in all of you *and* your abilities. Now, the question I ask of you is, are you ready?"

Each of the party members signaled their readiness and spent their last moments checking their gear to make sure all was in order. Once everything was ready, Thoman led the group to the entrance itself. The cave stood unassumingly before them, almost seeming to welcome the small band to its hidden depths. The entrance reached far above them and several feet wide as the opening slanted up out of the rocky earth of the mountainside.

The darkness in the cave looked menacing to Taryn at first glance. The stories of the first group to come here sprang to mind, making her glad to be surrounded by a larger group of skilled warriors. As she drew closer, she saw scattered equipment dotting the entrance, marking the failure and tragedy that met the last people who dared to set foot in the opening.

Bryn paled as he saw the scattered remnants of the group's gear and looked beyond it to find the brown and dried remains of blood, left from the last attack as the remaining members of the group fought for their lives, and lost.

Thoman stepped inside the cave and pulled out a pack that was on the ground. He opened the top flap and examined the contents. Inside were several blank pieces of parchment, a capped skin of ink, and two tomes: one a testament to the scriptures of Orn, and the other a simple diary that once belonged to Brother Tremue. The High Pallitine handed the pack to Bryn. "Here, this should be returned if there are any who would care to take it."

Taryn looked about the cave and was filled with a sense of disquiet by the lack of bones to pay testament to the men who fell here.

Bryn nodded solemnly and accepted the pack. He wished the group well before they took their final steps into the depths before them. "May Orn be with you all."

Taryn followed Thoman as the group entered the side of the mountain, filled with a sense of nervous anticipation. As they moved forward, the cave opened up and led to a sharp drop-off that ended twenty feet down, well out of reach of the last remnants of light filtering in from outside.

One by one, they looked into the darkness, lit their torches, and prepared for their descent into the mountain itself.

***

The dull roar of an underground spring whispered across the cold stone as the eight members of the party walked, greeting the group while they made their way through the subterranean passageways.

The cool smell of musty earth filled every step of their journey, only breaking once they felt the cool breeze that accompanied the rushing sound they had been hearing through the latter part of their travels. The group took a moment to rest as they reached the edge of the spring. Here they drank the refreshing, cool water it carried and consulted the map. Once they had refilled their flasks, the party moved on to head deeper into the earth.

Taryn wondered if anyone in the group felt as anxious as she did about the coming battle. The silence they embraced in the darkness of their underground hike was welcome and allowed her the chance to prepare herself for the task with little distraction.

"Hold," Derren whispered sharply while holding his fist up.

The other members of the party held their ground and paused, waiting for an explanation. It came quickly as a faint chittering echoed from some passage far ahead. They waited apprehensively as it grew louder, listening until it reached a crescendo as if a stream of vermin were heading for them. Just as it sounded as though the party would be overcome by the horde, the onslaught of noise diminished as the source of the noise traveled down another passage, away from the group.

Taryn shivered as her face twisted in disgust. "Rats," she muttered.

"They're gone," Derren said as he resumed course through the darkened passage.

"Easy enough for you to say," she retorted as a nervous shiver ran down her spine.

~~❧❈❧~~

Thoman carefully studied the creased map while standing several feet from the entrance they were looking for. Beyond the opening was a long, rocky cavern whose ceiling was lost amidst the darkness, stretching barely out of their lantern's reach. The High Pallitine reviewed their path with Derren and concluded that they had indeed arrived at their destination. He instructed his companions to stow their supplies to the side of the narrow passage and prepare their weapons.

The pallitine briefly went over their strategy again, revising it to match their new surroundings. "Okay, we all know the beast has heightened senses and likely already knows we approach." Thoman whispered to the group. "Once we've lit our torches, we're to toss them around the cavern to give us as much light as possible as we proceed inside."

Taryn flexed her fingers over the grip of her blade and focused her energy to the coming battle. She pushed all other thoughts aside and focused on her mentor.

CHAPTER 23

THE BEAST WOKE WITH A start as the faint clapping and scraping of boots echoed into his chamber. Slowly, he rose and stretched his legs, shaking the sloth of rest from his bones. He grew quiet and paid close attention to the sharp sounds that wove through the air and determined that soon, he would no longer be alone. The wyrm climbed the walls and moved across the ceiling to a stalactite, one with an advantageous view of the cavern. He resolved to wait, and gripped the stalactite's surface tenaciously as he looked below, waiting for the intruders to come.

Within minutes, the boot steps stopped outside of the entrance and voices muttered their savage whisperings, betraying both their intent and the uncertainty behind it.

***

The pallitine glanced at each member of the group, the feeling of excited vengeance burned with purpose in his breast. "Remember, this is his home. He knows it far better than we possibly could. Be prepared for anything. Are there any questions left unasked, or concerns to be had?"

Each member of the party shook their head or declined having any concerns. The members of the group each prepared their arms and readied themselves for the coming confrontation.

He continued, now satisfied that they were prepared for the coming battle. Conviction laced his words as he looked at each member confidently. "Be ready. We are a team. We strike as one, and we *will* win. *We* have the skill. *We* have the stones. And *we* have Orn on our side. Never again will this beast be free to hurt anyone else."

Bartholomew shook with a renewed vigor from the aging pallitine's speech and looked upon the group through eyes brimming with excitement for the coming battle. "By *his* sword this beast shall fall!"

While not as anxious as the young pallitine, the remaining companions each made their own exclamations and signaled their readiness.

A wall of warm humidity struck the group as they cautiously entered the cavern. The earthen floor contained the streaks of yellow, orange, and gray of various minerals. The stench of sulfur struck the intruders as it vented through several large channels that were carved through the walls and ceiling flowing up to the surface. On the far side of the cavern, steam jetted up from the earth's inner depths, slicking the walls and ceilings with a thin misting of sulfuric moisture. This plume followed its course up through an exceptionally wide vent that rested directly overhead in the ceiling above.

The group crept through the cavern looking for any signs of danger as one by one, they each tossed their lit torches about the stone floor. Once the torches were spread about the cavern and illuminated the the area, the light revealed scattered remnants of past meals, bones, rusted trinkets, and rotted cloth from the wyrm's victims. Torchlight flickered across the walls, revealing rich browns and yellows glistening amongst the drab gray of the cavern's inner walls. Thoman loosened the straps around his helmet and signaled the group to be ready for anything. He paused while surveying the cave and took a moment to adjust to the sulphuric heat before circling the area looking for any signs of their adversary.

⁓᭝᳙᭢⁓

Slowly, the wyrm blinked his eyes, watching the intruders as they spread their burning sticks throughout his home. He clung to the stalactite far above, watching his prey carefully while they wandered like lost insects seeking refuge on foreign soil. His tongue carefully slithered out, tasting the air. Fear was surrounding him, and it wasn't his. He waited patiently for one of the new arrivals to come close enough for him to pounce on. Excitement rushed through the hunter's veins as he flexed his claws and looked for the chance to strike.

The eight figures covered in leather and metallic shells spread out slowly as their confidence grew. He watched them move about, content with the wait for he knew that it wouldn't be long. He looked below in anticipation as two of their number walked close to where he clung while one fidgeted with the shell resting on its head and the second barked at the others. Instinct took over as he let loose his grasp upon the stalactite and dropped on top of his quarry.

⁓᭝᳙᭢⁓

Taryn looked around and found Harrold staring up at the ceiling above Thoman. She looked up to where he was and after a moment, she saw it. Curled around a stalactite was their prey. It clung above them, watching. Her heart skipped a beat and she turned back to Harrold who returned her glance with a face white as snow.

"Thoman!" He yelled out. "Above you!"

253

Taryn started at a run toward her mentor, but knew she would not be in time.

Both Thoman and Cirrus looked up to see the beast release his grip upon his perch and drop.

Cirrus pushed Thoman out of the way, but failed to get out from under the shadow of the large wyrm.

The beast landed with a crunch atop the bladesman and flexed its claws over the body it landed on and squeezed. Blood ran out in a pool, widening as the group stared in shock.

The creature from head to tail looked to be several yards long. Its light brown scales glistened from the steam that shot out of the vents. With the exception of one horn notably missing along its brow, several bony spines circled its crown and added to its threatening appearance. It bore intelligent eyes which seemed to calculate each move with precision. The wyrm acted with a speed and grace contrary for something of its size, and struck with a power to match.

Once she saw that her mentor was shaken, but relatively unharmed, Taryn slowed her run and looked at the others to coordinate the attack. She turned in time to see Hugh draw his bowstring back, and take measure of their foe. The ranger took careful aim as he looked the wyrm over for a weak spot.

Taryn glanced around and found Derren, who caught her gaze with his own. They nodded and proceeded to circle the beast on opposite sides as they discussed earlier.

In a concerted effort, the group engaged the wyrm while it turned its attention to the rest of the party. The beast flinched as arrows flew through the air and plunged into its armored neck. Derren and Taryn moved to flank their adversary while Bartholomew charged directly in to face the creature, drawing its attention on him.

Errol bellowed forth a frightening battle cry as he swore to avenge Cirrus before charging in after Bartholomew.

The wyrm swiped first at Derren, then at Taryn, knocking each off from their footing and onto their backs. It then fully ignored the charging men and bowled them over while it turned to run at Hugh. In a surprisingly agile maneuver, it stopped mid-stride and spun around to slap the ranger with its tail, sending his bow flying away from him while his body slammed into the cavern's wall.

Harrold's eyes tracked the High Pallitine, and now that he was safe, he pulled himself out of his initial shock and looked at the beast. He knew the stories well, but never expected them to be half as true as they were. In fact, the stories were underplaying its strengths.

The pallitine drew on his courage, knowing that the only way they were going to walk out of here was together.

He charged in, and swung at their foe, striking a glancing blow.

Fear surged through him as the beast turned a lazy eye in his direction. He backed away to run, only to feel the swift strike of one of the creature's claws pound his back and usher in darkness as he was smashed face first to the ground.

Thoman cursed his age while he staggered roughly to his feet. The wyrm literally had the drop on him, and he felt foolish for making the novitiate mistake of not looking up. Once he got his footing, he watched helplessly as the beast stopped its charge and spun to lash out at Hugh with its tail with a quickness that he had not witnessed before. The accursed beast was now turning toward Derren, who grunted in pain while trying to stand back up. The High Pallitine quickly ran over and helped Derren stand, and turned to realize that they were now facing the wyrm which had raised its head to watch them. He quickly took up a defensive stance and waited for Derren to ready his weapon. It was not until a full heartbeat had passed and he saw the creature's chest expand, that fear struck as he realized what the wyrm was doing.

⁓᠅⁓

The wyrm twisted his neck, growing annoyed with the prickling arrows as they dug into his skin between the soft scales on the underside of his jaw. He opened his jaw reflexively and was glad to find that the glands underneath were not hurt. Movement ahead distracted him from the pain as he saw one of the shelled men he swiped roll over from its back. He stepped forward and cocked his head curiously while the pallitine struggled to get up with the aid of another. His jaw opened to draw a deep breath as he tensed the muscles surrounding the glands which would feed the flames.

⁓᠅⁓

"Run!" Thoman shouted, ducking aside right as the beast's mouth opened.

The wyrm tracked Derren as it exhaled a broad stream of fire from its gaping maw, completely enveloping the pallitine in a column of flame. Screams bellowed forth from the column before the fire died down and the figure collapsed, falling on the ground to expose a still-burning and armored corpse.

Thoman, while quick to avoid the brunt of the blast, was still struck along the upper half of his body before escaping the flames. The stench of charred flesh hit his nostrils before it registered that the steel helm he wore was burning his face. As quickly as the realization struck, pain seared through his nerves, wracking the entire side of his head. The pallitine quickly discarded his now red-hot shield and yanked off the helm, screaming his own painful cry while thankful that the helm took the blast and not his head.

The wyrm growled in satisfaction at the fallen foe. The tantalizing aroma of burnt meat teased the senses, tempting him to stop and taste the spoils of battle, but he knew better. There were other enemies left to destroy. One of the shelled men, the one whose companion called it Thom-man, escaped the blast, and was only partially marked with the flames. The man's painful cries enticed him forward to continue the fight.

Taryn stood up from the ground in shock and horror as the flames surrounded Derren and immediately the vision of Pan Gorak came to mind, and once more she saw the sharp wicked smile cross his face while he brought his burning hand down on her. She stood watching, incapable of moving while her mentor barely leapt out of the barrage of fire and removed his helm, crying out in pain as he revealed deep burns and melted flesh along the left side of his head.

On the periphery, Hugh braced himself along the wall, recovering from the force of being knocked over as he clumsily regained his footing. He looked panicked as he held out his empty hands and began searching for his bow. In this moment, she knew that it was up to her to fight the beast. Again, she charged toward the beast and swung her weapon, only barely managing to scratch the thickened scales that covered its hide. The moment her blade connected with the wyrm, she cursed as she recalled the tactics they had so carefully gone over. She moved in time with her foe, slid the blade under one of the scales, and shoved the sword deep into her enemy with a powerful thrust.

Tearing pain rocked the wyrm's back as one of the intruders' weapons tore through his muscles. Incensed, he turned his head to find the assailant. He saw one of the shelled foes stabbing its back and flicked at her with his tail, knocking her over. The draconic beast watched her land on her back and now that he was convinced that the threat was dealt with for now, the hunter turned to find two more of the men charging forward and grew annoyed at the interruptions he faced at every turn of his claw.

⁓❧⚹❧⁓

Bartholomew and Errol both stood up, gripped their blades and ran in, furious from the death of their companions. The pallitine sought to distract the beast from attacking his leader and ignored the bladesman as he ran around to flank the creature. He reaffirmed the grip on his sword and screamed an unyielding battle cry. He moved as if inspired by the gods themselves, dodging a swipe from the beast's claw, and used the wyrm's own body for leverage to jump onto its shoulder. Once he found solid footing, the young pallitine buried his blade deep between the scales and within the flesh underneath.

⁓❧⚹❧⁓

The wyrm roared with a mix of rage and pain as yet another steel weapon ripped through his body and burrowed in his back. He saw only one thing that would help him, and this was something he could do now. The dragon-kin twisted his supple neck and lashed out, clamping his jaw on the offending figure. He encompassed the man's entire midsection within his teeth and bit down to rend his armor-covered foe. Almost immediately, the warm and inviting taste of coppery blood filled his mouth, and he lapped his tongue across the metallic surface of the armor. The hunter closed his eyes as he reveled in the

258

experience, and sucked one last time at the bounty of blood that poured from the now unmoving foe before spitting the figure out to focus on more immediate tasks.

Errol knew better than to waste a prime opportunity than the one that presented itself to him now. With the wyrm focused on the large pallitine, he skipped over the burning corpse and charged the beast. He sank his own blade into the other shoulder and reveled in the heat of the moment as he felt the muscles under the armored skin tear.

The large creature again roared out in a frustrated cry of pain as its leg toppled, and collapsed on its side, on top of the bladesman.

Errol felt his hip crunch under the weight of the beast and cried out in surprise. He looked down to find the creature's rough scales digging deeply into his midsection, compacting it far more than he knew was survivable. His back arched as a numbing warmth swept up his body. *Oh gods, not like this.*

Thoman's heart sank as his companions were dispatched one by one. He watched Bartholomew skid to a halt as he was spit out, and mourned the still body. The pallitine's armor, all but useless, barely contained the dark crimson that now poured out of his wounds.

He glanced toward the last of the bladesmen who lay crushed under the weight of the beast that was now struggling to stand back up.

It was then that he knew the folly of his quest for revenge. That truth struck him as much as the truth that it was his hate for this creature that now killed his friends and companions.

He also knew that he had no choice but to succumb to the rage that burned within. The High Pallitine let the deaths of his comrades fill him with an unbridled fury, and he raised his blade.

"In Hadrian's name, I will slay you!" He charged toward his prey and dodged a snap from the beast's jaw, ducked down, and slid past the slavering maw. The pallitine quickly scrambled to his feet and saw his chance. Thoman stepped forward and swung Orn's Razor in a wide arc, deeply gouging the beast's left eye, rupturing it. Vengeance flashed across the pallitine's burned face and filled him with the festering hate that he fostered since their last encounter. Wrathful elation blazed within as he saw the creature's defeat dangle before him, spurring him to press his attack on the vile creature.

❦

As loud as the wyrm roared earlier, nothing matched the ferocity that it wailed with now. Reflexively, the hunter swiped at the shelled man that struck him and knocked him over. He glared at the fallen foe with his one remaining eye and seethed with primal hatred, snarling at the glint of steel from the weapon that took his eye. The dragon-kin flicked at the blade with his claw, sending Orn's Razor careening across the cavern, far out of the reach of his foe. He pushed himself up on all four legs, cursing every moment of pain. The hunter moved in for the kill, full of hate for this puny being, and stomped a foot on top of Thom-man's chest, leaving only his shoulders and head exposed. A fount of blood rushed out from his quarry's mouth, filling the wyrm with a frenzy as he clenched his jaw around the gasping figure's head with a snap. Throbbing pain shot through his destroyed eye with each pulse of his heart and fed the rage as he summoned forth flames to roast the head he held within his clenched jaws. Now charred to his satisfaction, he chewed the morsel and swallowed the remains. If it weren't for the pain thrumming throughout his body, he knew how much he would savor the moment. He knew how much the delightful taste of the fallen enemy's charred flesh would satisfy the craving that now stoked his need to finish off the remaining intruders.

⌁⌁⌁

Taryn stood in horror and disbelief as she watched the wyrm kill Thoman. Rage burned within her at the sight of her mentor's death. As much as she wanted to lose it and charge headlong at the beast, she knew she could not. Her eyes flew to the weapon gifted to Thoman for this battle and then back to her enemy. With the beast distracted, she knew the time was now. She ran to pick up Orn's Razor, ignoring the arrows flying past her head as they slammed into the beast's armored hide. Once close, she leapt up to the creature's maimed shoulder and used two of the swords still embedded to climb on its back. She held on to the neck and braced a foot on one of the swords as the wyrm rocked to the side when it realized the danger it was in. The rocking paused long enough for her to scrambled up to the wyrm's neck and grip Orn's Razor with both hands. Taryn mustered her strength and swung the blade with the power and conviction of desperation. Blood splashed around her in a violent eruption as the body quaked from the blow and sent her flying off to crack her head on the cold stone of the cavern floor.

⌁⌁⌁

Taryn's eyes flickered open. Her raspy breath came out painfully while she assessed her surroundings. The quiet that surrounded her was a stark contrast to the violence she last witnessed. It took only a moment for her to clear the fog from her thoughts and realize that she was on the stone floor of the cavern and covered in blood. She raised a hand up to her head and tried to stave off the throbbing that was slowly making itself known. The pain that pulsed through her skull intensified as she struggled to recall what happened. The last thing she remembered was watching the creature's blood fly as Orn's Razor struck its neck, and then she was in the air, flying off to where she now rested. In a panic, she rolled over and pressed her arms to the floor as she tried to get up. Her efforts were met with a darkness that enveloped her senses as she succumbed to the agony of the effort.

When she woke again, Hugh was kneeling over her checking for signs of life. Gradually, she rolled over and stared blearily up at the ranger. She sat up and looked over at the beast. Its head rested on the ground half-severed from the huge body which lay strewn across the cavernous floor as it twitched, dying in a pool of blood.

Cautiously, she stood up, only vaguely aware that she instinctively picked up the weapon that felled the mighty beast. Still numb from the battle, she surveyed the area around her. When the half-burned corpse of her mentor caught her gaze, shock took over and she dropped the sword. Taryn staggered mindlessly to Thoman's now lifeless body. Grief took hold as she saw his maimed form up close, weeping while the depth of the loss began to dawn on her. Her friend, her instructor, the example that she tried to live up to for so many years lay before her, no longer there to comfort her, no longer able to guide her. For the first time in years, she felt alone.

Hugh came to her side and held her while they both mourned their loss.

And then it struck her. She looked up and saw Hugh standing with her, mourning the same man she did. She wasn't alone. The single most important thing that Thoman left her with was knowing there were others she *could* rely on, and who could rely on her in return. Not only Hugh, but Illya, who she had grown close to in their travels. Even Harrold, the man who risked as much as she did to help Thoman in his quest, had garnered her respect.

A harsh, raspy moan whispered out from several feet away and broke her thoughts.

Both figures backed up in shock and turned to look at Bartholomew. Surprised by his unexpected survival, they rushed to the fallen pallitine.

"Ho, lad. Don't stir too much." The ranger cautioned the fallen pallitine as he examined his still-bleeding form. "We thought ya dead."

Coughing up blood, the pallitine retorted, "Thy thoughts were mine own naught moments ago, friend. 'Twould seem to be that Orn hath more left in store for this pallitine indeed," he said with a pained smile. "Derren hath been lost, that I saw. Is anyone else...?" He left the question unfinished as his eyes brimmed with a sorrowful hope.

Taryn looked away, unable to answer the question.

Compassionately, Hugh rested his hand upon Bartholomew's shoulder. "I'm 'fraid so, friend." He paused to compose himself as the truth caught in his throat. "Thoman is also lost ta us, as are the bladesmen. Now rest still. I must see ta yer wounds, otherwise we might lose another."

"And Harrold?"

"He's still out, but alive."

The Arturian simply nodded and looked away.

Hugh started to unfasten the clasps which held what was left of Bartholomew's armor in place. "I'm afraid that yer still bleedin'. I'm goin' ta need ta take off yer armor ta better look at the damage and bandage your wounds."

Wincing in pain, the pallitine nodded.

Taryn assisted Hugh as he removed the young pallitine's armor, revealing several gouges along his abdomen, most of which had started to clot.

Hugh frowned at the sight, and left Taryn to care for the wounded pallitine. When he came back, he set his pack next to the young man and fished out a pouch of bandages. The ranger tended to the pallitine's wounds, wrapping them to help the man as best as he could. Once he dressed the multitude of wounds, Hugh sat back and allowed the young man to rest.

"How do you think he'll fare?" she asked, trying to distract herself from Thoman's fate.

"Aside from his armor bein' rendered all but useless, he seems ta have several broken ribs. I doubt there's anythin' a few weeks of rest won't mend. My worst concern is the amount o' blood that he's lost. If he makes it through the next couple o' days, he should be fair. Time will tell. We should let him rest for a day before tryin' ta move him." The ranger glanced up to the vents that wound out from the ceiling as his eyes widened with inspiration. "I'm goin' ta try and start a fire here, but it might not last long. If it goes out, light up a lantern, and save as much fuel as possible. I'm goin' ta get some help. There's two skins of my home-brewed mead that I'll leave ya with. Be sure ta make him drink it. Not only will it ease his discomfort, but it'll help him ta recover and get his strength back before we dare move him. If I'm not back within a day, take Harrold and Bartholomew with ya and get out."

Hugh moved around the cavern and gathered a handful of torches together to form a small fire and doused the rest in order to save them for the journey out. Satisfied that all was in order, he came back and reassured Taryn before leaving. "Ya'll be all right, I swear. Take care, and watch him. He'll need plenty of fluid so be sure ta give him the mead."

Taryn's worried eyes conveyed her understanding as she swept her gaze in the pallitine's direction.

Bartholomew nodded briefly to Hugh as the ranger came over to make sure that all was well before he departed. As soon as the ranger turned to gather himself for travel, the fallen pallitine struggled to look to where Thoman had fallen. His face twisted in a grimace as the agony from his efforts overcame his resolve and he fell unconscious.

Hugh knelt down to check the still form. "Good, he's breathing." His stern gaze barely hid the pain of loss they both felt that the victory had brought them. He stood and nodded curtly to Taryn before departing.

Taryn waved solemnly in farewell as she wished the ranger a safe journey and urged him to hurry. Once Hugh had left the cavern, she gazed upon her mentor, moved over to kneel next to his maimed body and openly wept for his loss.

CHAPTER 24

BARTHOLOMEW WOKE AND SAW THE orange flicker of torch-light sweep across Taryn, who sat next to him. He struggled to lean up, but as he tried to speak, his lungs revolted and coughed up the acrid, coppery taste of dried blood.

"Don't try to get up," Taryn urged as she placed a hand on his shoulder.

Bartholomew reluctantly gave in to the weakness that consumed him and turned to face Taryn. The dull pain he felt upon waking grew sharper, forcing him to wince and further aggravate the injuries he suffered. He looked to the shadows, his lips trembling as his mortality faced him now more than ever. Never had he been beaten so soundly. Never had he faced such a fearsome foe. Never had fear consumed him as it did now. The cavern that once felt so humid and warm, was damp and frigid as he laid sprawled out and helpless. He brought a trembling hand to his forehead and found it moist with cold sweat. A single notion pushed all other cares aside as he sunk further into the stone floor. *I am going to die here.* The apprentice caught his attention, a stark sadness tainted her mask of compassion as she reached into a nearby sack. Her emotions triggered nothing inside him but an abstract recognition. He found himself unable to commiserate with her; his once bountiful fount of compassion lay dormant in the shadow of his imminent death.

"Here, drink this." The sole angel who stood near to watch him die offered a pouch and held it to his lips.

Gratefully, he opened his mouth and waited. He felt the honey-sweet mead trickle down his tongue and struggled to recall anything tasting so sweet, yet so foul. What should be a soothing and comforting drink in his time of need filled his thoughts of all that was wrong and foul in this world. He gulped the last drop and mouthed a thanks to Taryn before turning and succumbing to another fit of pain. The torture quickly passed, followed by a numbing warmth that enveloped his legs. His eyes panicked and he turned back to Taryn, silently pleading for relief while his face contorted into a twisted mask as he kicked out, trying desperately to feel his legs. The icy touch of death reached out to grip his feet and crept upward as he kicked. Each of his wounds cried out with the jerk and ripped under a mask of dried blood from the exertion, rewarding him for his movement with a new brand of agony until the welcomed kiss of oblivion gave him the relief he so desperately sought.

⚜

Flickering torchlight met the pallitine's gaze as his eyes fluttered open. Another wave of cool sweat greeted him, breaking his thoughts from the nightmarish visions of being held within the beast's jaws and crushed within the prison of sharp teeth as each spike pierced his very core.

The sound of boots echoed in the cavern and distracted him, urging him to turn his head. Weakness permeated his still form, making the movement much harder than it should have been. By the time he moved his head, more of the cold sweat beaded across his brow and trickled down the side of his face.

The movement cruelly reminded him of his current state. Pain wracked his senses with each motion, forcing out the painful moans he fought hard to prevent. The agony he felt made him ask why fate would be so cruel to drag out his torture and not, for the love of Orn, let him die. He tried to steel himself with thoughts that his sacrifice would not have gone in vain. He tried to find comfort in the fact that Taryn felled the beast and quelled the evil that would have continued to be wrought upon countless innocents if it went on unchecked, but he could not. Silently, he swore to himself that should he survive this trial, this flirtation with death's call, he would search for what was wrong with this world and right those wrongs, no matter the cost. The pallitine swore to Orn himself to be ever more vigilant against the forces of darkness wherever they might dwell should he live another day. His silent, desperate plea for Orn to find mercy and give him this one chance to live left him in such a state of despair he could do little but watch the congregation of people that walked toward him.

Hugh led the march toward the pallitine, followed by both Bryn and Illya.

Once the elven sage saw the fallen pallitine, she swiftly moved to the prone figure and knelt next to him. She gingerly placed a hand on his head and one upon his chest, and examined the pallitine carefully.

Bartholomew winced from the touch, and grew worried when it dawned on him that he could not feel her hands on him whatsoever.

Illya looked upon Bartholomew in concern and moved more gingerly, trying to avoid hurting the fallen Arturite.

Bryn walked up behind her and nodded at Bartholomew in greeting before turning to look at the remains from the battle. Sorrow visibly consumed him as he looked at his former companions and walked to where they lay.

Bartholomew turned his gaze back to Illya, and looked up to her hopefully.

Once she finished examining the wounds, she placed a hand upon his brow and held a green crystal in the other.

The pallitine watched in wonder as the crystal flared to life for an instant and began to fade while Illya closed her eyes.

Wearily, her head dropped and she began to wince in pain as she muttered phrasings from some light, lyrical tongue.

Immediately, the Arturite's vision began to grow fuzzy as a faint warmth flowed throughout his being and touched the crushing numbness that engulfed his body, replacing it with a new torture that joined the chorus of pain he so desperately sought relief from. His teeth ground while he fought the fire searing in his every nerve. It was at this crescendo of agony that he felt both of the healer's hands upon him as they pressed down on the wounds which closed under her touch. The pain diminished as the chanting continued, teasing the faintest hint of strength back into his limbs.

Time lost all relevance and passed only with each pulse of the dulling pain until the soft chanting finished and she leaned back. Sweat beaded on her forehead and she slumped her shoulders. The exhaustion from her efforts wore heavily upon her slender form.

Taryn walked closer from where she stood as she watched the ritual. "Is he going to be all right?" She cautiously asked.

The sage nodded, "Yes, I used what knowledge I have of the power of Vitae to help him replenish his lost stores of blood. He is by no means fully healed, but he is doing better than he was. We must let him rest to regain what strength he can before we set out."

Bryn walked back from the bodies and shook his head, looking as if he were unsure how to react to the sight. "They were good men. All of them."

Hugh looked at the scout. "Your men fought bravely 'til the end. They died as they lived, as honored warriors."

He nodded in response, and turned to his fallen comrades.

Illya stood up and turned to the ranger. "Where are

the others?"

Hugh pointed out the bodies to the sage. The loss still painted heavily in the creases of his brow and tainted his gaze.

The sage embraced Hugh, her actions betrayed the unvoiced reluctance to view the bodies. Once her resolve solidified, she turned and moved first to Thoman. She held her hand above his chest and mourned. After a moment of silent reverence, she turned to Derren and knelt next to his body, placing her arms upon the cool and charred armor and wept, embracing the figure that she grew to care so strongly about in such little time.

Bartholomew watched the display with a detached respect. He recognized he should be feeling more for the loss of his companions, but the realization that they gave their lives to end this threat filled him with a strong comfort that pushed him past the sense of loss. Although still weak from the loss of blood, he no longer feared death and looked up to the cavern's ceiling, thanking Orn for this second chance and reaffirmed his promise that he would do whatever it took to cleanse the world of its evils. Exhaustion drifted through the pallitine's bones, but this time Bartholomew welcomed the rest, taking comfort as the blanket of conviction wrapped him in its warm embrace.

When Bartholomew awoke, he saw that the men had made three makeshift litters, two meant to take the lifeless bodies back for a proper burial on the surface, and the other for himself. He turned to find Bryn walking from another part of the cavern holding a flawless orb colored the purest shade of night, filled with only the faintest wisps of gray which swirled with a life of their own within the mysterious globe. The orb was bound by a broken ring of crimson metal, which marred the otherwise flawless surface.

"Hugh, what do you make of this? It was in the pile of trinkets in the corner." He jabbed his thumb vaguely behind him, in the direction he came from.

The pallitine strained himself to get a better look at the orb, and found his efforts solicited less pain than he felt earlier.

Harrold sat nearby and set a hand on his arm. "Take it easy, save your strength, my friend." His face looked much like Bartholomew felt, his nose appeared broken, and the side of his head marred by the violent confrontation with the cavern's floor.

Hugh stepped over to Bryn and shook his head as he looked at the mysterious object. "I have no idea, my friend. Illya, what do ya think?"

Illya stirred from her mourning, and looked grateful for the distraction. She stood from her seated position which she kept faithfully next to Derren's remains and walked to the guide. "Interesting, I've not seen the like before," she whispered while taking the item from Bryn. The sage sat on the ground and looked deeply into the orb while she slipped into a trance. As she stared, the gray wisps within came alive, thickening as they swirled inside the globe. Her face turned into a scowl and darkened visibly. Haunted tension echoed from behind her eyes as she shoved the orb into the guide's hands. "This is something I do *not* want around me. It carries a negative aura, and dark omens abound in its wake. It may be worthwhile to have someone else skilled in the arts divine its purpose, but that will *not* be me." Fear edged her gaze as she looked upon the object and backed away to return to her rightful place beside Derren.

Bryn dubiously accepted the orb from Illya and wrapped the artifact with a strip of cloth before stowing it in his pack.

Once the preparations had been completed, and Illya was sure Bartholomew would survive the journey, the two men moved the pallitine to his litter.

Everyone took a final look about before they set out to leave the cavern. Each member of the party wore the consequences of the battle heavily in their actions as they dealt with the loss of their companions.

Bartholomew's conviction rose with each step taken as he was carried from his place of defeat. He knew that he was chosen to survive this battle for a reason, and he was bound to make sure that he would see his purpose through to the end.

CHAPTER 25

A CHILL BREEZE SWEPT OVER THE barren hilltop as it skirted the mountains and brushed through the party while they gathered to pay their last respects to their fallen comrades. Taryn placed the final stone upon Thoman's grave and stood back to contemplate her friend and mentor's life. As she remembered his dedication and impact on her life, she vowed to uphold the values he worked so hard to instill within her.

Tears slipped down her cheek as the hole Thoman left grated against her very core. She raised a hand to her face and despaired that she would no longer be able to rely on his compassion, no longer hear his voice, and would no longer have the nearest thing to a father she'd ever known.

The group stood in a circle around the four graves and took turns sharing memories or feelings they had for their companions, honoring the departed and wishing them well as they started their journey into the afterlife.

Hugh rested a hand upon Taryn's shoulder as he moved in to stand next to her while they paid their respects. "I'll make sure the church builds a proper shrine ta respect his sacrifice, that do

I swear ta ya. We've both lost someone dear ta us, but let's not sink in the mire of grief. He would want us ta move on and do good in his name."

Taryn agreed with the barest of nods and tried to compose herself. "Yes, he would." She turned to Hugh, forced a half-smile and embraced him, wishing she could change the fate of her now-departed friend and mentor. She turned to the others, grateful for each member that survived, thankful that there were others she could share Thoman's memories with, and who would also share in the mourning.

Harrold stepped near. "We have both lost someone dear to us in this journey. If there is ever anything you need, do not hesitate." Sadness washed his profile in a depth of loss as he knelt and touched one of the stones over Thoman's resting place. "Goodbye, Thoman."

Illya stood across from Taryn, faint tears drying on her cheeks as she stood near Derren's grave with her hands clasped in front of her. Her head lifted and she acknowledged the apprentice's gaze. A mournful smile flashed before she looked down at the grave to pay her silent respect for her fallen comrade and love.

Bartholomew stubbornly stood, with Bryn's assistance, and bore a grim but proud look on his face. He seemed to recover, emotionally at least, much quicker than Taryn anticipated. He truly was an Arturite Pallitine as Thoman said on the outset of their journey.

Bryn bore the cold look of someone who had lost others before and while he did mourn, this was not unfamiliar territory for him.

Hugh's face wore the same distraught sense of loss Taryn felt. He squeezed her shoulder before turning away from the graves and headed down the hill away from the makeshift memorial.

One by one, the band broke rank and moved downhill to the field where their camp was set up. Each member mournfully prepared for the long journey home. Taryn sighed as she looked past the graves to the mountains they traveled out of and looked up into the sky, watching the sun set over the horizon before joining the others. *Farewell, my friend. You shall sorely be missed.*

⌒ℑ※Ⅎ⌒

The grandeur of the Prime Temple of Orn felt somewhat less impressive than Taryn recalled as they approached the holy compound. She wasn't sure if it was the heavy heart she carried which changed her impression, or the mere fact she no longer had Thoman to show her the hidden truths of the temple; the sight lacked the same feeling it inspired when he first rode with her toward the ornate structure all those weeks ago.

As the party drew near the building, they were greeted by a small cluster of priests and their assistants. The group was quickly ushered into the temple they had left so many weeks ago, and shown to a waiting room off the foyer. Shortly after, the High Seeker walked briskly to where the party gathered. He greeted them warmly, asking for word on their success.

Taryn and Hugh stepped to the forefront of the group, both with somber looks upon their faces. "We were successful in our quest, High Seeker, but not without cost. We've lost the bladesmen, and both Pallitine Derren, and High Pallitine Thoman ta the beast before we slew the foul creature." Hugh went on to describe the battle, telling how each of the members valiantly fought the beast before falling in the battle. He went on to describe Bartholomew's bravery, and finally Taryn's courageous charge as she climbed the beast's back and killed it.

When the story was done, Taryn produced Thoman's blade and presented it to the High Seeker. "I believe this gift should be returned, now that he can no longer wield it."

The High Seeker placed his hand upon Taryn's and looked compassionately into her eyes. "My child, if ever a man had someone to bequeath his most prized possession upon, Thoman had you. He was given the blade as a gift to aid in the quest, and by all accountings of the battle, it aided greatly and you were the one who wielded it. The blade is yours."

Taryn bowed in thanks to the High Seeker, not finding the words to convey the gratitude she felt.

"Yer grace," Hugh interjected. "There's the matter of the burial for our friends that've been lost in this quest. They're buried on the edge of the Untarian Mountain Range. I would humbly request a shrine be built out of respect of their sacrifice and ta mark their deeds."

The High Seeker readily agreed. "Yes, yes, of course. I shall have it seen to immediately. There is also the matter of contacting the Order of Guardians so that the Prime Pallitine can be advised of the loss. And there is the matter of a vacancy in the order itself." He looked meaningfully at Taryn. "Long have I known Thoman. And long have I trusted his judgment. He placed his faith in you for many years and trained you to be who you are today. Although I have no formal say in the matter, I will sponsor your inclusion within the ranks of the Order as a fully vetted pallitine."

Confused, Taryn protested. "But I haven't gone through the trials! That wouldn't be honorable to skirt the requirements merely because of who tutored me!"

"Oh, dear child." The High Seeker looked Taryn in the eyes, smiling softly to reassure her. "Do you not think the journey you've embarked on has been a trial? Do you not think the beast *you* slew properly demonstrated your skill? Do you not think the fact you willingly chose to return such a fine weapon you rightfully had claim to demonstrated your honor? I would think you've gone through a much tougher trial than the Trials of Honor you've put so much stock into could *ever* be. The very reasons you protest only further reinforce my opinions in the matter." A narrow, but sad smile parted his lips. "Yes, my child. In my eyes you are already a pallitine in all but title." The High Seeker paused to collect himself and turned to address the rest of the group with sorrowful eyes. "I must give you all my sincerest thanks for your sacrifices in this journey. Your rooms were kept for you, and I would request that you stay with us so we may pay proper tribute to the fallen heroes."

The aged figure held his hand up in blessing for the group and turned again to Taryn and rested his hand upon her arm. "As much as I dislike doing this, there is a matter I was planning on discussing with Thoman when he got back that must now be dealt with." He looked away and paused as if in contemplation before looking into her eyes to speak again. "Take this time to reflect upon our friend and come to terms with what you must. Once the memorial is done, I will send for you and we can talk then. Just be prepared for your duties as a pallitine to start early."

He looked upon the group in a mournful gaze and politely excused himself to reflect on the news and to begin preparations for the tasks that were now his to fulfill.

Unsure what to make of her unexpected sponsorship into the ranks of the pallitines, nor of the ominous meeting mentioned, Taryn turned back to the group.

⚜

The memorial service was much grander than Taryn expected. The service was administered by Erik, which of course meant the memorial lasted half again as long as it otherwise might have. Several times during the ceremony, his words broke as he looked to the heavens with a sorrowful gaze. Though the service was long, not a single soul betrayed any annoyance or showed impatience as each remembered the heroes in their own way and appreciated the kind words spoken.

Once it was over, she was introduced to the Arturian and Irlinian High Pallitines, along with a slew of other ranked officials, political and otherwise, who all wished their condolences. It was a parade of figures, half of whom she forgot in the blur of being whisked to meet this person, or pulled to talk with another. Among the most memorable in these meetings was the introduction to Illya's father, Koryn. He seemed an odd fellow, Taryn thought, but a warm enough person and she could see why he would have been friends with Thoman. He had spoken several times of going out with Hadrian and Thoman, and fondly recalled how well Thoman dealt with the worst of situations and stood as a shining beacon of the best of traits.

Taryn politely made small talk with the abundance of well-wishers until she found an opportunity to break away and hide out with Hugh on the far side of the communion hall. Relieved to be out from the center of attention, she turned to the ranger and motioned to the gathering of people in the hall. "I knew he was well respected, but in the years I've been with him I've never even seen most of these people."

Hugh chuckled and took a long pull from a flask he brought with him before offering it to her. "Our friend has had many years ta help many people. He drew much attention and made a number of friends since we were kids. With as many favors owed ta him, it's a small wonder he never went inta politics." He grinned and winked knowingly at Taryn.

Taryn laughed at the thought. "Yes, I can see it now, Tramirian Chancellor Thoman refusing to give up his sword as he *mediates* disputes between baronies." She gratefully accepted the flask and took a drink before handing it back. The apprentice glanced around the grand hall, looking for her other companions. "I've seen Bartholomew, Harrold, and Illya when I spoke with her father, but not Bryn. Have you seen him? How is he doing?"

Hugh took another pull from the flask. "Bryn was here during the service, but once the processional left he saw fit to leave. Illya followed soon after." He turned to look her in the eyes. "He seems fine, but didn't look as invested in either of the losses as we were. Illya, on the other hand, has taken Derren's loss harder than I would've expected. I mean, it was obvious the two were drawn to each other, but I hadn't expected her feelings to run that deep." He turned his gaze back to the crowds and capped his flask before putting it away. "Give her time. I expect that's what any of us could use. The thick-headed pallitine, on the other hand, is a hard one ta read. There are moments when I suspect he was affected the worst of all, but then he seems ta come back and stand even taller." He shook his head, still gazing out nowhere in particular. "I'm not sure if that one is proud, crazy, or too dedicated ta care, but I'll tell ya something. Coming that close ta death would shake *my* nerves, if even for a bit."

Streaks of orange and red broke the morning sky as Taryn came out to the stables. Straw greeted her footsteps as she neared the deceptively large outbuilding. Two bundles rested next to the entrance, near a unique burnt-leather saddle and a couple of saddlebags filled to near-overflowing with food and supplies. She waited for a moment until Bryn came out, leading his horse to where his gear waited.

"I heard you were leaving. You sure you don't want to stay a bit longer? There is no shortage of friends here."

The guide smiled as he loaded his gear upon the mount. "Thanks for your kindness, but it's time I moved on. I have other... dealings to pursue. Maps to make, people to help, the usual," he said evasively. He started to move toward his horse, but paused midway and turned back to Taryn. "I know I haven't been around much since we got back from the mountains and I *did* want to say I'm sorry for your loss before I left. He was a good man." His eyes betrayed a hint of the sadness and discomfort his words could not express.

"Thank you. Good luck in your journeys. May we meet again."

He looked sidelong at her while securing his gear. "I have no doubt in that. None at all."

Taryn watched as he mounted his horse and rode out of the temple grounds. With this part of her journey complete, her thoughts inevitably wound their way back to the Absolutionists and the threat they posed. The hole left in her heart by her departed mentor ached as memories of him pushed those concerns aside. *Gods, Thoman. Why did you have to die?*

ABOUT THE AUTHOR

RODERICK DAVIDSON LIVES IN THE Pacific Northwest with his wife and has three awesome children. His imagination runs rampant, and he writes to help focus the stream of creative chaos that he views through his mind's eye. He has been a fan of fantasy and science fiction works since he can remember, and enjoys reading books from authors such as Piers Anthony, Isaac Asimov, and David Eddings, among others. His other interests include drinking copious amounts of coffee and gaming; his favorites being role playing as well as strategy games.

OTHER BOOKS BY THE AUTHOR

PALLITINE'S PATH

Book 1: Pallitine Rising
Book 2: Pallitine Fallen (in progress)
Book 3: Pallitine Lost (in planning)
Book 4: (title not set) (in planning)